'A mystery with heart and soul, and a poignant picture of a family living with loss. Highly recommended'
Frances Quinn

'A compelling and powerful debut, laced with mystery and full of heart'
Alison Moore

'Powerful and raw law, like the sea she describes so evocatively. Really wonderful writing'
Amanda Berriman

'Poetry in prose. Written with warmth and wit, this astutely observed study in grief is balanced by an exploration of faith, friendship and love'
Fiona Erskine

'A heartbreaking exploration of grief and faith, with undercurrents of unease and intrigue, this is a tender, poignant and compassionate literary thriller'
Philippa East

'A stunning debut: evocative descriptions, strong characterisation and a simmering tension which builds to a thrilling finale. Fans of *Broadchurch*, in particular, will love it'
Sarah Linley

'Utterly engrossing and atmospheric, *Sea Defences* is an extraordinarily accomplished debut novel with its bare but beguiling prose and poignant expl
Jane Jesmond

..... .ylo..... a gra..... of Edinburgh University and lives in Suffolk, where she taught for almost twenty years. Her short fiction has won or been listed in competitions including the Bridport Prize, Bare Fiction and Flash500, and has been published in magazines and anthologies. *Sea Defences*, her first novel, began life as a prize-winning short story, placed third in the Bath Short Story Award.

Sea Defences

Hilary Taylor

Lightning Books

Published in 2023
by Lightning Books
Imprint of Eye Books Ltd
29A Barrow Street
Much Wenlock
Shropshire
TF13 6EN

www.lightning-books.com

ISBN: 9781785633355

Cover by Nell Wood
Typeset in Garamond and Baskerville Cyrillic LT

British Library Cataloguing in Publication Data
A catalogue record for this book is available from the British Library.

For Emily

He stares at the empty sea. His wet clothes cling to him and weigh him down. Wind gusts around him and he can't stop shaking. Waves crash, on and on, the sound that sends him to sleep every night. He rocks backwards and forwards, and a moaning sound mingles with the cry of the wind.

'Help. Oh, Mumma, help,' he hears himself whisper at last.

Waves in the Margin

Rachel never stopped loving the sea. Even after it happened. The need to blame someone consumed her, but she never blamed the sea.

She had always longed to live in a place where she could hear the crash and suck of the waves through the open window at night, where she could smell the salt in the air, where there would always be sand stuck in the soles of her shoes. She loved to walk that ever-shifting boundary between land and ocean, that magical seam, where neither world claimed her. On that smudged line, the stitching is loose. The fabric pulls. No one can say the ocean ends here and the land begins here. Or the other way round. You could fall between the cracks.

February. A bleak Friday afternoon. Whose idea was it to hold a PCC meeting at such a time? Rachel's pencil meandered down the margin, forming intricate curls and spirals, creating a border of waves for the agenda. Her feet were freezing, and the musty smell in the vestry made her feel sick. Some of the fabrics – the cassocks and altar cloths and those tapestry kneelers – must be twice the age she was. Bat droppings nestled in the corners of the window sill. They would have met in the vicarage if it wasn't located in the most distant of the four parishes, six miles inland from Holthorpe. She had considered offering her house, but it wouldn't be fair on the children, not to mention Christopher. Besides, it was still five months till her ordination and it wouldn't do to get ahead of herself.

She ticked off the items. The Christmas Fayre had made over eight hundred pounds, the Scout Hut had been booked for the Easter bake sale, and everyone was in favour of putting an extra thousand towards the Parish Share.

'Maybe we'll manage more than half this year,' Gail said.

Rachel glanced at the clock on the wall. Five past four. Jamie would be all right for a bit on his own at home, but Hannah needed collecting from Friday Club at half past. She might make it, if she could avoid being grabbed for 'a quick word' after the meeting. They'd have to go to Tesco on the way home. She made a mental list. Loo roll, cereal, bananas, cheese. Something easy for tea. Pasta. Again.

'Finally,' Gail said, 'we come to the summer concert.'

'Ah, yes.' Clearly, Thelma had been waiting for this last agenda item, and now set her jaw and shoulders for battle.

Rachel closed her eyes.

'I still don't understand,' Thelma went on, 'why we have to give half the proceeds to the RNLI. When we had the Saffron Singers, we always got all the money, and a jolly good fundraiser it was. And since this is a replacement for that event, I can't see why it has to be a different arrangement.'

Rachel opened her eyes, but was careful not to meet anyone's gaze. Instead, she looked at her paper. The pencil lines were thick and dark, and the dainty curlicues had grown into towering waves.

'We agreed this last time,' Gail said. 'It's in the minutes. The proceeds will be split fifty-fifty.'

Rachel noted Gail's relaxed yet authoritative posture, the kindness in her eyes. Am I kidding myself, she thought, imagining I can do this? She was good at the intellectual stuff, but the patience needed to negotiate these petty personality clashes was beyond her. Putting on a dog collar couldn't change that, and she wasn't sure the training was doing anything to improve her people skills. But then, Gail had been a vicar for over thirty years. She'd had a long time to get good at it. Maybe Thelma's 'got issues', Rachel thought now, as some of her colleagues would have said about their students, and this quarrelling is a displacement activity.

'I know it was agreed,' Thelma said. 'But could someone explain why?'

Martin, next to Rachel, exhaled sharply. 'The lifeboat group approached me,' he said, with exaggerated patience, 'to see if our band could play for their summer fundraiser, and then it turned out the venue was double-booked, and it was agreed to hold the concert here and split the proceeds between both worthy causes.'

Gail held up her hand. 'Thank you, Martin. As I said, it's settled. And of course, Thelma, we'd be most grateful if we could leave the refreshments in your expert hands as usual. Savoury nibbles, I think we said.'

'I always did scones when we had the Saffron Singers,'

Thelma said. 'With cream.'

Rachel drew a hard line across the page under Any Other Business. And back again. Twenty past four. They should have finished half an hour ago. Even if she left now, she'd be late. She fished her phone from the bag by her feet. The relative merits of savoury nibbles and cream teas were batted back and forth around her.

'Sorry,' Rachel murmured. 'Sorting out Hannah.'

No one took any notice.

Christopher agreed to collect Hannah. 'No problem,' he said. No one at his school stayed late on a Friday.

'I'll do a quick shop and be home in time to cook,' Rachel told him. 'We can all eat together.' She ended the call, let out a long breath, and gave her attention back to the room.

'I'm sure there's someone else who'd be perfectly capable of masterminding a savoury buffet,' Thelma said. 'It doesn't have to be me.'

'Okay.' Martin's voice took on a brisk jollity. Rachel couldn't believe he was calling Thelma's bluff. 'I'll ask Mick and Louise. They do most of the RNLI catering. They'll be glad to step in if it's too much for you, Thelma. They always do a grand spread.'

'Well, I don't think—' Thelma began.

'Thank you.' Gail let him get away with it. 'Please do ask them. Now, it's nearly half past four. Any other business? No? Let's say the Grace.'

Thelma caught up with Rachel at the lych gate. It was almost dark, and the wind gusted round them. Rachel shrugged herself further into the collar of her coat and headed across the lane towards her car. Her feet were like ice blocks. Her hand was on the door handle when Thelma said, 'It's such a shame about the Saffron Singers, isn't it? Disbanding. People came from all over Norfolk.'

Would it be kind to mention the reputation of Thelma's delicious scones, or would it add fuel to her fire? Before she could decide, Thelma said, 'Still, it's just as well, I suppose, in the circumstances.'

Pastoral care, Rachel thought. People skills. No excuse, now I'm not rushing off for Hannah. She let go of the handle, touched Thelma's arm. 'Is everything all right?'

Thelma burst into tears.

It was four years since Rachel had heard the first whispers. Not a call, then. It was too quiet, too easy to ignore or misinterpret. There were flashes of a desire to study theology, to read more, to write, to explore ways of making church more relevant in today's culture. As an RE teacher, she had deep philosophical and theological discussions with her students, and when one of them asked her why she wasn't a priest, the question wouldn't go away. A few months later, the parent and baby choir she attended with Hannah was rehearsing 'Feed The Birds', from *Mary Poppins*. She sang the words, over and over, pictured the scene from the film, and then she made the connection with what Jesus had said to Peter in the Gospel. Feed my lambs. The whisper became a call.

She argued against it. How could she feed his lambs? She wouldn't have the patience, she was too rebellious, she had the family to think about, and she already had a job she loved. There was that dark time after Hannah was born. Surely that disqualified her. And deep down, though she hardly dared admit it, lurked another, deeper fear. Sometimes, when she stared up at the night sky and imagined the size of the universe, or when she remembered the sound of her mother's last breaths, she felt she was on the edge, a step away from losing all certainty. What if she became a priest, and her faith deserted her?

'But that's what faith is,' Gail told her. 'Carrying on in spite of the uncertainty. Show me a priest who's never had doubts.'

'It's not exactly doubts,' Rachel said. 'It's not about God, or his love, or his power. I know he's there. I've seen him answer prayers, change people's lives – he changed mine, even. I do believe in all of that. But this faith – it came to me – I didn't go looking for it. What if one day I wake up, and it's just…gone?'

'Look,' Gail said. 'To be honest, I'd be more worried if you felt completely confident, sure of yourself. A little bit of self-doubt will keep you grounded. It's not a reason to turn your back on this before you've given it a chance. Give it time. Reflect. Pray.'

Rachel couldn't imagine Gail suffering from self-doubt. From her sleek grey bob to her Skechers boots, she radiated confidence, but she inspired it too. You got the feeling she knew what she was talking about, was comfortable with who she was, and she had a way of seeing beyond any problem. Rachel knew she couldn't – and didn't have to – become another Gail, but she longed to share her certainty, her steadiness, her solidity. She spent hours in prayer, staying up all night sometimes. She talked to Christopher too, and even to her friend Izzy, who didn't believe in God, and two years later, after much exploring and examining, she was accepted as an ordinand.

Perhaps, she thought now, inviting the weeping Thelma to sit in her car, out of the wind, she'd been right to question the call, should have questioned it more. Sometimes she wondered why they had accepted her.

She hadn't imagined they would still be sitting in the car half an hour later. She'd been right about the issues. Family issues, as it turned out – a daughter-in-law who refused to let Thelma see her grandson. 'Don't grandparents have any rights?' she wailed. 'I feel like I've lost him. He'll grow up not knowing who I am.'

Rachel listened and made understanding noises and talked about faith and prayer and the loving arms of Jesus – concepts she believed in with all her heart – and yet somehow the words sounded hollow. Eventually Thelma blew her nose and said thank you for listening; it's really helped. So she must have done something right.

In Tesco, Rachel grabbed a trolley, rummaging in her memory for that mental list. Pasta, cheese, cereal. What else? She reached the bread aisle. Was bread on her list? She threw a sliced white into the trolley. Bananas. She'd forgotten the bananas. Better get some grapes too, and a jar of sauce. If she fiddled about with tomatoes and made one from scratch, it wouldn't be ready till after Hannah's bed time. Chocolate mousses would do for pudding. She dashed to the checkout and back to the car.

Leaves swirled around the little car park behind the store. Trees swayed, and as she pulled away it started to rain – great, fat, heavy drops. There were sandbags outside some of the shops, and even one or two of those proper floodgates. At the bottom of the high street a sheet of cardboard blew across the road and for a terrifying moment clung to the windscreen. Rachel slammed on the brakes but the wind caught it up again and she drove home slowly with a hammering heart.

Crow's Nest

They had moved to Holthorpe seven and a half years ago, on a wet day in July. It was the summer before Jamie started school, the year before Hannah was born. When the removal van had gone, the rain stopped and the sun broke through. Rachel was making up the beds when the light changed. She dropped the sheets and ran downstairs. She found Christopher in the kitchen, unpacking baking tins and saucepans. Jamie sat in a square of sunlight by the back door, parking his toy cars in rows against the step.

'Let's go to the beach,' she said.

Outside, wisps of cloud criss-crossed a blue-washed sky. Steam rose from the pavements. The tide was out, and the wet sand glistened. On the horizon, the wind turbines shone silver, and the water sparkled in the sunlight. After a mile or so, they passed an old pillbox, half-buried at the top of the beach. It must have been built eighty odd years ago at the beginning of the war, on top of the squat cliff, to protect the land from invaders. Rachel wondered when it had fallen victim to the fragility of this part of the coast, and whether anyone had watched as this slice of land detached itself from its moorings and slid to the shore below. How long would it be before every trace of it was swallowed up? Evidence of past landslides littered the jumbled, sloping cliff; furrows and gullies ran between steep, grass-topped banks and scattered hummocks. It looked like solid ground, but it was an illusion.

Another mile and they reached a tumbled wall of dark granite boulders stretching across the beach and into the sea. At the end stood a groyne marker, with two outspread arms, and a basket shape on the top.

Jamie pointed. 'Look! A robot!' he said. They let him take off his shoes and socks to paddle in a shallow pool. The cliff was higher here, its face almost vertical, towering over the beach, as close to a headland as there could be on this straight coastline.

Christopher took her hand. 'Happy?'

She smiled up at him and nodded. 'I feel like a different person,' she said. 'Like the me I was meant to be.'

He leaned in and kissed her on the mouth. She tasted salt.

'We'll build a room in the roof,' he said. 'With lots of glass. We'll see the sea from up there.'

'A look-out,' she said. 'A crow's nest, like on a ship.'

But you cannot always see when a storm is on the way. And when one hits, and changes your life, it is impossible to see the time before as it really was. You will always view it through the prism of that event and what it has done to you.

Holthorpe nestled in a dip in the cliffs, a bustling magnet for tourists from Easter to October, with its cafés and galleries and gift shops, and its long, award-winning beach. The last bank branch had closed years ago, the post office was a tiny counter at the back of the newsagent's and the nearest dentist was twenty miles away, but there were three care homes, as well as a hairdresser, a Tesco Metro and, much to Christopher's delight, the best bike shop in Norfolk. Rachel took to running on the beach, and she swam every week, even through the winter, joining the hardy few with their dry robes and flasks. The cold water made her feel alive in a way that nothing else did. The town was quieter in winter, but still people came – walkers and birdwatchers, fossil hunters and seal lovers. There were days, though – even bright, cloudless days – when the beach was almost empty. And over it all stretched the huge expanse of sky.

The loft room had been finished the year after they moved, in the Easter holidays. Rachel found a second-hand French chest of drawers with carved cabriole legs. She sanded it and painted it a soft grey-blue. Together, she and Christopher built the framework for the under-eaves storage. She bought a job lot of pine doors in a reclamation yard, sawed them down to fit, and painted them all in the same muted colour. A rag rug and a wicker chair came from a charity shop, and on the wall above the bed were three framed paintings by Jamie – a sailing boat, a shell and an ice-cream. She made cushion covers from old jeans and put a basket of beach stones by the window. She painted a driftwood sign and hung it on the door. *The Crow's Nest*.

'Let's not have curtains,' Christopher said. 'Let's just have the sky.'

'Romantic.' Rachel laughed. 'But how much sleep will we get in the summer?' They settled on blackout blinds of midnight blue.

On the first night they were to sleep up there, they peeped into Jamie's room, where he slept with his limbs flung out like a starfish, then crept up the new stairs like a couple of guilty conspirators, whispering and giggling, fingers on lips. They stood at the window, with their arms round each other, looking out over the lights of the little town. Clouds hung low in the sky and the strip of sea was invisible.

'Bed?' Christopher moved his hands to her hips.

Rachel let her body slide against him, felt herself begin to melt at his touch. She closed her eyes. 'Mmm. Why not?'

'I've got something to tell you,' Rachel said afterwards. She lay in the crook of his arm in the half dark of their new bedroom.

'What?' He turned to look at her.

'I knew this morning,' she said. 'I've been saving it up to tell you. I did a test.'

'What? After all this time? It's just...happened?'

'Yes.' She knew she was grinning like an idiot, and she thought she would never stop. 'We're having another baby.'

'And you let me...?'

'Let you? I wanted it. It's perfectly safe.'

'So when...how far on are you?'

'Five and a half weeks. December the tenth.'

The call came at lunchtime the next day. Christopher had taken Jamie to the playground down by the promenade, and

Rachel was in the garden, sowing a row of lettuces in the tiny raised bed she had squeezed in beside the shed. They hadn't bothered with vegetables in their dreary patch of garden in Norwich. This wasn't much bigger, but sunnier and south facing. The other house had always felt temporary – the layout was impractical and the rooms were dark – but this was a place to put down roots. A place to make a home.

It wasn't just the house – a 1920s brick semi with a bay window and a green front door. It wasn't just the sea and the sand, the sky and the cliffs. She had fallen in love with everything about Holthorpe – the crammed-in yards and lokes, the brick and flint buildings and higgledy-piggledy roofs, the tinny sound of the town hall clock, the smell of fish down by the slipway, the old men calling 'Y'orrite, bor?' across the street to each other, lifting their hands in salute. She loved the brightly painted beach huts and the fading murals on the sea wall. Moving here had felt like coming home.

She'd built a cone of bamboo canes for her climbing beans, and in a few weeks she would plant out the tomatoes from their pots on the kitchen window sill, where their warm, savoury scent promised aromatic salads for the end of summer.

She brushed soil from her fingers and ran into the kitchen, picked up her buzzing phone from the table. Her mother. Cathy.

'Hi, Mum. I was going to call you tonight. I've got some—' What was it that made her stop? A sound? A catch in her mother's breath? She gripped the phone tight. 'Mum?'

'Hello, love. I'm sorry. It's not good news.'

And so, as the baby grew inside her, she had watched her mother fade.

He must have stood there a long time, because it's dark when he finds himself at the top of the beach. The tide has already covered the mudstone. He hears voices. Silhouetted figures call to each other down by the sea defences, waving torches and poking about on the rocks. Blue lights flash up there at the end of the lane. People climb up and down the steps.

And then the fear hits. There will be shouty policemen and a prison van. He's seen it on the telly. Angry crowds with roaring mouths. 'You'll pay for this.' Holding up signs. Banging on the van. The police will ask questions and he will get in a muddle and say things he doesn't mean to say.

They will take him away from Mumma.

He crouches in the shadows at the foot of the cliff. At last, the blue lights have gone and he creeps up the steps to Wetherley End, hidden by the gorse.

Bead Things

Rachel cooked the pasta, stirred in the sauce, gathered her family round the table and flopped into a chair. Friday night. She had made it through the week.

Hannah refused to pick up her knife and fork. 'It's got meat in,' she said. 'An animal has been killed to make this.'

Rachel sighed. 'Sorry, darling. I forgot. I was in a hurry. Give me your plate and I'll pick the meat out. You can have extra cheese.'

'No. There'll be bits of meat you can't see. Like germs. I don't want it. Not any of it.'

'The cow is dead anyway,' Jamie said. 'You're not saving its life.'

'Leave her alone,' Christopher said, but it was too late. Hannah set up a loud wail, her eyes screwed up tight.

'I'll do some beans on toast,' Christopher said. 'I was on the point of doing it anyway. I didn't realise you were going to be this late.'

'Sorry,' Rachel said. 'I got waylaid by a weeping parishioner.' A wave of guilt swept over her. How could she make light of Thelma's troubles? Was this the kind of priest she was going to be?

Christopher spooned beans into a bowl, and put it in the microwave. 'Well,' he said, 'now you've got a weeping daughter to concern yourself with.' He put two slices of bread in the toaster and pushed the lever and looked across at her. Rachel could read the reproach behind his eyes.

'So, how was Friday Club?' Rachel said, when Hannah had calmed down and was tucking into her beans.

'We had marshmallows and we made bead things.'

'Bead things?'

'For praying. Where is it, Daddy?'

'Marshmallows are made of lambs' ears,' Jamie said. 'Didn't you know?'

Hannah's eyes widened and her lip wobbled.

'That's enough, mate,' Christopher said. He reached across the worktop and found a bracelet made of coloured beads threaded on to thin elastic, and put it on the table.

'He's teasing. It's not true.' Rachel picked up the bracelet. 'Oh, that's lovely. How is it for praying?'

'We had to choose colours to show what we were praying for. Mine's about my family.'

'Can I have Hannah's pasta?' Jamie asked.

'Go on then.' Rachel pushed the plate across the table. There was no fat on him. When he took his top off you could count his ribs, and his arms were like sticks.

'This green one's for Daddy,' Hannah said, 'because he likes forests and recycling. The blue one is for Jamie because his bedroom is blue. Purple is for you, Mummy, because of that perfume you smell of.'

'That's a smell, not a colour,' Jamie said.

'I know, but it starts with the same sound. Purr. Anyway, it reminds me of Mummy.'

There were two more beads on the bracelet, a yellow one and a brown one.

'This one is me because I like chocolate.'

'And the other one?' Rachel said.

'The dog.'

'The dog?'

'I'm praying for a dog. It's yellow because I'd really like a golden Labrador like Harvey. Anyway, you can wear the bracelet or keep it by your bed and then you can move your fingers along the beads like this and they remind you what to pray for.'

'Can we have pudding now?' Jamie said. 'It's not going to work – praying for a dog. You know we can't have one. That's why we take Harvey for walks.'

This time, no one could stop Hannah's meltdown. In floods of tears, she jumped off her chair, shot round the table, and beat her fists against her brother's chest. 'You can't say that! It is going to work. It is!'

Jamie grabbed her wrists, and then Hannah fell into Christopher's arms, sobbing.

Rachel snapped. 'For heaven's sake, you two. That's enough. Go to your rooms, both of you.'

'But you got chocolate mousses. I saw—'

'Enough! Go!'

Christopher took Hannah, and Jamie stomped up the stairs

after them. Rachel leaned her elbows on the table, put her head in her hands, felt tears prick against her eyelids. Why did all of life have to be a fight?

She put the shopping away, loaded the dishwasher and wiped the surfaces. All was quiet upstairs.

Christopher appeared in the doorway. 'Hannah wants to say goodnight. Jamie's apologised.'

He stood aside for her to pass and they didn't touch.

'By the way,' he said, when she was halfway up the stairs, 'there's no loo roll. Did you get some?'

'Oh, I knew there was something else.'

'I'll go now. Anything else we need?'

'Don't think so.'

But there is, she thought, as the door closed behind him. There must be something else we need. Something to make all this work. Let me know if this is the right path, she prayed silently, and oh, please, help me to be better at it.

She looked in on Jamie first. 'All right?' she said.

He nodded, without looking up from his game.

She stepped inside the door, waited till he did look up. 'Thanks for saying sorry to Hannah,' she said. 'And God always answers our prayers. Remember? Sometimes it's yes, sometimes it's no, and sometimes it's wait.'

'Yeah,' he said, and gave her a sideways grin before going back to his game.

Hannah was curled under her jungle duvet, cuddling Floppy Rabbit and Puff-Puffin.

'Here. I brought this up for you.' Rachel held out the bracelet but Hannah didn't take it, so she left it on the pillow and knelt down, stroked Hannah's cloud of hair.

'Look. We'll ask Val if we can take Harvey for an extra long time on the beach tomorrow, shall we? And then we'll get pizza and go bowling. How about that?' It was a twenty-mile round trip for bowling, but it was something they could enjoy together.

Hannah popped her thumb out of her mouth. 'And can I hold Harvey's lead? By myself?'

Rachel smiled. 'We'll see.'

Perhaps, if they had a long tramp across the beach, she and Christopher would be able to have a proper talk. Find a way to make this all work better.

'Did you tell Jamie off?'

'Now, Hannah, that's none of your business. He said sorry, didn't he?'

'Well, he's still mean. And I still hate him. I wish I hadn't put him on my prayer bracelet.'

'Hate is a very powerful word. He hurt your feelings but he said sorry. Now, forgive and forget,' Rachel said.

'What's that monstery sound? Outside. That roaring and tapping.'

'It's just the rain on the window. And the wind. It's all right.'

'I don't like it.' Hannah's voice wobbled.

'Tell you what. Let's sing that song we're doing at choir. The one about how God has the whole world in his hands. Even the wind and the rain. And you and me. It might sound a bit scary out there, but you don't need to worry about storms, or anything else. Because you're in God's hands. Safe as can be.'

Diane, the health visitor, had introduced her to the parent and baby choir. 'Singing is good for the soul,' she had said. 'It might be just what you need.' And it was. It had saved her, in those desperate weeks, and now, six years on, they both still loved it. Besides, she wouldn't have Izzy if she hadn't joined the choir.

They sang the song through twice.

'There. Now it's time to sleep. You're tucked in all nice and cosy. Snug as a bug in a rug.' She kissed her daughter, moved the bracelet further along the pillow so she didn't lie on it, and turned off the lamp.

She went upstairs and looked out at the sky. Hannah was right. The wind did sound like a monster, howling round the house, with the rain finger-tapping on the windows. She pulled the blinds down, then sat on her bed and called Izzy.

'Do you think it could have been a mistake,' she said, 'thinking I was called to be a priest?'

'Why? What's happened?'

'Clash of priorities.'

'That happens to all of us. It's because everyone is more than one thing.'

'What do you mean?'

'We all have more than one role. You know. You're a mother, a daughter, a wife, a sister, a trainee vicar, a friend. There are bound to be tensions.'

'But there's more to it with being ordained. It won't be just a role. It's deeper than that.'

Christopher saw her calling as a choice, but it wasn't – not really. He had supported her in the way he would have done if she'd gone for a deputy headship, or enrolled on a post-graduate course. But it wasn't the same. It wasn't a job. Being ordained changed who you were. She found it easier to talk about this with Izzy – someone outside the church, who didn't even believe in God. Izzy took her as she was – beliefs, doubts, the whole package. But she wasn't afraid to challenge, and was unshockable – an essential requirement, she said, for her job as welfare officer at Jamie's school.

They'd met at choir when Hannah and Lenny, Izzy's son, were a few months old. Rachel had thrust Hannah into Izzy's arms one afternoon in the Scout Hut, in the middle of 'Top Of The World'. 'Here. I can't look after her any more. I can't keep her.' She had run all the way home in tears to find that Christopher had called Janet, his mother, to come and take charge.

That was Janet's speciality – taking charge. A small, energetic woman, all sharp angles and neat lines, she had been widowed young and had adopted a busy capableness as her way of coping with everything life threw at her. She had clear-cut opinions on how things should be done, and was not shy about sharing them.

'She's just here till you get better,' Christopher said, and went to retrieve the baby.

Better? What did he mean? Better at being a mother?

'But,' Izzy said now, 'being a priest won't stop you being all those other things.'

'No.'

'Did you have a row?'

'Not really.'

'Come over. I've got ice cream and two spoons.'

Rachel imagined the two of them in Izzy's tiny living room with a tub of Ben and Jerry's cookie dough – it was never any other kind. Rachel would curl up on the threadbare sofa and Izzy would sit cross-legged on the rug in one of her hand-knitted creations, her wild hair tied up in a bright strip of cotton.

'Can't,' Rachel said. 'Christopher's gone shopping. Anyway, it's a bit crazy out there. I might get blown away.'

'Tomorrow then. After the kids have gone to bed.'

She'd have sorted everything out by then. But it would be a good end to the day. Something to look forward to.

'Okay. Thanks, Iz.'

The wind woke her in the night. A bluish light filled the Crow's Nest, and she was alone in the bed. Christopher was standing by the window, and the blinds were up.

'Christopher?'

'Come and look,' he said. 'It's wild.'

She joined him and they stood in their glass nest while outside, clouds boiled up and rolled across the sky. The wind roared and rain lashed against the window.

She stood close to him, their arms touching. 'I wish this afternoon had gone differently,' she said. 'Sometimes I don't know how to get the right balance.'

'We're both responsible for finding a balance. Not just you. Sorry I made you feel bad.'

'Oh, I do love you,' she said, and then paused. 'Most of the time.'

'Imagine,' he said, 'being in a crow's nest on a ship, seeing a storm blowing in when no one else knew it was coming. They used to send people up there as a punishment sometimes.'

'I was driving through town today,' Rachel said, 'and a piece of cardboard stuck to my windscreen. Just for a moment. It was terrifying. Not being able to see.'

When they went back to bed, they left the blinds open and their hands moved over one another's skin, and when his mouth found hers, she thought, *it will be all right*. The light turned their bodies silver, and the howling of the wind and the beating of the rain drowned any sounds they made.

Sea Urchin

'Galvanised clout nails. Fifteen-millimetre.' Adam repeated the words each time he passed a street lamp. After he'd got the nails, he would go down to Molly's kiosk for the pasties, then walk home along the beach. He might be able to get on the reef.

What he really wanted was a sea urchin. Hundreds of living things made their home in the gullies and arches of chalk below the surface, but sometimes, at low tide, the reef's edge was exposed along the beach, and it was here that Adam loved to search for the fossilised remains of long-dead inhabitants of the ocean – bullet-shaped devil's fingers, neatly ridged lampshells and sea urchins like hearts, imprinted with a perfect, five-pointed star.

He stopped outside the fossil shop. 'Echinoid.' He rolled his tongue around the sounds. That was the proper name for a sea-urchin. There were two in the window, the size of pound coins. Four ninety-nine each. He would never pay for a fossil that someone else had found. He knew he'd find one. Sooner or later.

Next to the urchins, an ammonite sparkled in the pale, winter light. It was made of iron pyrites, which turned from black to gold when you polished it, like magic. Its other name was fool's gold. It made him think of those fairy tales where someone sets off to seek their fortune and is granted three wishes in return for a good deed. Adam had three ammonites on his shelf, but he'd never found a golden one. He knew he'd find something good today, though. It felt like bubbles inside him. As long as Danny Goodrum wasn't about. Adam chased the fear away before it burst the bubbles, and pushed open the door of the hardware shop.

It was an old-fashioned shop with nails and screws and hooks loose in tubs, and spools of wire and string that could be cut to any length you wanted. Mr Bright stood behind the counter in his brown apron.

'Galvanised clout nails, please,' Adam said. 'Fifteen-millimetre.'

'What's she up to now?' Mr Bright scooped nails into a bag. 'How many?'

'Fixing the shed roof. Before Erik gets here.'

'That'll be plenty, then.' Mr Bright put an elastic band round the bag. 'Erik?' He frowned and then his face cleared. 'Oh, you mean Storm Erik.'

'Yes, I do. Mumma doesn't want him to rip the felt off the shed roof so she checked for rusty nails and some of them were rusty and when she looked in the tin she didn't have enough fifteen-millimetre galvanised clout nails and she asked me to get some more so she could carry on with her jobs in the garden and I'm getting pasties too so she doesn't have to cook anything for our tea.'

'Blimey! Don't forget to breathe, mate.'

'Thank you. I won't.' Adam took the bag and paid. If I did forget, he thought, I'd die. Anyway, you don't have to think about breathing. It's automatic. Perhaps Mr Bright didn't know that. Or maybe he was making a joke. Adam smiled as he turned to leave, just in case. He could try this joke on Molly. He liked it when she laughed. Her eyes crinkled and the sound made him think of that little waterfall at the dip in the cliff.

The wind was stronger now, and there were little dots of rain in the air. Rubbish blew in spirals in the lokes, and everyone was walking with their shoulders hunched and their heads down. Not that there were many people about. Adam liked it in the winter, when the town belonged to people who lived there, and the pavements weren't crowded with visitors. There were sandbags outside some of the shops. Adam glanced into the amusement arcade, hoping Danny might be there, because then the way to Molly's and the beach would be clear, but the place was empty.

If I do see him, Adam thought, I'll look straight ahead and keep going even if he shouts at me and I'll go and tell Molly my breathing joke and I'll get beef and onion pasties and maybe even butterscotch buns if there's enough money and then I'll go to the beach and find my treasures. His fist tightened round the bag of nails in his pocket. What if Danny was at the playground with his mates and what if they shouted even ruder words than the ones Mumma used? His heart hammered, and sweat prickled his back.

'Ignore them,' Mumma would say. She'd been saying it ever

since the first time Danny called him a moron at school. The names got worse and now it was four years since they'd left school and Adam had mostly stopped telling Mumma about it because she always said the same thing. It wasn't that she didn't care. She just didn't understand that he wasn't like her. Ignoring wasn't a thing he could turn on or off, like she could. If she didn't want to think about a thing, she switched it off.

Danny worked for his uncle who was some kind of handyman, but he still had lots of time to hang around the town looking for trouble. Adam had been to college for a bit and then started an apprenticeship in hospitality. He'd enjoyed working in the café until the incident with the knives when Mark turned the kitchen radio up to full volume. He didn't go back after that. Mumma said she'd always look after him, so what was the point of him being educated till he was eighteen. Anyway, she said she could always inform any busybody officials that she was training him as a gardener in the family business. And she did take him with her to clients quite often, especially if there was heavy work like laying a path, or lots of digging, but no one ever checked and now that he was twenty, it didn't matter anyway. That's what Mumma said.

His real job, though, was being a fossil hunter.

In spite of the cold wind, two children were playing on the slide – a big girl and a smaller boy – and a man was sitting on a bench smoking and looking at his phone. Adam stopped and watched. The big girl was helping the boy to climb up the steps, going up behind him to make sure he didn't fall, but what if he did fall and she couldn't save him? She wasn't much bigger than he was.

The man looked up from his phone. 'Time to go, kids,' he called.

It was only after they'd gone that Adam spotted Danny, sitting on a picnic table by the boating lake, swinging his legs. He was alone, but Adam's heart still jumped. Molly's kiosk was on the other side of the playground, on the sea front. Adam would have to go right past Danny to get there.

'Oi, Brain-dead, how's it going?' Danny shouted.

Adam decided not to answer this. Mumma said it was okay not to answer people if you didn't want to. It was part of the ignoring strategy. But not answering didn't make the horrible words vanish. They were still there, in your head, like bruises and scratches on the inside of you. Miss Finlay, one of his teaching assistants at primary school, had talked about unkind words hurting you on the inside. Adam had seen her being hurt on the outside once. A boy she was helping had scratched her arm with a pair of scissors and there had been lots of blood but when she came back to school she still helped the boy and smiled at him the same way. There must have been consequences though. There were always consequences. If you did something wrong, you had to make amends. That's what Mumma said.

A ball with no air left in it was floating on the lake. There were dead leaves and sticks and rubbish on the water too, and the wind was whipping it up into little waves. Danny jumped up and stood on the table.

'I said, how's it going? You deaf as well as brain-dead?' he shouted. Then he pointed at the ball. 'Get my ball for me, will you?'

I'm not brain-dead, Adam said inside his head. If I was, I wouldn't be standing here. But he didn't want to speak to Danny out loud. He didn't want to get the ball either. It was right in the middle, too far to reach from the edge. Probably wasn't Danny's anyway.

He wished he was already on the beach, but his legs wouldn't move. He gripped the nails more tightly until they dug into his palm. Molly's wasn't far. He couldn't smell the pasties, though. Maybe she hadn't opened today. She sometimes didn't in the winter, especially if the weather was bad. Danny jumped off the table and came towards him.

Adam turned and ran into Cobbler's Yard, through the loke at the end, down the steps and across the beach to the water's edge, where he stood, breathing hard, bending forward, his hands on his knees. He didn't look back.

When he'd got his breath again, he walked along the sand, scanning the groups of pebbles, hoping Danny hadn't followed him. By the time he felt brave enough to think about going back to Molly's, he realised it was too late. She'd be shut. It would be dark soon, and the mist in the air had turned to proper rain, slanting in from the east. Waves crashed, but the edge of the reef was still exposed.

He picked up a piece of green glass, worn smooth like a pebble, and put it in his pocket. Then, all at once, there it was, lying on the sand by his foot. Exactly what he'd been hoping for. A stone with a delicate star shape imprinted on the surface. A fossil sea urchin. He gasped, bent down and picked it up, ran his fingers over the pattern. It was like a flower, with five fine, pointed petals. He held it in his palm, feeling its weight. It was beautiful. There were no broken bits, and the stone was a perfect heart.

'Yeah!' He punched the air and ran round in circles. A wave soaked his feet, but he didn't care. 'I knew I'd find one. I knew!'

He marched on towards home, leaning into the wind, with a satisfied warmth in his middle. He never got tired of this walk and he didn't care about the weather. After another twenty minutes it was too dark to look for any more treasures. He made his way diagonally across the beach and then trudged over the bank of stones towards the steps that led up to Wetherley End. Mumma would be cross about the pasties, but it didn't matter. He had found his sea urchin.

'Oi! Moron!'

Adam's throat closed. He held his breath, didn't dare turn. It was hard to keep your balance on these great cobbles – impossible to move quickly. He heard the stones shifting under Danny's feet.

'Must be worth a lot, your fossil collection. What was it you found today? I heard you with your crazy shouting, watched your little happy dance.'

Run. Not too fast. Don't fall over. Up to the steps. Hang on to the rail. Don't let him follow me up here. Don't let him come up. Oh, Mumma, please.

'Bet that fossil shop in town would take them. What d'you think? Worth a try?'

Now he did turn, stood on the steps, flashing with fury. 'You keep your hands off my fossils, d'you hear? Now get lost, bloody Danny Goodrum.' He used the word Mumma would have used and felt the bravest and most terrified he had ever felt. He pounded up the rest of the steps, his heart racing.

Behind him, on the beach, Danny Goodrum laughed.

Winterbloom

Mary stood on the step ladder at the side of the shed and eased the claw of the hammer under the nail head. She yanked out the rusty nail, hoping it wouldn't rip the felt. She ought to tear the old felt off and start again. But that was a job for several dry days in a row. Now, all she could do was to get these new nails banged in so the wind didn't sneak under the loose edge and rip the whole thing off, leaving the bare wood exposed to this foul weather.

She dropped the nail into a jar, took a new one from the few that rolled around in the bottom of a tin, and hammered it in. The next one wasn't too bad, though it was hard to be sure when you couldn't get anything in focus. Then two more that had to be replaced. She climbed down and moved the ladder along, heaved herself back up, and examined the next few nails, trying to ignore the ache in her head from all this eye work. That was how she thought of it now. Eye work. Making sure the thing she wanted to look at was outside the blurry patch in the middle of her vision. Not-focusing in order to focus. No wonder it gave her a headache. Best not to think about it. Maybe she'd pick up some glasses next time she was in town.

'Why are you looking at me sideways?' Adam had said this morning, when she had asked him to buy more nails.

'I'm not.' She stopped trying to focus on his face. After all, every inch of it, every curve and line was etched within her. He was hers, and always would be, whether or not she could see his ear-to-ear smile and his untamed mop of hair. Instead, she looked towards the window, the square of light, the strings of shells that hung there, and the spidery yellow fronds of the witch hazel in the coffee jar on the window sill. 'Did you hear me? Fifteen-millimetre galvanised clout nails. Got that?'

'Yes, Mumma.'

'And get some pasties so I don't have to cook. I've got a lot to do out there before this bloody storm comes.'

And she had done most of it. She had dragged the driftwood bench to her new rock and shingle garden, a couple of metres from the cliff edge. Perfect view of the sea. She had put the grasses in – stipa and blue fescue. The rest of the planting would come in the spring – sea holly and tree lupin. Yellow-horned poppy, maybe, and fleabane. During the week she'd made an inventory of her seed packets and cuttings, and a shopping list, for herself and for her clients. She had cleaned the pots and tools and labels, and reorganised the storage inside the shed. It was tidier than the inside of the house, with its shelves and pegboard and hooks and bins, its drawers and racks and tins and jars. She should have done more outside work really, because of this storm. Erik. Ridiculous, giving names to storms.

She hammered in the last nail. Adam should be back soon, with the new ones. She'd only done one side and the wind was getting stronger, whipping her hair into her eyes, and swishing through the grasses. The tamarisk branches whispered behind her driftwood bench. Foul weather it may be, but she wouldn't want to be anywhere else. This was her place – Wetherley End, where the ocean met the land. A mile and a half to the west, Holthorpe lay in a dip in the coastline, out of sight from here. To the east, the cliffs climbed to their highest point – the Bluff, as everyone called it, towering over the sea defences below – huge imported granite blocks. She stood on the ladder, looking north over the ridge of the shed roof. You didn't need eye work for this. There was the sky and the sea, the turbines on the horizon, sometimes clear and shining, sometimes ghostly figures or not there at all, the strip of sand with its ever-changing dips and pools, the shifting banks of pebbles, and the knobbly chalk reefs. She would never get tired of it. It was what had drawn her to the house when she had been thrown from the wreck of something she had thought would last a lifetime. Perversely, perhaps, she felt anchored here, where earth and water met. And it was for Adam that she needed an anchor.

It wasn't long after he started school that she noticed the whispers at the school gates, watched how the other parents steered their children away. She thought back to the time when one of the mums had approached her, smiling, suggesting a coffee, and she had been on the point of softening when the question came – friendly, bright, sympathetic. 'He's such a sweetie – Adam. What's wrong with him, exactly?' Even one of the school staff had used the word *problems*, before covering up with a stammering apology and talking about *needs* instead.

Nothing is wrong with him, she wanted to say. He doesn't have problems. He has this wonderful ability to see the world and to relate to it in a way that you and I don't. It's not something that needs fixing and it's only part of who he is. She did say it, a few times, but in the end found it easier to keep her distance, and it wasn't hard to persuade Adam to do the same.

She resisted assessments and labels for as long as she could. 'No point,' she said. 'I'm perfectly capable of giving him the tools he'll need to get through life in one piece, to defend himself.' She wanted to protect him from making the mistakes she had made. In the end, though, Miss Finlay convinced her that Adam would benefit from some help in school, and she had to admit he did seem to enjoy working with her.

If the view had drawn her here, the land across the lane had clinched the deal. The house, a ramshackle, single-storey affair, and its long back garden, stood between Wetherley Lane and the cliff edge. On the landward side of the lane, opposite the front of the bungalow, stood a paddock of just over an acre. Bit by bit, she transformed it into a nursery for her gardening business. At that time, beyond the garden fence was the coast path and four or five metres more clifftop. Wetherley Lane had curved down all the way to a small car park, with a path from there sloping down to the beach. A few years ago, the car park had been closed for good, and last autumn a ferocious storm had blown in from the north, with record-breaking winds, torrential rain and a tidal surge. The power had failed, and, while the house rattled around them, Adam sat in the flickering candlelight, and Mary paced from room to room, a knot of helpless dread tightening inside her. In the morning, they found that the lane ended in a sheer drop. A huge landslide had buried what was left of the car park. But Wetherley End and its garden had escaped.

Now there was a barrier at the end of the lane, and a huge danger sign. All the other residents of Wetherley Lane had gone, tempted by some crackpot council scheme, their houses demolished and the remains of the gardens left to run wild. She and Adam were the last ones here and they weren't going anywhere.

There were things that could be done. She knew that. Before her life had changed, before Adam, before she came to Wetherley End, Mary had worked in coastal engineering. She knew the forces at play. She had seen communities threatened, livelihoods endangered. She and her colleagues had met with marine ecologists and councils and investors. Risks and benefits were balanced, stakeholders consulted, schemes drawn up. Decisions trickled through the web of proposals and arguments and bureaucracy. Huge ships moved rock armour from Scotland and Scandinavia. Enormous dredgers pumped millions of cubic metres of sand on to beaches. Eco-warriors called for planting programmes to stabilise fragile slopes, for natural solutions, for soft engineering.

But along this stretch, where she had come to roost, it was all about managed retreat. In other words, letting it happen. Letting the sea win.

'Over my dead body,' she said to herself.

She put the hammer and the empty tin in her tool belt and climbed down the ladder, holding the jar of rusty nails. She would check the weather strip on the shed door while she waited for Adam. The mice had been at the hinge section. She peeled off what was left and cleaned the jamb. She should have asked him to get another mouse trap while he was at Bright's. She stuck the new length of tape down and peeled off the paper, then closed the door. The floorboard just inside the door rocked under her feet. Hopefully, not too much of it was rotten. She stuck some weather strip round the window frame. She'd intended to make a shutter this year, but the bench had obsessed her.

It was one of the best things she'd ever made. She'd trawled the beach day after day, waiting for the sea to cast up its treasures – beautiful pieces, worn smooth and bleached, some of them lumber and some simply bits of trees, twisted into the most wonderful shapes. She had challenged herself to use proper peg joints so it had taken her weeks to finish. But it was more comfortable than all the indoor chairs, and certainly a thing of beauty.

She closed the shed door behind her and trudged round to the bench. She loved watching the light fade in the sky. She sat with her legs stretched out, rotated her aching ankles. There, that was better. No point giving houseroom to aches and pains. Where had Adam got to? They had to get this roof secure.

It began to rain, thin, sharp needles carried on the wind. As Mary sat, breathing in the salt air, letting the rain sting her face, gazing out to sea, a ship loomed out of the murky grey, a storybook ship, in full sail, floating, not in the sea, but in the air. It was magnificent. She stared, hardly daring to breathe, knowing it wasn't real, but able to see ropes, flags, tiny figures on the deck, and those huge, billowing, wind-filled sails.

If I move, if I breathe, if I blink, Mary thought, it will vanish.

For a second or two, she hung on to it, and then she blinked.

The ship was gone.

This was not the first time she had seen things that weren't there. Grids and patterns appeared from nowhere, and one morning a pair of blue clockwork beetles had scuttled under the stove. But there was no point paying any attention to it. She would be fine. Absolutely fine.

Still no sign of Adam. She got up and went back to the house. By the door of the lean-to, the witch hazel offered her the most exquisite scent, a sweet, spicy fragrance, with a hint of citrus. She snapped off a sprig, with its wispy yellow flowers blooming on the bare, leafless wood.

'Winterbloom,' the nurseryman had told her when she bought it not long after Adam was born. 'That's its other name. Special powers, some people say. It's supposed to give protection.'

Load of rubbish, of course. You had to build your own protection, in ever-hardening layers, around you. Keep people at arm's length.

Even without special powers, the witch hazel flowers were pretty and she liked the scent. She took the sprig back to the shed and went inside, cut a length of twine and tied the twig to the door handle. Then she went back up the path, and the sweet smell went with her into the house.

Footprints

Water dripped down Adam's neck and the rain stung his skin. Danny had gone away, but what if he was planning his next move?

Mumma came in from the garden, stamping her feet on the mat, and bringing with her a sweet, spicy smell. Her hair hung in tails about her face.

'About time,' she said. 'Have you got the nails? It's already blowing a gale out there. Don't take that coat off. Come and hold the torch. Otherwise I'll be tacking my thumbs to the roof. Put the pasties in the oven first.'

'I didn't get the pasties but I got these.'

Adam found the bag of nails and handed it over. He wished he could tell her about Danny following him all the way from Holthorpe, but her crossness had wriggled under her skin and made her hard and sharp.

'No pasties? For heaven's sake! We were going to have them for tea. Now come on out and bring that torch.'

Adam followed her out. Wild rain lashed against him. The door banged and then swung open. He grabbed it and yanked it shut. The wind whistled through the bushes and grass, whipping them into a mad dance. The felt on the shed roof slapped against the wood underneath.

While Mumma hammered the nails in, Adam thought about Danny creeping up behind him and threatening to sell his fossils. What if he broke into the house, stole the treasures and took them to the shop? What could Adam do? He'd have to hide them. But where?

'Last one.' Mumma banged in the nail and huffed down the ladder. 'Can you get the ladder back in the shed? I want to get the pots indoors.' She picked up a heavy pot with a big, spiky plant in it, and carried it up to the house.

Adam hung the ladder on its pegs on the back wall. In the doorway, the floor sank under his foot. He shifted his weight. A loose floorboard. Like the one under that dip in the carpet in the corner of his bedroom.

Yes. That was the perfect place for his fossils. He would hide them under the floor. Danny Goodrum would never find them there, even if he did break in. He grabbed the torch and the hammer on his way out, locked the shed and ran back to the house.

'Come and help with these last ones,' Mumma said. 'I'll have to leave the agapanthus. It's too heavy even for the two of us. And never mind about the pasties. We'll go and get chips later.'

Once the pots were inside, Adam left Mumma in the kitchen rubbing her hair dry with a towel, hurried into his bedroom and put all his treasures in a shoebox. He lifted the edge of the carpet and hooked the claw of the hammer under the nail in the middle of the loose board, yanked it out. As he levered the board out, his finger scraped on a splintered piece of wood. 'Shit!' He dropped the board and put his finger in his mouth, tasted blood.

When the board was removed, he shone the torch into the hole. Nothing but dust. He had to turn the shoe box on its side to get it into the gap. Then he balanced the board back in place without replacing the nail. He folded the corner of the carpet back down. His finger was still bleeding, so he went into the bathroom and ran it under the cold tap, then pressed a towel against the cut while he found a plaster.

He went with her in the car to get the chips. Rain beat down. The top of the lane was flooded, and they drove through at walking pace. In town, rubbish and leaves and cardboard boxes were blowing round the streets. Back at home, they hung their wet things by the stove, and ate their chips in front of the telly. Afterwards, he leaned against Mumma on the sofa. She felt soft again now. She took his hand.

'What have you done to your finger?' She put it to her lips and kissed it where the plaster was. 'Magic kiss,' she said. 'My wounded soldier.'

When Adam was in his pyjamas, he turned out his light, knelt on his bed and looked out of the window. It had been windy for two days, and the rain had hardly stopped, but Mumma said it wasn't Erik it was just his advance guard and when the real thing hit them they'd know about it. The window rattled and the wind howled. Ragged clouds raced across the sky. Waves crashed and clattered back through the stones.

Storms like this uncovered all sorts of treasures. It was

called scouring. He'd read about it in one of his fossil books. What might he find tomorrow? Whatever it was he'd have to hide it under the floor. Because of stupid Danny Goodrum. The excitement faded and he closed the curtains and got into bed.

A clattering sound woke him. Then a thud. He sat up and switched on the lamp. His pencil jar was rolling on the carpet, the coloured pencils scattered. It must be Erik, shaking the house like a toy. He pulled the curtain aside and looked out of the window. Rain lashed against the glass, and all he could see was the reflection of his room. He turned the lamp off.

Sheets of rain slanted across the garden, hammering into the grass, bouncing off the paving stones, gusting with the wind. And oh! There was Mumma, standing at the cliff's edge. Her coat flapped like wings and her hair whipped about her head. Adam held his breath. She lifted her arms and shook her fists at the sky, and he saw her shoulders lift and her body lean. Her back was to him, and the wind drowned her voice, but he knew that her roar was like the roar of a tiger.

'Mumma,' Adam whispered, his face almost touching the glass, his fingers fluttering against it. 'Don't stand there. You'll fall. Come back inside. Oh, Mumma, please.'

Should he go, pull her back from the edge? Did she think she could stop the storm? He got off the bed, put on his coat and shoes, went through the lean-to and opened the door. Rain pelted into his face, stinging his cheeks. The wind tugged at him, sucking him into its grasp. He caught hold of the door frame, hung on, scrunched his face against the lashing weather.

'Mumma,' he called. 'Mumma, come inside!' But his voice vanished into the sky. He let go of the door, leaned into the wind and started towards her.

She didn't look at him, but she let her fists drop and gripped his arm. Her fingers dug in through his sleeve. He looked down. Waves crashed on the beach, and the wind whipped up huge clouds of spray.

By the time they went inside, the sky had lightened to a pale grey, streaked with yellow and pink. Adam went back to bed, but he didn't sleep. He could hear Mumma moving about in the kitchen and then he heard the telly. When he eventually joined her in the living room, she was drinking coffee. *Homes Under the Hammer* was on, but he could tell she wasn't watching it.

By lunch time the rain had eased. Mumma said she wasn't hungry, so he helped himself to a crusty bread roll, with a packet of crisps and a jam tart. Then he swooshed the crumbs off the table and looked at the clock. It would be low tide in an hour or two. Time to go and see what treasures he could find.

He climbed down the steps and turned towards the Bluff and the jumble of rock armour below it. The wind was still gusting, but with longer lulls in between, and the sky was clearing, allowing a pale sun to shine through. At the water's edge, he scanned the clusters of pebbles. He was almost at the rock armour when he spotted the unmistakeable black triangle of a shark's tooth. He picked it up, stared at it in the palm of his hand before putting it in his pocket. He'd forgotten to bring plastic bags. He climbed over the sea defences. It was a while since he had searched on the other side.

He scrambled down and stopped and stared. He couldn't believe it. What was normally a small patch of mudstone had become enormous, stretching away from him, flat and glistening, its covering of sand washed away by the tide.

He walked across it, and an unexpected pattern caught his attention – brighter patches reflecting in the sun. They were little puddles, dotted across the surface, twenty or thirty of them. He stooped to look more closely, ran his fingers round one of the outlines.

He thrust his hand in his pocket for his phone, and then remembered he'd forgotten to bring it. He'd have to come back to take photos, but he couldn't leave it too long, or the tide would have covered them again.

His mind raced. Was it...? Could it be...? He had read about fossils of dinosaur footprints. Huge dents in the rock. But these were the size and shape of human feet. Was it possible? Could real people from hundreds of thousands of years ago have walked here and made these prints? Some of them were so small a child must have made them.

And no one but him knew they were here.

There's an ambulance and three police cars and blue lights flashing. He stands, helpless, watching. Mumma's face is covered in earth and blood and rain. Her eyes are shut. They're putting a blanket on her and he hears them say hospital.

Her eyes flicker open as they lift her into the ambulance.

'I couldn't reach it,' she whispers.

And he knows that she tried to save him.

A policeman tells him to get into the car, puts a hand on his head.

They are taking him away.

Holy Stone

Navigating those months of waiting, anticipating Hannah's birth and her mother's death, had sapped Rachel's strength. The days unfolded and she ricocheted between hope and dread.

'Don't think of it as the end, love,' Cathy said. 'It's the same as what's happening to this little one.' She put her hand on her daughter's growing bump. 'Getting ready to leave the only world you've ever known, to be born into a new one. One that will be beyond anything you could ever have dreamed of.'

'Oh, Mum.' Rachel took hold of Cathy's thin hand. 'It's hard to see it like that. I know it's true. I do. But I…I can't bear it that you're going.'

Faith had come to Rachel and Cathy together, when Rachel was fifteen and her father, Ed, had finally left, after drinking his way through the previous five years. The mother of one of Rachel's schoolfriends supported Cathy through the worst times, found her a counsellor and invited them both to a series of discussion evenings at her church on the other side of Ipswich. They asked questions. They began to pray. They found answers. 'Life's beginning to shine again,' Cathy said. Tim, Rachel's older brother, was dismissive of the idea of believing such rubbish, of 'finding God,' but Cathy said, 'I didn't find God. He found me.'

For Rachel, it was more about finding someone she could trust. Someone who would never let her down. A few months after they started going to church, she was walking home from school after a drama rehearsal one December evening, when a group of boys from the year above began to jostle around her, shoving into her and laughing, making suggestive comments. She glanced around, looking for anyone who might have noticed, who might help her. A man jogged past on the other side of the road – didn't look her way. It wasn't far to her road, but to get there she had to cross the green, and even if she went round the long way, she'd be walking beside the long brick wall which surrounded the grounds of a posh hotel. No one else was about, and fear gripped her. She began to shake. What could she do? How could she get rid of them?

'I'm meeting my dad,' she said. 'He'll be here in a minute.' But her voice wobbled and she knew she hadn't convinced them. Please, God, please, she whispered in her head. Help me. Do something.

'Hey, I thought it was you.' A woman's voice. Loud, friendly, assured. Quick footsteps from behind her, drawing level. The lads fell back, left her alone.

'Hello, you.'

There were two of them, a man and a woman, in their

thirties perhaps.

'Haven't seen you for ages. How are you?'

Rachel couldn't find her voice and the shaking wouldn't stop. But the boys had gone, vanished into the December darkness.

'You looked like you needed help,' the woman said. 'Are you okay? Can we walk you home?'

Rachel always thought of them as angels sent by God.

'Just humans,' Tim said, 'looking out for other humans.'

'Humans can be angels,' Rachel said.

By the time the baby arrived, Cathy was in the hospice.

'We'd like you to choose her name,' Rachel told her when she introduced them to each other one dark December afternoon.

Cathy smiled. 'What if…' – pause for breath – '…you don't like it?'

'No problem,' Christopher said, with a gentle brightness that made Rachel want to hug him. 'Her middle name will be Catherine, so we'd just use that instead.'

Cathy closed her eyes and a shadow crossed her face. 'Hannah,' she said, when the pain had passed. 'Hannah Catherine.' She paused, concentrating on breathing. 'Thank you.' A whisper now. 'It's…an honour.'

'Oh, Mum.' Rachel lifted the baby closer, held their hands next to each other, skin to skin.

Cathy died on Christmas Eve, when Hannah was three weeks old.

And Rachel felt herself falling.

'Mummy, my bracelet's gone.'

Rachel's mouth felt thick and her lips stuck together. 'What? It's not morning yet. Go back to bed.'

'But it's gone. My prayer bracelet that I made at Friday Club.'

Hannah stood by the bed in her pyjamas, her hair standing round her head in a great cloud.

'Oh, Han, we'll look in the morning. You don't need it now.'

'I did need it. I woke up and I wanted you and I thought if I prayed I'd feel better. But it wasn't there.'

'It's probably fallen down the side of the bed. We'll find it in the morning.'

Hannah began to cry – sniffly little sobs. Christopher stirred. The wind howled round the Crow's Nest, and rain beat against the windows.

Rachel sighed, struggled out from the warmth of the duvet, and they went down the loft stairs together. Screwing up her eyes against the brightness of Hannah's lamp, Rachel knelt on the floor and felt about between the bed and the bedside table. She pulled out a damp, blue sock and Floppy Rabbit.

In the end, she moved the furniture away from the wall, and lifted the duvet and the pillow off the bed. But although she found an assortment of toys and books and clothes, the bracelet did not come to light. Once Hannah had gone back to sleep, Rachel padded back to her own bed. Her feet were freezing, so she put them on Christopher's legs, curling herself to fit against his body. But she was wide awake now, and found herself mulling over the irritations of the day. She had hoped that last night meant she and Christopher were reconciled, but she couldn't forget his comment about the weeping daughter. He had meant to wound her, but the sadness in his eyes had hurt her more. Did he think this new direction of hers had taken something away from their life rather than enriching it? They needed to talk it through. Today. On the beach. The children would be happy, they'd have the dog, and there would be the sea. The sea always made things better.

Eventually, she eased herself away from him and slid out of bed, found her thick socks and her long cardigan, and crept downstairs to make some tea.

'Can't we just go home and watch *Star Wars* instead?' Jamie rolled up his napkin and brandished it like a lightsaber, with zingy noises to match. 'No normal person would go for a walk on the beach in this weather. Or hasn't anyone noticed the water falling out of the sky?'

'There's a patch of blue up there,' Rachel said, but it was wishful thinking. The window was steamed up. Rain dripped down the glass. Everything was a blur. It had poured all morning, so they'd swapped their plans around and after choir they'd driven ten miles inland, had three games at the bowling alley, all won by Jamie, and a long, late lunch at Pizza Hut. But no time yet for a proper talk with Christopher. Cooped up indoors, under artificial light and with the heating turned up too high. She pressed her fingertips to her temples, closed her eyes for a moment. Why couldn't Christopher bounce them out of their stupor, make them laugh, get them going? She was tired of always being the one to jolly things along. But he was tapping the menu card against the table, staring at nothing, disengaged.

'What about Harvey?' Hannah said. 'He needs his walk.'

'We all do.' Rachel stood up, scooped her bag from the table. 'Val's expecting us. And the rain is supposed to stop mid-afternoon, so by the time we get back it'll be dry. I'll go and pay. Come on. Get your coats on. Zip them up. We're braving this wet stuff as far as the car. Don't forget your lightsaber, Mr Skywalker.'

'Mu-um. F'sake.' Jamie dropped the napkin into an empty glass.

'Language, Jamie, please,' Christopher said.

'What? I didn't say anything.' Jamie flung his hands in the air and marched out into the rain in front of them.

Not the best start to a fun-filled family afternoon on the beach, Rachel thought, as the door swung to behind her. Still, no one could stay grumpy for long with Harvey running round their feet, then dashing off to dig up some phantom bone from the sand. Maybe she should arrange for Hannah's prayers to be answered in the form of a little rescue dog, a border terrier, perhaps. If her theory was right, and dogs had this un-grumpifying effect, perhaps it would be worth it.

It proved true this afternoon, although the upturn in the general mood might have been as much due to the improvement in the weather as it was to the crazy yellow animal that was Harvey. By the time they came down the hill into Holthorpe, the rain had stopped and the sky had begun to clear.

Before long, the dog was lolloping across the stone-strewn sand, dashing in and out of the shallows, while Jamie and Hannah chased about, laughing and shouting and throwing Harvey's well-chewed red ball.

Slowly, they made their way east, away from the town, towards the Bluff and the sea defences. Everyone knew the cliffs were unstable. There were notices all the way along the path at the top. Half way to the Bluff they came to the pillbox buried in the beach under the cliff, its concrete roof slanting up, and its steel doors stuck fast in the shingle bank. Hannah ran to the doorway, got down on her hands and knees, but stopped short of crawling inside. Once, a year or two ago, when the spring tides came, it was completely submerged.

The beach was almost empty of people, and awash with a golden light, but the waves were still high, and the wind still wild. Out at sea, the wind turbines were emerging from the grey shroud, and a single ship was visible on the blurred line of the horizon. Turnstones scuttled among the gulls at the water's edge, and a cormorant swooped low before alighting on a rock and spreading its wings. It would be dark in a couple of hours, but for now, this was just what they needed.

Rachel put her arm through Christopher's. 'I wanted to ask you,' she said, 'how you think things are going?'

'What things?'

'For us, as a family, since I started this course.'

'Why? Isn't it what you expected?'

'I'm asking what you think.'

'I do support you, Rach. I said I would.' He squeezed his arm against hers, but his gaze was directed out to sea, away from her.

'I know, but you seemed cross yesterday when I got held up.'

'Everyone was cross. We were all tired. Hannah was ready for her tea and I didn't know whether to wait for you. And when you said that about what's-her-name crying on your shoulder, I just thought Hannah needed your shoulder more. That's all.'

'But you were there. You're her parent too. We share that job.'

'I know, and I've said I was sorry I upset you—'

'Look!' Hannah ran up to them. 'Look at this! It's got a hole in.'

It was a white stone, the size of a hen's egg, with a hole all the way through. In her other hand she held a length of frayed blue rope.

'Wow!' Rachel and Christopher said at the same time, and then laughed.

'Can you thread it on here, Mummy? See – it's like my beads that I threaded. I could make a big one with these. Can you thread it and look after it for me? I'm going to look for more holey stones.' She darted off to a line of shingle further up the beach, walked slowly along it, eyes down.

Watching her made Rachel think of the fossil hunter – Fossil Boy, Jamie had called him.

The first time she had seen him was before Hannah was born, that first summer at Holthorpe. It was a blue and white and golden day, with a fresh westerly breeze, and sunlight sparkling on the water. She and Jamie walked barefoot at the water's edge.

The boy, fifteen or sixteen, tall and skinny, wearing shorts that came to his knees, was walking on the chalk reef, where it stuck up in little islands above the rippling waves. Every now and then he would crouch down, pick something up, examine it, and either discard it or drop it into his rucksack. He was intent on his search.

Leaning against the wooden groyne, two lads watched him. They laughed, nudged each other, and then charged across the beach and pushed him. He lost his balance and splashed into the water. One of them snatched his bag, and they ran off across the sand, whooping.

Rachel's first instinct was to run to him, but she checked it. She didn't want to embarrass him. He got to his feet, came off the reef on to the sand.

'Why did they do that?' Jamie said. 'Did you see them? They pushed him in the sea.'

'Perhaps they were playing a game.' Rachel hoped it was true.

When they came nearer, she saw that he was wiping his sleeve across his face and muttering to himself. Blood dripped from his hair. There were sharp flints in among the chalk where he had fallen.

'Are you all right?' she said. 'You've hurt your head.'

He touched the blood, looked at his hand, wiped his sleeve over his face again. He sniffed back tears. 'I'm not all right but I think I will be soon. They took my bag but I know they don't really care about fossils like I do.'

'Oh, fossils! You collect them? Jamie, did you hear that?'

'I found a belemnite,' the boy told them, 'and some fish bones and bits of fossilised wood and a green stone that was really glass which is not a fossil but it's still a treasure and they were all in my bag so they're lost now.'

'Did you know them?' Rachel said. 'Those boys?'

'Yes.'

'Is your head okay? Shall I have a look…?'

'No thanks. I have a mirror at home and I'll have a look and if I need a plaster I'll put one on.' He turned and trudged away towards the sea defences.

Later, Jamie found the bag, half buried in the sand, with the fossils – the treasures – still inside, but the boy had gone. They took it home and hung it on a peg, hoping they would get the chance to give it back. The green glass was beautiful – a pale, frosted teardrop, not the usual dark green of modern bottles. How long had it been in the sea, turned by the waves, worn away by countless stones, before the ocean gave it up?

'A holy stone.' Christopher laughed, now, looking at what

Hannah had found. 'That's a good one. A holy stone to pray with.'

The stone fitted in Rachel's palm, smooth and cold. She twisted the frayed ends of the rope, pinched it between her finger and thumb, and poked it into the hole, pulled it through and tied a knot. 'There.' She held it up in front of her and it glowed pale gold in the light from the low sun.

A cry came from behind them, back along the beach towards the pillbox. 'Harvey! Harvey! Come back!'

They turned. Jamie was running in the other direction, waving his arms and shouting. Far beyond, Harvey was darting in circles round a group of people and two small dogs.

Rachel shoved the stone in her pocket and ran towards him.

'Wait for me!' Hannah ran after her. 'Harvey! Harvey!'

'Stay with Daddy!' Rachel pounded across the sand, and renewed her resolve not to get a dog of their own.

By the time she reached the group, one of the other dog owners had caught Harvey and was bending down, rubbing the dog's head and talking to him. Jamie stood awkwardly to one side.

'Sorry about that.' Rachel took hold of the lead.

'It's okay. No harm done.'

'He just dashed off,' Jamie said, as they walked back. 'It was those little dogs. They were yapping and jumping and he was only being friendly. He wanted to join in.'

'Never mind.' Rachel had the dog on the lead now. 'It wasn't your fault.' She wrapped her scarf higher round her neck. The wind was stronger, and it had turned cold. Down near the water, Christopher was skimming stones over the waves.

'Where's Hannah?' Rachel called as they came near.

'She went with you. To get Harvey.'

'No, she didn't. I told her to stay with you.' Rachel scanned the beach, both directions, and up towards the cliffs. 'Where is she? Where's she gone?' Her heart filled her chest, pressing against her ribs. 'Hannah?' she shouted. 'Hannah, where are you?'

They sit in silence for a bit. Although they're sheltered from the worst of the weather, it's cold, and both of them are in wet clothes.

'If you really aren't going to go home,' he says eventually, 'I know a place that's a lot more comfortable than this. It would be safer, too.' He thinks of the heavy padlock, and the key in his pocket. 'I could take you there, and I could get you some things. A sleeping bag, maybe, and something to eat.'

He crawls backwards out of the doorway. 'Come on. You can't stay here.'

Cormorant

The orange glow in the sky had gone by the time the police came. Blue lights flashed on the lane at the top of the cliff. Uniforms. Questions. Radios crackling and voices calling instructions. The couple with the yappy dogs had joined the search. Others had gathered, running from the town end of the beach when they heard there was a lost child. What can we do? Can we help? Rachel wanted to shout at them. Go away, so I can see where she is! So I can find her. How can I see with all of you crawling across the beach?

'A yellow coat,' Christopher kept saying. 'She's wearing a bright yellow coat. You can't miss her. She's only…only six.'

She heard the catch in his voice and her throat closed.

Miss her. You can't miss her. The words thumped in her heart against her ribs. Can't miss her. Bright yellow coat. Only six. Please, God. Please, God, please please please. Fist curled tight. Fingernails digging in.

More questions. A woman police officer. What else is she wearing? How tall is she? Hair colour? Had something upset her? Had there been an argument? Why did she wander off? Might she have gone home? We'll need your keys. Someone at the house.

Red shoes. Spotty trousers. I think – yes, she had her penguin socks on. She's this high. Six years old. Blonde hair, frizzy, like a cloud. The dog had run off. She wanted to…I told her to stay with Daddy. He thought she was with…oh, I can't, I can't. Where is she? Where's she gone? What's happened to her? We need to keep looking. What if she…?

'It's our job to look for her now, Rachel.'

'It's our job!' Rachel felt herself explode, felt her face stretch into a shape she didn't recognise. 'She's our daughter. I'm her mother. It's my job to look for her!' And then, straightaway, in a whisper, 'Sorry. Sorry. I just…I can't…'

'I know. I understand it's hard to let us take charge. But we have officers searching the whole area – the beach, the town – and we'll have people at your house, too, in case she does make her way home.'

'What about the rocks?' Rachel said. 'Over there? Someone got stuck there once. Their foot. It was on the news. What if she's stuck and the tide comes in and…?'

'We've got officers there right now. We're doing everything we can. If she's in there, we'll find her and get her out. The coastguard helicopter and the lifeboat are on standby.'

Her radio crackled and she moved away.

Another officer, a man, older. 'Has she climbed on those rocks before? Is she likely to have done that?'

'No. I don't know. She might have done.'

'She's not scared of things like that,' Christopher said.

'She's a good climber.' Jamie's voice was small and wobbly. 'Remember, at High Trees, Mum, on the climbing wall? And at the park.' He burrowed against her, but she was hollow, useless, empty of any shred of comfort for him, even when his shoulders shook and he gave way to tears.

'She wouldn't have climbed on the cliffs, would she?' the officer said. 'It's tempting.'

'No. She knows it's dangerous.' Rachel put her hands over her face. 'I just want her back. Get her back! Oh, please, get her back.'

They stood on the beach, while the sea rolled in and the wind blew and the gulls cried. Christopher thrust his hands into his pockets and hunched his shoulders against the cold, his face pinched and closed.

Spray flew up as the waves crashed against the rocks at the foot of the Bluff – those lumps of granite shipped in from somewhere, great blocks tumbled across the beach to protect the land from the ocean. Even at low tide you couldn't get round them on the beach. The end was marked by one of those posts with a basket on the top and two horizontal arms. Robots, Jamie had called them when he was little. A dark shape flew across the sea and landed on one of the arms – a cormorant. The bird stood there, like a figurehead on the prow of a ship, its wings outspread, a silhouette against the darkening sky beyond.

The police made them climb up the steps and sit in a patrol car parked by the barrier, a little way along from a rundown bungalow on the cliff edge. They waited.

More radio talk. Words jabbed the fog that had settled around her. They didn't make sense. Nothing made sense.

'Rachel?' Christopher's hand was on her arm. 'Rachel? We're going home.'

She looked down at the sea defences. The cormorant was still there, wings outspread, standing guard.

When they got back to the house, Rachel put her hand in her pocket for her key, but instead her fingers closed around the holy stone that Hannah had given her to look after. The door opened. There was someone in her hallway.

'I'm Lucy. Family liaison. If anyone's hungry, there are some sandwiches in the kitchen. I can make some tea.'

'We should eat something.' Christopher's voice was flat.

Jamie flopped into a chair, stared at the food.

'I can't.' Rachel stood in the doorway.

'At least have some tea, Rach. Come on.'

Rachel sat down, put her head in her hands. 'I can't,' she said again. 'I'll be sick.'

Lucy was talking but the words wouldn't knit themselves together. *Photograph. Search. Toothbrush. Dog.* Then she went out of the room, stood at the bottom of the stairs, talked on her phone or radio. 'Where?' Rachel heard her say, and her heart leaped. They'd found her! But when Lucy came back in, she sat down at the table, put her hand on Rachel's. 'They've found a sock,' she said.

Rachel's mouth filled with a horrible taste. She shoved her chair back, put her hand over her mouth, stumbled from the room and heaved herself upstairs, clinging to the rail. Hannah's bedroom door was open. She went in without turning on the light and lay on the bed, curled herself on her side, still in her coat and shoes. Her fist tightened around the holy stone, and she held it against her heart, its rope rough on the skin of her wrist.

When she closed her eyes, all she could see was the cormorant on the robot's arm.

And a wet sock, abandoned on the sand.

No little girl in a shiny, yellow coat.

Oh, please, dear God. Please.

Sheep Cushion

Eventually, after Adam had gone out, Mary stirred from her inertia in front of the telly and went back into the garden. At least the shed roof had held. And her cliff had survived. It took her almost an hour to lug all the pots outside again, and tidy everything up, and then she crossed the lane to the nursery. The storm had ripped through the polytunnel, and the flapping bits of polythene that remained would be useless. She'd have to replace the whole thing before spring came, dig a new trench probably. She cleared up what she could and it was dark before she trudged back to the house, aching all over. Lights flashed by the barrier. Police cars, it looked like. There must have been some trouble on the beach.

Adam wasn't back. She closed the curtains, put sausages and frozen chips in the oven, and settled down in front of *The Chase*. After a bit she heard the cars drive away, and a little later the door of the lean-to creaked open.

'Adam, is that you?' She went to his bedroom, put her head round the door. 'There's sausages and chips in the oven keeping warm. There's a couple of jam tarts left, too. What's the matter?' He was soaking wet and shivering.

'Nothing, Mumma.'

'What's this?' Mary picked up his jacket from the floor. 'It's soaked. It's not raining again, is it?'

'I fell over.'

'Bring it in the kitchen and hang it up.'

'Okay. In a minute.'

She dished up the meal, and took the plates into the living room. It was probably something to do with Danny Goodrum – that bloody pest – picking on him again. It wouldn't be the first time he'd given him a soaking. She kept telling Adam to ignore him. It was the only way to deal with a bully. With most things, really. You got by, then. Survived.

Once he had got into dry clothes, Adam wolfed down his sausages and chips and then spent half an hour in his room with his bashy music before wandering back to watch *Midsomer Murders* with her. He sat picking at the loose piping on the arm of the sofa.

There was the sound of a car outside. Wedges of ice-blue light swept across the ceiling and then disappeared. Headlight beams.

The television screen showed a murky underwater shot, but then most of what she watched was murky these days. It didn't matter with the quiz programmes, but she found it difficult to follow these murder storylines. The camera closed in on something that could be a body folded into a lobster pot. Outside, the engine stopped. Car doors slammed. Moments later, a sharp knock at the door.

Mary heaved herself up. She shouldn't have stayed outside so long. Her ankles and knees were killing her and a dull ache had settled in her lower back. She would have a good hot soak in the bath once she'd got rid of whoever this was. She shuffled to the door, dragged the curtain aside, turned the key and opened the door.

Two police officers, a man in uniform, and a woman in a black padded jacket. Mary couldn't tell what expressions they wore and she wasn't about to squint at them.

'I'm DI Sally Lincoln and this is DS Jack Stone. Mind if we come in?'

'Why? What do you want?'

'We need to talk to you. It would be easier if we came in.'

'What about?' Mary took a step back. 'Come in here.' She took them to the kitchen, and stood by the stove without asking them to sit.

'And you are?' The uniformed officer took out a notebook.

'Mary Farthing.'

'We're investigating a missing child, Mrs Farthing,' DI Lincoln said.

Mary didn't correct their assumption about her marital status. It was none of their business. 'What do you want to know?'

When he was almost four, Adam had wriggled free from her hand in a supermarket car park, and been found a mile away and one hour and seventeen minutes later playing on the slide in a park he had only ever been in once. She knew how it made your insides hollow and your head light, how all the weight went into your limbs like sand. How sounds flew out of people's mouths and buzzed in the air like insects, refusing to form into words or sentences that meant anything, and you just wanted everyone to shut up and let you think. Let you make a plan and get on with it. Let you find your child. Because that was your job. Keeping him safe. Defending him. No room for failure.

'Could you tell us what you've been doing today? Where you've been?'

'I haven't been anywhere. I've been here.'

'In the house? All day?'

'Yes. And the garden.'

'And did you see anyone on the beach, Mrs Farthing?'

'I had storm damage to sort out. I wasn't looking at the beach.'

'So you didn't see anyone.'

'No.'

The sergeant looked up from his notebook. 'Do you live here alone, Mrs Farthing?'

'Adam's watching TV. My son.'

'We'll need to talk to him.'

They followed Mary to the living room. Adam sat in a corner of the sofa, hugging his sheep cushion, with his knees up to his chest.

'Adam, the police want to ask you some questions.'

'Some questions,' Adam said.

The two police officers exchanged a glance.

'Do you mind if we...?' The woman nodded towards the television.

Mary picked up the remote, muted the sound. 'I don't want him upset,' she said.

The other officer stepped forward. 'Adam, my name's Jack. Do you mind if I sit here?' He put his hand on the back of the other chair, a cane one that used to be in the lean-to before the plants took over.

At least he had a kind sort of voice, Mary thought. Friendly. And he knew to use Adam's name at the beginning of the sentence. Was it instinctive? Or was it training?

'Sit here,' Adam said.

The policeman hesitated, his hand still on the chair back.

'It's okay,' Mary said. 'He does that sometimes if he's nervous. Repeats things.'

Jack Stone sat, and Mary sat down beside Adam on the sofa. She didn't touch him. Only the sheep cushion would do when he was like this. 'Adam,' she said, 'the police officers want to ask you a few things. It's okay.'

DI Lincoln remained standing.

'Adam,' – Jack Stone leaned forward – 'have you been out today?'

'Yes.'

'Where did you go?'

'The beach.'

'Was anyone else there?'

'Danny. He wants to sell my fossils.'

'Danny?'

'Danny Goodrum,' Mary explained. 'Lad he was at school with. Gives him a hard time.'

'He followed me,' Adam said. 'Yesterday.'

'Yesterday?' DI Lincoln said. 'Did you see anything today?'

'Yes.'

There was a silence.

'What did you see?'

'A shark tooth.' Adam paused. 'And footprints.'

'Where were the footprints?'

'On the beach.'

'Do you know who made them?'

'No.'

'Can you describe them, and where they were exactly?'

'Yes.'

Mary decided not to intervene. Would they understand that he wasn't being deliberately evasive, but was simply answering the question?

DI Lincoln sighed. 'Tell us what they were like. Do you think they were trainers? Boots?'

'No. The footprints were made by bare feet. They were down by the water when the tide was out.'

'Where were they going?'

'Nowhere. They stayed where they were.'

Mary smiled to herself.

'Did you see the person who might have made the footprints?'

Mary had managed to focus on Adam's face now. He looked puzzled and then a nervous grin spread across his face.

'That's a good joke,' he said. 'Do you want to hear my joke? It's about breathing.'

DI Lincoln sighed again. 'Was anyone else on the beach?'

'Dogs and people I didn't know. And birds. Gulls and turnstones mostly. If Danny tries to get my fossils you could make him stop because it would be stealing which is against the law.'

'Adam, we can talk about that later.' Jack's voice remained calm. He paused, and to Mary's surprise, Adam looked at him. 'A child is missing,' Jack said.

Mary felt Adam's body tense beside her. He screwed his eyes shut, buried his face against his cushion.

'I'm sorry.' Mary stood up, adjusted her gaze so that she could read DI Lincoln's expression. 'I know you need to do your job, but you won't get any sense out of him now. Can't you see he's in a state?'

'Mrs Farthing, it's entirely possible that he's in a state, as you put it, because of something he witnessed on the beach, something he's not telling us.'

'He would have told me if he'd seen anything out of the ordinary.'

'He tells you everything, does he?'

Mary didn't answer. Her back ached. Her ankles were stiff. She wanted a bath. She wanted a good night's sleep. And then she wanted to stand on this edge of land where she had made her home, to stand there and say to everything that threatened it, Stop! This far and no further!

'We may need to talk to you again,' DI Lincoln said. 'Both of you.'

After they had gone, Mary locked the door and pulled the curtain and went to run her bath. Adam followed her as far as the hall, still hugging the sheep to his chest. It was a threadbare thing now, white with a black face. She had knitted it in the weeks before he was born, with great, chunky, rope-like yarn.

'I smiled at the joke, Mumma,' he said.

'Yes, Adam. You did.' And because he didn't turn away immediately, she put her arm around his shoulder and he leaned against her.

He imagines Mumma looking at him through the rain, strings of wet hair flinging themselves about her face.

'What have you done?' she would say. 'What have you done?'

He has to get to her. Has to explain. He climbs back up the gully, not caring about his soaking feet, and comes to the lane. Oh, Mumma, what are we going to do? He forces himself to keep going, whispering inside his head. It wasn't my fault, Mumma. I wanted to tell you, only... He longs to cling to her, to hide his face in her chest. If only he had never seen the million-year-old footprints or the girl with the dandelion hair.

Blue Holdall

Rachel fell asleep at four in the morning, her muscles aching, her eyes sore from weeping. She woke from a restless, dream-filled sleep before dawn, to find Christopher clinging to her, his body heaving with sobs. His face, a mess of tears and snot, was buried hard against her shoulder and the top of her chest. She eased her free arm round him, and stroked his hair, the back of his head.

'Oh, my love. My love,' she murmured, and eventually he calmed and they lay together, waiting for daylight.

They wanted to go to the beach before Lucy arrived in case she told them not to go. Janet, who had driven over from Ipswich late last night and slept on a child-size inflatable bed in the box-room office, was pulling towels from the washing machine. They should have some toast first, she told them. She would stay with Jamie, who was still asleep.

The storm had blown itself out, leaving a dull, grey shroud over land and sea. Lines of searchers were dotted along the slope of cobbles, as well as up on the cliffs. Members of the public had joined the police. But it was almost high tide, and most of the beach was underwater. The second high tide since Hannah had… Rachel couldn't bear to see the faces of those strangers who were looking for her daughter. Or for any other evidence. She thought of the sock that had been found, and put her hand over her mouth.

'Let's go home.' Christopher reached for her hand, and they trudged back over the stones.

Izzy phoned. 'Shall I come?'

'Yes. I don't know. I can't… Later. Tea time. Then I won't have to…' She thought of Janet, of the toasted sandwiches or the pasta bake, whatever it would be. Sitting round the table. She couldn't. Not without Hannah.

But they sat round the table all afternoon anyway and the hours squeezed and stretched into unfamiliar shapes. Janet made cups of tea. Lucy popped in for chats. Jamie was in the sitting room, watching *Star Wars* for the hundredth time, losing himself in another world. The music and the sound of marching throbbed through the house, but no one told him to turn it down. Rachel fidgeted, sitting down, standing up, walking from doorway to doorway, up and down the stairs, as if eventually she would stop at a threshold and there would be Hannah, colouring furiously, her tongue sticking out in concentration, or creating something fabulous out of an egg box or a ball of wool. Rachel itched to be busy, but at intervals a heavy exhaustion washed over her and she sank to a chair, the floor, the stairs, unable to move.

'There's got to be something,' she said to Lucy. 'Something we should be doing.'

But there wasn't.

She drifted into the sitting room and slumped on the sofa next to Jamie. His face was a blank, staring at the screen.

'You okay, love?' she said.

He looked at her. His eyes filled with tears and he shook his head.

Her arms went round him, and he leaned into her embrace, but she had nothing to give. She was empty.

'I'm sorry, Mum,' he said. 'If I hadn't called you when Harvey ran off...if I could have stopped him...'

'Hey! Don't say that! It's not your fault. You mustn't think that.'

'They will find her, won't they, Mum?'

'Yes. Yes, of course they will. It won't be long now.' She stroked his wrist. He was bone-thin, and his skin still so perfect. 'What happened here?' she said, looking more closely.

'What?'

'These scratches.' There were two of them, half healed, parallel lines above the knobbly wrist bone.

'Oh, nothing. Paper cut or something.' He took his hand from hers.

She watched the film with him for a while. The sounds and images floated through her senses, but underneath she kept hearing her words to Jamie. *It's not your fault.*

Fault. The word burrowed into her and made a nest deep inside.

Late in the afternoon, Lucy left. 'You've got that number,' she said. 'You can call any time.'

Rachel went back into the kitchen, stood in the doorway. Janet and Christopher sat staring into empty cups.

'Someone's taken her,' Rachel said. 'She wandered off and someone took her.'

Now that she had voiced it, the possibility took hold in her imagination. Her stomach churned. How could you ever hope that your child has been abducted? She pushed the nausea down because she wanted it to be true. Outside, darkness was falling. Another long night lay ahead, and to think of Hannah, alive somewhere, was better than…

'Don't torment yourself, Rachel,' Janet said.

'I'm not.' Rachel couldn't find the energy to explain. It wasn't torment. It was hope.

'The police are doing everything they can.' Janet. So capable. So sensible. So just like last time.

'It's more than twenty-four hours.'

'Rach, don't.' Christopher's voice was flat. He didn't look at her.

'I'll start tea.' Janet got up and went to the fridge.

It was called golden time. She'd read about it. After the first twenty-four hours, the chances faded. But they didn't go away altogether. And if someone had taken her, then surely…

The phone rang.

Rachel's heart jumped, thumped against her ribs. She squeezed her hands into fists. It would be him. Her. Them. Whoever had taken Hannah. It would be a demand for money. A ransom. Come alone. Don't tell the police. Unmarked notes. She couldn't move, couldn't breathe.

'I'll get it.' Janet wiped her hands on a tea towel.

It was Gail.

Rachel dashed up the stairs, both flights, dived into the

Crow's Nest and opened all the doors of the cupboards under the eaves.

Maybe it wouldn't be a phone call. Maybe it would come in the post. Or by hand, through the letterbox. She had to be ready. Where was it? She hadn't used it since... These cupboards went back a long way at the bottom. It would be buried right at the back, where the roof sloped down. She burrowed in, threw things out behind her – shoes, bags, old duvet covers. Ah! Here! She dragged it towards her, and backed out of the cupboard. She sat on the floor, leaning against the bed, hugging the blue holdall to her chest like a shield. Or like a child.

'Oh, dear God, please let her be alive. Please. Let her be safe. Bring her back to me. Please.' She whispered the words, but then her prayer unravelled into a web of nameless fears, tangled through with threads of possible scenarios. A woman had taken Hannah – one who had lost a child and never got over it. Or a scheming couple after money. The ransom note would come today, tomorrow, and she would pay – of course she would – stuff the money in the holdall, leave it in a litter bin. Oh, let it be someone who will look after her. Please let them take care of her. Let her not be cold or hungry. Let it not be someone who will hurt her.

And all the time, behind the images that flashed across her mind, was the endless sound of the sea. Her arms tightened around the bag. Oh, please, dear God, let it not be that.

Footsteps on the stairs. A tap on the door.

'Rachel? It's me...'

Izzy.

'So I thought,' Rachel said, 'I'd better be ready.'

They sat on the floor side by side, leaning against the bed, with the contents of the cupboards strewn across the rug in front of them.

'You mean…the bag is for the money?' Izzy said.

'Yes. Used notes, they always say, don't they?'

'Have the police said they think she was abducted?'

'No, but she could have been. It's quite likely. Don't you think?'

Izzy reached over, squeezed Rachel's hand. Then she said, 'I wish I…' Her voice cracked. 'Oh, Rachel I'm so sorry this is so terrible I can't think what… Sorry I'm just… I'll just be here with you and shut up, shall I?'

Rachel felt her face relax almost into a smile and then the tears came again and she let the bag go and leaned against her friend and Izzy took her in her arms and held her.

When the tears had passed, Rachel said, 'You know the last time I even saw this bag?'

'No.'

'Remember when I gave you Hannah? At choir? Just put her on your lap and went away?'

'Yes, but you weren't yourself. You were —'

'I packed it when I got home. Ready to run away.'

'You were ill.'

Rachel shrugged. 'I know. But that's what I did. I packed it. Pyjamas. Underwear. Socks. Spare jeans and a fleece. My passport, even. Money. I went to the bank and took out six hundred pounds in cash. It made me feel safe. I had an escape route.'

'But you didn't go.'

'I did. A week or two later. Shoved the holdall in the car and drove all the way to Peterborough. Janet was still in the house, so everyone would be all right. But I didn't even get out of the car. I just came back.'

'Why Peterborough?'

'I don't know. I just went in a straight line.'

'What did they say when you got back? What did you tell them?'

'I don't think they knew. It was the middle of the night. I was back before they woke up.'

It had been midsummer, a clear, cool night. She had gone up to bed while it was still light, as soon as Hannah was settled, but had been jolted out of sleep when Christopher came up. She lay there beside him, unable to relax, and a terrifying darkness pressed in from all sides, crushing her until she thought she would break. Her heart banged, pounding in her ears and shaking her body. She couldn't get her breath. I can't, she thought. I can't get out. Her body lay straight and stiff, and she wanted to move but she couldn't. In the end, with a supreme effort of will, she climbed out of bed. All she could think was that she had to get out, get away, or some unthinkable disaster would occur and she would be to blame. She opened the cupboard, slid the packed holdall out from behind a crate of shoes, and crept from the room.

In the car, alone, under the stars, with the shadowy landscape unfolding past the windows, she felt strangely light, as if everything that had weighed her down had suddenly been lifted from her and she was floating into a future where none of it would matter. She could be someone else. She found herself laughing uncontrollably until tears ran down her face. She was drunk with relief.

But when she stopped the car outside the first hotel she

came to on the outskirts of Peterborough, she couldn't get out. It was the middle of the night. She would have to stay here in the car until morning. She thought of the sun coming up in a couple of hours, and of people getting on with their normal lives while she checked in, showered, ordered something to eat. And then what? The fear rushed back. She pulled out of the car park and headed for home. By the time she arrived, she felt numb. She had tipped the contents of the holdall into a drawer and stuffed the bag into the back of a cupboard.

They stayed quiet for a bit. Then Rachel said, in a small, tight voice, 'I didn't just put her on your lap.'

'It's all right, Rach,' Izzy said, squeezing her hand again. 'You were ill.'

'I said I didn't want her any more. I remember. I said I didn't want her.'

'You didn't. You said you couldn't keep her. Couldn't look after her. And anyway, whatever you said, no one blames you. You mustn't do this to yourself.'

'But what if this is some kind of payback? How could I say such a thing? How could any mother? My baby...and now she's not here, and I need them to find her. I don't care if someone's got her. I hope someone has. If he came here now and gave her back to me I would kneel down and kiss his feet. I would. Oh, please, let her be, let her be...'

Izzy's arms tightened round her and she rocked her and sang. A low, sweet lullaby.

He sees her from the bottom of the steps. She's poking at the mud with a stick, down by the jumble of sea defences – those great blocks of dark stone that Mumma calls rock armour. The tide is on the turn and an orange light flows over everything, like it's been washed in gold. It will be dark in an hour.

'Are you looking for fossils?' he says, when he reaches her.

Cold Water and Vinegar

There was a stretch of damp, mild, dull days. Low cloud hung heavy in a sky that refused to lighten. When it wasn't raining the air was full of mist. Now and then a half-hearted breeze tugged at the grey blanket, but failed to shift it. Mud slicked the paths, and in between tides the sand remained under a sheen of water. Lethargic waves rolled in, sucked back.

On Friday, a week after the storm, the weather changed. A cloudless blue sky stretched over a sparkling sea. Frost glittered in the sunlight, and the bite in the air made Adam think of spearmint toothpaste. He felt clean and fresh and full of energy.

He took his fossil bag, and some money for buns, climbed down the steps, across the stony ridge, and set off at a run along the hard sand. The sea was calm and sparkling. On the horizon a big block of a ship glowed red in the sun. People were out walking their dogs and everyone smiled and said lovely morning or isn't it glorious and Adam said yes and smiled back.

Molly was wearing a purple scarf with white spots and her hair was a new shade of orange, done up in a spiky bunch on top of her head.

'Hi, Adam. Isn't it a lovely day? Makes you glad to be alive, doesn't it? What can I get you?'

'Two butterscotch buns, please, Molly.'

'Freshly made this morning.' She picked out two with her tongs, dropped them into a paper bag and handed it to him. 'One eighty, please. How's your mum? Haven't seen her lately.'

'Good, thank you.'

'Have a nice day.'

'You have a nice day, too.' Adam put the buns in his rucksack and turned to go back down to the beach. Don't look, he said to himself as he passed the children's playground. But he couldn't help it. His head turned and he scanned the scene. No Danny. Thank goodness. A couple of mums were there with toddlers, and an old man was operating a remote control boat on the lake. One of the mums unstrapped her child from the buggy, and he ran over to watch the boat. His mum chased him and grabbed his hand. The wall around the lake wasn't very high, and a sign said the water was a constant depth of three hundred and eighty millimetres. The boat chugged across the water, churning up a froth of bubbles.

Although the tide hadn't yet covered the sand, Adam decided to walk home by the base of the cliff. It was hard work trudging over the huge cobbles, but the heavy rain might have exposed fossils embedded in the cliff, or even washed them out, down to the stones. He found a few bits of blue sea glass, and there were hundreds of dead starfish, but no fossils.

He came to the dip where the stream trickled down the cliff in a mini waterfall, and spotted a bottle, half-buried at the edge of the little pool. He crouched down and unearthed it. It wasn't broken and it was heavier than he thought it would be. The glass was cloudy, and the bottle was half full of a yellow liquid, and sealed with a rusty metal cap. It looked like wee, but the yellow was too bright. Anyway, why would someone wee in a bottle, put the top on and leave it there? If you needed to go on the beach, you just made sure no one was looking, and did it. Besides, it was one of those crown caps that would have to be sealed by some kind of machine. The glass looked old, too; dull and worn, a whitish colour. Adam stood up, rubbed the sand and grit off the glass, and put the bottle in his bag. You could call it treasure. Of a sort.

When he was home, he washed his new treasures, and lined them up on his shelf. He wondered if he should hide them under his bed. Just in case. Maybe tomorrow. Or the day after that. It would be a shame not to display them for at least a little while. He went into the kitchen, where Mumma was stirring something in a pan on the stove. He put the paper bag on the counter. 'I got us some of Molly's buns. Butterscotch.'

'Lovely,' Mumma said. 'Tomato soup first. Can you butter a couple of those crusty rolls?'

They took their lunch on trays into the living room. The kitchen table was cluttered with layers of newspapers, seed packets, and a heap of earth-covered parsnips.

The local news came on. A reporter in a beach car park under a cloudless blue sky.

'That's Saltbourne, isn't it?' Mumma said. 'What's happened there?'

The reporter, a young woman in a bright green coat, said a body had been found washed up on the beach early that morning and was believed to be that of Hannah Bird, aged six, who had gone missing at Holthorpe a week ago.

The tray on Adam's lap pinned him to the sofa. He was squashed in by the sheep cushion on one side, and by Mumma's bulk on the other. The picture changed. A school photo. A smile like sunshine. Dandelion hair.

Adam jumped to his feet. The tray flew off his lap and an arc of bright orange shot across the sheep cushion. The bowl and the plate and the tray landed on the floor.

'Adam!' Mumma shouted, getting up. 'Look what you've done! For heaven's sake, whatever's the matter?'

Adam rushed to his room, threw himself face down on his bed, his hands over his ears. He didn't want to think about it, didn't want to remember.

When Mumma came to see if he was okay, he said he was. He wanted to tell her about that day. He wanted her to put her arm around him and say everything would be all right and she would always look after him. But what if she couldn't? What if she said they had to tell someone?

'Come on, Adam. I know it upset you, seeing that about the little girl and everything. But there's nothing we can do. Accidents happen.' She rubbed his shoulder. Her hand was warm and firm. 'You can't stay here getting yourself in a state. Come and eat something. I've warmed up some more soup for you. And we've got the buns. We can watch Antiques Road Trip instead of the news.'

Adam followed Mumma back through the hall. As they passed the kitchen, he saw the sheep cushion cover on the draining board, a huge orange stain across its middle.

'It's all right,' Mumma said. 'Cold water and vinegar. A long soak. That'll get it out.'

'Okay,' he said, and went into the kitchen.

But she laughed and squeezed his shoulders. 'Don't worry,' she said. 'I'll do it later.'

When he was small, he had taken the sheep cushion into the garden for a picnic and fed it chocolate cake and blackcurrant juice and left it out in the rain all night. Mumma was cross and went on about taking care of things and making amends. She had shown him how to unbutton the cushion cover at the back, and made him soak it, and then wash it in soapy bubbles until the stains had almost gone. The chocolate and the mud had disappeared easily enough, but the blackcurrant had left a faint bluish blob by the ear.

Mumma gave Adam his soup in a mug this time, and they watched some people driving round the country in an old car, buying antiques and then selling them again, which reminded him of what Danny had said about the fossil shop. And when he pushed that fear away, all he could think about was the little girl being washed up on the beach. Hannah. That was the name the reporter had said. Hannah Bird.

He put his mug on the side table. He couldn't finish the soup. His stomach churned. On the telly, a lady was talking about paying for something. It was as if she was talking to him. *Pay for this. You'll pay for this.*

Adam lay awake, certain that his dreams would be of Hannah. Eventually, he fell into a troubled sleep, and dreamed of roaring monsters and crashing thunder. At last, light crept round the edges of his curtains. He knelt up on his bed to pull them open.

Oh! What was this? Sky filled his window. Where were the bushes? Where was the shed? Where was the garden?

He stumbled to Mumma's room. How could she sleep when huge chunks of the world were rearranging themselves? He threw himself on to her.

'Mumma! Wake up! Wake up!'

'What? What is it?'

'It's gone! There's just all sky!'

'What's gone? What do you mean – all sky? Get off. Let me move, will you?'

Mumma rolled over, slid off the bed. He grabbed her sleeve, pulled her into his room, and they looked out of the window together. 'Sheesh,' Mumma said, and then went quiet for a long time.

'Bloody rain,' she spat out at last. 'Filthy, stupid, bloody rain.' She stomped into the lean-to and put her wax jacket on over her pyjamas, pulled on her wellies. 'Come on,' she said. 'I suppose we'd better inspect the damage.'

He followed her out. More than half the garden was gone. They stood at the new edge of the cliff. A great slice opened at their feet – raw, rust-coloured earth, with a fringe of grasses and vegetation, their secret root tangles on display. Beyond, lay the tumbled slope of what had been their garden, scattered with plant debris and broken bits of the shed.

Adam heard the words again, echoing in his head. *You'll pay for this.*

Without going inside to get dressed or have breakfast, Mumma climbed about gathering up broken plants, and some of the scattered contents of her reorganised tubs and shelves. Adam helped her for a bit, but by mid-morning he had had enough and was itching to be off on his own. He climbed back up to the house to fetch his bag and then came down the steps. There were people on the beach now, taking photos. Some of them, in blue helmets and yellow jackets, were measuring and tapping at their iPads. Mumma was halfway down the new slope. It was as if the cliff had turned to liquid and poured across the beach. Now that he was down here, looking up, he could see that what was left of the garden, together with about ten metres of the cliff intact each side, was sticking out like a mini headland. On both sides, great curved chunks of land had broken off and slumped down the face of the cliff.

One of the officials spoke to the people on the beach and another went to talk to Mumma. She flung her arms in the air, and he could see she was arguing, but eventually she stomped down to the beach and came along to the steps.

'Ordered me off my own land,' she told him. 'Said the council would be in touch about the house. Bloody ridiculous. My garden. My house. None of their bloody business. They've put danger signs up all over the place. Still, at least they've sent the gawpers away.'

She grabbed the rail and huffed and puffed up the steps, still swearing.

Lancashire Hotpot

Rachel agreed, in the end, to a bath.

For three days and nights she lay in Hannah's bed, buried under the duvet.

'Try to eat something,' Christopher said. 'At least drink some water. Please.'

She drank a little. And there was toast. Or soup. Something. She was sick, then empty. She went to the loo a few times, clung to the walls, the door, the side of the bath.

There were sounds. Voices. The phone ringing. Doors. Footsteps.

The smell of Hannah, warm, sweet, like the smell of the skin on the inside of your elbow. The cotton sheet.

They had found her. But found was the wrong word. Advise you not to see her, they said.

The bathwater was hot. There were bubbles. The scent

made her think of purple.

'Do you want me to stay?'

She shook her head, closed her eyes. Lowered herself, let her hands float, slid down until her head was underwater. She let the breath go out of her and waited. Slowly, she pushed herself back up. Water dripped from her face, her hair. Steam billowed round her and there were long gaps between her breaths.

She struggled into joggers and a big jumper, went downstairs. In the sitting room, cards crowded every surface. Flowers stood in vases on the floor and the bookshelf and the coffee table – white ones mostly, and the heavy, sweet scent made her feel sick.

It was a foreign land. She could not be here, with all this.

'I'll make some tea,' Janet said.

Rachel followed her into the kitchen. Outside, grey branches, grey roofs, white sky. Perhaps there had been snow. Or would be.

'Here, why don't you sit down?' Janet pulled out a chair. 'Christopher's gone out for a bit. He'll be back soon. Jamie's at Anthony's. Films, I think. Do you want anything to eat?'

'I don't know. I'm not hungry.' Hollow. That's what she was. Hollow. A huge, gaping emptiness. But not hungry.

'Oh, Rachel, dear, this is…' Janet put her hands over her face and her breath came in rough, rasping sobs.

Rachel drank some tea and ate half a biscuit, but it was hard to swallow. Her throat was sore.

The doorbell rang.

It was Gail.

'I'll be in the other room,' Janet said.

Gail sat opposite and reached across the table, took Rachel's hands in both of hers. Her skin was cold and rough. The other half of the biscuit lay among scattered crumbs.

'I'm so, so sorry,' Gail said.

Rachel looked up, met her gaze, then looked down again.

'I can't begin to imagine what you're going through,' Gail said. 'But I can listen if you want to tell me, or if you'd like to talk about Hannah, or what happened. Or I can just sit with you if that would help.'

'Thank you.' Rachel's voice was a whisper. She was unable to say any more. After a while, she withdrew her hands from Gail's grasp and let them fall into her lap. She thought about Hannah running across the sand, about the dog and the stone with the hole in. She thought about the warmth of Hannah's skin, the sound of her laugh, the way she beat her fists against her brother's chest. But she couldn't say any of it.

They sat in silence and Rachel had no idea how much time passed before Gail said, 'If you want to talk, any time, I'm here for you, Rachel. I'll do anything I can to help you get through this.'

'I don't want to get through it. I don't want to…' Rachel pushed her chair back, sprang up from the table. 'I just want it not to have happened. I want her not to be dead. I want her back. I want her back.' She burst from the room, across the hall, shoved her feet into trainers, fumbled at the door handle and flung her way out. She ran across the road, through the estate and down the steps. She pounded across the sand and did not stop until she reached the sea defences. She threw herself face down on the beach and dug her fingers into the sand. Her mouth stretched wide and her jaw ached and the only way she could get her breath was to let it out in a high, keening wail. Over and over. On and on and on under the cold, white sky.

Someone brought a pie. Chicken and leek. It was creamy and hot and came in a chunky pottery dish. Janet made mashed potatoes and steamed some broccoli. She had pulled the blinds down and laid the table with napkins and a jug of water. Rachel felt like a guest. She had changed out of her wet clothes and wore clean pyjamas and one of Christopher's hoodies. She smoothed her hair. Grains of sand fell on to the table and she brushed them to the floor.

She ate a few mouthfuls, drank some water.

Jamie picked out the mushrooms and left them on the side of his plate.

'Good pie,' Christopher said.

'Thelma, I think it was,' Janet said. 'Called while you were both out.' She paused, looked at Christopher. 'The vicar came too.'

Christopher put his knife and fork together, wiped his mouth with his napkin. 'We'll need to talk to her. We have to decide about—'

'No!' Rachel said. She kept her voice under control, placed her hand, palm down, flat on the table. 'No. Not yet. We don't have to decide anything. I can't. It's…' She stood, moved to the door. 'No,' she said again, and left the room.

Christopher followed her up the stairs, into Hannah's room. 'Oh, Rach.' His voice cracked and he caught her hand. 'Please. Please let me in. Talk to me. I can't get through this without you. I've lost her too. Please, Rach.'

'I didn't lose her,' Rachel said. 'I left her with you.'

Rachel woke in the night, stared into the dark. She reached up, felt about on Hannah's bedside table until her fingers closed around the holy stone, with its rough, frayed rope. She drew it towards her, under the duvet. She eased her thumb into the dip where the hole was.

Where are you, God? Where were you? How do you expect me to keep on?

In the morning, she put the stone in her pocket and went out. She walked up and down between the sea defences and the pillbox, back and forth, again and again. She needed to be there, alone, putting one foot in front of the other, with the sand under her feet, the salt in the air, the swish of the waves, and the mewing of the gulls. After a time, she stopped, faced the sea, took in a huge breath and let it out in a great roar. She stood there, shouting and roaring until her throat was sore. Then she charged up and down between the water's edge and the bank of cobbles, and hurled stone after stone as far as she could, watching them splash and vanish.

The holy stone lay against her hip. She pulled it out of her pocket, held it with the blue rope hanging, drew back her arm, made ready for the throw, twisting her body, tensing her muscles. But when the roar came she could not let the stone go. Look after it for me, Hannah had said.

She threw herself face down and wept into the sand until she was empty and numb and the waves splashed over her legs.

She got to her feet eventually and turned towards home. She came past the groyne and the reef where, years before, she had seen those boys push the fossil hunter into the sea and run away with his bag.

She had carried that bag with her on several trips to the beach before she found him again, and gave it back. He opened it while she watched, checked his treasures, then slung it over his shoulder. 'Thank you,' he said, and then walked away.

She'd seen him a few times over the years, plodding up and down the beach, but she wouldn't have recognised the other lads. They'd have left school some time ago. What would they do for kicks, now they were adults? She shivered and pushed the thought away.

Christopher and his mother didn't like her going out on her own.

'At least take your phone,' Janet said.

But you don't understand, Rachel thought. I want to be alone. Cut off.

'Jamie needs you,' Christopher said. 'He's lost his sister. We have to face this together. As a family.'

I don't want to face it, Rachel thought. I can't.

More cards came, more flowers, more casseroles and pies, gentle hands on hers, sympathetic eyes, soft murmurs, meaningless swirls of sound. She didn't read the cards or the notes on the casseroles.

Gail came again. 'You're not on your own,' she said.

Rachel felt herself unravelling. The foundation she had built her life on was crumbling.

Izzy came, and Christopher brought her up to Hannah's room. She lay down with Rachel on the bed, wrapped her arms around her, sang to her again.

'Rach,' she said, gently, 'don't shut your family out. Please. I know you must feel...I mean. Christopher. Jamie. I've seen him at school. He... They—'

'Please.' Rachel pulled away, sat up, tried to control the shake in her voice. 'Not you too. Don't tell me what to do. Don't tell me how I must feel. I know you want to help. But there's nothing...' Her voice became a whisper. 'Nothing.'

She went back to the Crow's Nest, to her own bed, lay down beside Christopher, held the holy stone. His arms went round her and she smelled mint. But when she woke, their bodies were no longer touching and the space between them was like a wall.

She watched films with Jamie, felt his skinny frame lean against her, stroked his hair. Words wafted in the air around her, sometimes landed and stayed long enough to arrange themselves into some kind of sense. *Inquest, adjourned, funeral, counselling.* She shut her ears against them. She wrapped layers around herself, big jumpers and scarves and blankets.

Thelma brought more food in a casserole dish with a pattern of daisies. 'Lancashire hotpot,' she said, handing it over on the doorstep. 'Simple and wholesome. We're all praying for you, dear.'

Rachel thought of Thelma weeping in the car that night. Of Hannah waiting at home. How cross and tired everyone was. The barb in Christopher's words. Now you've got a weeping daughter.

She barged past Thelma. 'Hannah doesn't eat meat!' she shouted, and hurled the dish down the path. It smashed on the paving stones. Dribbles of gravy snaked among chunks of meat and slices of carrot and shards of daisy-patterned china.

Thelma stood with her mouth open.

Rachel went back into the house and shut the door.

From the kitchen, later, she heard Christopher apologising

on the phone, and he went out to clear up the mess. He came in with a plastic bag, tied in a knot, and put it in the bin under the sink. A line of blood oozed on his finger, and he held it under the cold tap.

'Sharp, that broken china,' he said.

The next time Gail came, she sat with Christopher in the sitting room, and the murmur of their voices filtered through the ceiling to Rachel, lying in Hannah's bed again, in her clothes, holding the holy stone, smelling Hannah's skin on the sheets, surrounded by her books, her toys, her clothes. The words had a grey, spongy texture, and they stuck together in blobs, attached themselves to the walls and carpet like fungus. It hurt to breathe. She pulled the duvet over her head and it was a long time before she felt it was safe to emerge.

When she went downstairs, Christopher wasn't in the room, but Gail was still there, sitting quietly among the sympathy cards and the fading white flowers. Over her grey clerical shirt, she wore a lilac-coloured jumper which reminded Rachel of one her mother had worn. Rachel hesitated, then moved forward, closed the door behind her, and perched on the edge of the sofa, ready to take flight.

When she looked back to that Friday – to the PCC meeting, the impromptu counselling with Thelma, the supermarket dash and the drive through the storm, she was tormented by the idea that God knew what the next day would bring. She had tried to imagine the everlasting arms holding her close, ready to carry her through. But it was impossible. All she could see was betrayal.

And yet, she could not let go.

'The thing is,' she said quickly before she changed her

mind, 'it shouldn't have happened. It was all wrong. There was the dog, and Jamie, and I left her with… But I didn't check and he said… And what I want to know is why do we teach all that stuff about God's protection? It's nonsense. I keep wondering… Was she on the rocks or the beach, and was anyone else there, and did someone…? And God just watching. Letting it happen. And now…all this about his loving arms… I just can't… She should still be here. She should be here.' Her clenched fist came down hard on the arm of the sofa.

Gail listened. She waited. And then she said, 'I get the feeling you want to blame someone.'

Rachel put her hands over her face.

'Perhaps you're not sure who,' Gail said, 'but it sounds like sometimes it's Christopher. Sometimes it's yourself. And sometimes it's God.'

Mermaid

After the landslide, Mary rescued what she could from the collapsed cliff, ignoring the warnings of the council officials. The weather remained cold, and the sky clear. The air was crisp and sharp and the soil was hard and unyielding. She knew, though, that underneath this frozen surface, the rest of the cliff was biding its time. Groundwater seeping through the sandy layers was pooling in the clay, and it was impossible to predict which section would collapse next, and when it might happen. It was all about where the cracks in the clay might be, where the weak points were. To the east and the west of her property, it was as if a monster had bitten great chunks from the coastline, while here, miraculously, her house and half her garden stood on a blunt nose of land above the landslide below.

Near the foot of the slope, she sensed the instability beneath her feet, and it was here, a few days later, that she stumbled across shards of the agapanthus pot. She picked one up, a sharp triangle, with a green metallic glaze on the outside, and plain red earthenware on the inside. She poked at some of the other pieces with her foot. Lumps of soil clung to them, with a tangled mesh of broken roots. A couple of the seed heads lay crushed at her feet. She never cut it back, the agapanthus. She loved how the winter made miniature sculptures of the frail structures, how the bronze stems and the black seeds glittered in the hoarfrost. This year, though, since the fog had eaten a hole in the middle of her vision, it was more a remembered joy than a present one.

What other treasures lay buried in this froth of mud and soil, ripped from the layer that anchored them between earth and sky, earth and sea? She despaired of finding anything she could salvage, anything she could revive or replant. Snapped bits of tamarisk, clumps of fescue grass, woody stems of rosemary lay scattered across the slope among panels of her shed and half-buried tools and boxes. And here was the door. She caught a waft of spicy citrus, found the bedraggled sprig of winterbloom still attached to the handle.

'Bloody storm.' She kicked the door, and tears of rage and frustration spilled over. She sniffed them back, wiped her face with her hand. She wouldn't give in. She would save what could be saved. And she would find her bench, even if she had to dig over the whole sorry landslide. She put her hand up to shade her eyes and surveyed the slope. Where would she start?

There, in front of the broken skeleton of a tamarisk bush, stood a tiny figure.

Mary gasped. It was a woman, no taller than a pencil, in a burgundy-coloured crinoline and a black top hat, twirling a furled umbrella in her hand. As Mary stood staring, the woman pranced about, her wide skirts swaying, her head high, and her umbrella spinning. Back and forth she waltzed, dipping and whirling among the damaged stems. Then, in one quick movement, she unfurled her umbrella and held it over her head, tilting it against a barrage of tiny falling needles, bright and sharp, like metal rain. Mary blinked and the vision vanished.

She thought about the ship that had floated from the mist, and the blue beetles under the stove, and the strange grids and patterns. I can't let myself go mad, she thought. She put the unwanted images out of her mind, adjusted her focus, and climbed up the slope to enlist Adam's help. They would make a start on looking for the bench.

And while she worked, she would make a plan for saving her cliff, her house, her future.

After an hour of digging, Mary straightened, steadied herself with one hand on the spade, pressed her other hand to her back. Her bones stood hard and solid like a line of rocks under a thin skin of earth, and the heat of her aching muscles seeped into her cold fingers. Under her boots the avalanche of sand and topsoil and root-clumps and tangles of plant matter had altered the seam between land and sea, had unpicked the stitching and tacked it back askew. She stood, feet apart for balance, on the innards of the cliff that were now laid bare, exposed and bright under the winter sky.

A little way off, Adam poked about with his spade, throwing up sprays of rust-coloured earth, and sending a clatter of stones down the slope. She adjusted her gaze, bringing his figure out of the blurry centre of her vision, and watched him – the slack of his shoulders, his restless focus, shifting from the sky to the sea, and then along the crumbling landslide that had once formed the foundation of their garden.

What was the bloody point? He didn't care. The bench could be anywhere. Buried under this lot. She thought of the wood, bleached grey-white, smooth and cool under her palm. She had scoured the beach day after day, until the tide had offered her the right pieces. She had fitted them together, judging the weight and balance and the look of the thing. She had engineered the joints, and found the perfect spot at the edge of the rock garden, facing the ocean, with the tamarisk behind it.

'Oh, don't bother,' she called to him. 'If you can't put the effort in, just don't bother. I've seen little kids put more elbow grease into building a sandcastle.'

He might as well go off on one of his fossil-hunting forays. Treasures, he called them, the things he found. She wasn't convinced of the value in any of them. Bits of glass and stones with vague patterns on. An old glass bottle had appeared on his shelf the other day, with some cloudy yellow liquid in it. Why he saw that as treasure, she couldn't imagine.

He grinned. 'Okay. See you later.' He let the spade fall and half ran, half slid down the slope, and then loped across the beach. His limbs had always been too long for him. When he was born, it was days before his legs had unfurled after being folded tight inside her body. In his early teenage years he had fallen over himself and crashed around the house knocking into things. His jacket flapped in the wind and he stopped to zip it up. He turned to wave at her, shouted something she couldn't hear.

You, Mary thought. You are the bloody point. He wasn't looking any more, but she waved back and then thrust her hand in her pocket when she realised she was shaking her fist at him. She kicked at a clod of yellow soil, then lifted her spade and pushed it deep into the earth, heard the clink of stones hit by its blade. Us, here. Me, trying to save my bench, my garden. The cliff. The house. You're the bloody point of it all.

She stumbled down the foothills of the fallen cliff, and marched across the wet sand towards the water's edge. She would get back to her rescue mission when she'd calmed down.

She didn't see it at first. One minute the beach was empty – the glistening sand with its scatter of stones and criss-cross ripple pattern, the fringe of surf and the grey-green swell of the ocean beyond. The next minute, down where the waves were breaking – a dark shape. It could have been a rock, but she knew all the rocks along this stretch. A seal, perhaps. She had found a dead pup a month or so ago, not far from here.

She stood still, fixed the creature in the middle of her gaze, and stared. It vanished. She blinked, looked sideways. There it was again, a curved, uneven form, lumpish at one end, and tapering towards what could be a long, shimmering tail. An image flashed across her mind of the mermaid carved into a pew end in the church, with its oddly masculine face and its flat, round breasts. What if...? She shook the thought away. She had read of hoaxes. Photographs posted on social media – not that she had anything to do with that rubbish. Waste of time. It did look like something washed up, though. She swallowed, thought of the drowned child, found a few days ago.

She took a step closer, and another. A piece of driftwood, maybe. Or was she seeing things again? Was this another of those things that weren't there, like the ship and the umbrella lady, the blue beetles and the grids? Would it vanish when she looked away or blinked? And if it didn't, what would she find when she came nearer?

But why should she go any nearer? She turned, looked up towards the broken cliff, to her house on the top, its garden sliced off just metres from Adam's bedroom window. That was her business, not this.

But when she turned again, and found the creature in her fickle, treacherous vision, it was a mermaid she saw. She went closer. Ah, no. It was nothing more than a bundle of dark clothes. Its sodden edges, that she had thought could be a tail, lifted and lowered with the lapping of each wave. The tide was coming in. Then she noticed the hands, blotched red and purple, and the wet hair, a pale crescent of skin visible underneath. A body, then, after all. Legs, no tail. And not a child, this time. Would she have to…? She couldn't just leave it. She bent down, found herself reaching towards the shoulder, then hesitated. Was that a movement? The fingers, there, in the sand? Was it the sea washing over them that made them curl like that? No. There it was again, a feeble clutching motion, as if to grasp at something that wasn't there.

The person was alive. She crouched down, put her hand on the shoulder and shook it. A strand of hair fell away from the face. It was a woman. Her eyes were closed and her lips were tinged blue. There was no response. Mary shook again, harder.

'Can you hear me? Are you all right?'

A groan this time, and a shrinking movement, curling in on herself.

'Come on. I need to get you out of the water. Are you hurt? Can you get up?'

Another groan, and a wave washed over the legs and feet. Mary hooked her hands under the armpits and heaved, while snatches of first aid advice flitted through her memory. *Don't move the casualty. Keep them warm. Recovery position.* Bollocks, she said to herself. Tide'll be over her in minutes. She'll drown if I leave her. The woman's head flopped against Mary's legs. Then her eyes opened and her feet moved as if she was trying to stand up, to get her balance, but there was no strength in her and she let herself go again.

'Come on,' Mary said. 'Let's get you up here.'

After a few metres she had to stop and rest, but at least she had got her out of reach of the waves. For now. She sat, getting her breath back, with the woman leaning against her. On the horizon, five or six of the turbines shone white in a patch of sunlight. The others were a dull grey against the pale sky. Low, ragged clouds scudded westwards, hustled by a temperamental wind. Better get this done, Mary muttered to herself, and got to her feet again. By the time they came to the bottom of the steps, the woman was making some attempts to walk, though still leaning heavily on Mary. She had begun to shiver.

'Up here,' Mary said. 'To the house. Get you warm. Some dry things.' The sooner you're back to rights and gone, the better, she thought. And I'll get back to rescuing my plants and digging out the bench, once I've located the bloody thing.

'No, no. I…' The mermaid woman gave in with a sigh, and let Mary help her up the wooden steps set into the slope of the cliff. They had been closed a few years ago, declared unsafe because of the unstable ground, but Mary had dragged the barrier aside and no one seemed to notice. Not many people used them though – dog walkers, sometimes, and the occasional birdwatcher during migration season. They were her steps, as this cliff was hers – this cliff that was now a mini headland with her house on top of it. Its violation by the storm was something suffered in her body, her bones. It was an attack against Adam, too, against all that she had promised him when she came here after Evan's betrayal.

Mary had fallen in love with Evan because of the way he laughed and because he listened and was kind. They would walk the cliffs or sit in the candlelight after a meal or lie awake in bed long into the night, and talk for hours. He was in the finance department in the coastal engineering company where she was the only female engineer. By the time she found out he was married, it was too late. She was in too deep. There was no going back. He said the marriage had been dead for years and it wasn't her fault. It should have been a warning, she thought afterwards.

He left his wife, moved into Mary's flat in Norwich.

It was only a few months earlier that Fiona, Mary's younger sister, had moved out, after a long and slow recovery from a breakdown in her mental health. She was still a frequent visitor, sometimes turning up at the door in her pyjamas, her hair in tangles and her face streaked with tears, but more often bursting with confidence and optimism, her eyes sparkling and her hair shining, and laughter spilling from her beautiful, treacherous mouth.

Evan never seemed to mind her intrusions and Mary loved him all the more for his acceptance of her unpredictable, needy sister.

It wasn't until after the accident that she discovered the truth.

Fiona had become increasingly distant, and hadn't been to the flat for more than a month. 'I appreciate your support,' she said to Mary. 'Of course, I do, but I'm trying to be less dependent on you, see other friends, use my coping strategies when I feel fragile.'

It was early summer. A Friday. Evan told her he was going to an old friend's stag night in Birmingham. 'I'll be back around six tomorrow. It's supposed to be warm on Sunday. Let's spend the day at the beach.'

He didn't come home.

They died at the scene, Evan and Fiona, on the coast road near Wells. Someone at Fiona's funeral told her the affair had been going on for three months. Two weeks later, at the age of almost forty-four, Mary was amazed to find that she was pregnant. A month before Adam was born, she moved into Wetherley End, the house that would be her stronghold, her defence against the treachery of the world.

At the house, Mary pushed the door open, and, with her arm still around the woman's shoulders to keep her from falling, took her to the kitchen, where sheets were drying on a clothes horse in front of the stove, and strings of shells hung at the window. No sign of Adam. If he'd gone off on one of his fossil hunts, he wouldn't be back till dark.

The woman stood shivering in front of the stove by the steaming sheets, her hair and clothes dripping on to the mat. Mary went to the cupboard in the hall, took two faded blue towels from the shelf and carried them into the kitchen, laid them on the bench. The woman had not moved. Like a child, Mary thought. Without speaking, she eased the wet coat off the shivering figure, and undid the buttons of the shirt, peeled it down her arms, off her back, helped the woman to step out of her shoes and trousers. She was soaked through to her underwear, but did nothing for herself.

Mary hesitated. 'Shall I help you with these, too?'

When she had taken off the wet clothes, she wrapped the woman in a towel and lowered her on to the bench.

With the second towel she rubbed at the wet hair, smoothing it away from the face. Then she laid this towel over the woman's shoulders, filled the kettle and set it on the stove. From her own room, she brought a green cotton shirt and a pair of work trousers she could no longer get into. They'd do, with a belt. She found socks and a jumper and when the woman was dressed, Mary made a mug of instant coffee, with warmed milk and two heaped spoons of sugar. She pushed a pile of newspapers and seed packets and some jars of nails across the table to make space for the mug.

'My name's Mary,' she said. Then she folded her arms, and stood leaning against the stove, letting its heat warm her aching muscles.

When the empty mug was back on the table, the woman looked up at her. 'Rachel,' she whispered. Her expression was one of such bleak despair that Mary looked away, but in that moment when those eyes had met hers, a realisation ambushed her. Thrust itself upon her with a physical force as something shifted inside her, slotted into place. She knew who this woman was and why she had lain down on the cold sand in the depth of winter and let the waves wash over her.

Mary's fingers tightened and her shoulders tensed. She pressed her lips closed. This woman's grief did not belong to her. She'd suffered her own losses, built her own defences. How could she – why should she – share in the sorrow of another? What was this woman doing in her kitchen, wearing her clothes and looking at her with those haunted, deadened eyes? I saved her from the sea, she thought. Why should any more be required? But she found she had to speak.

'I know.' She paused. Was that enough? Was more expected? In the warm kitchen, the silence waited. Mary sniffed, let the words line up, order themselves, and then, at last, spill over. 'Hannah,' she said. 'Hannah was your little girl.'

The woman who was not a mermaid sat on the bench and tears ran down her face and her hands clutched at each other in her lap until they leaped up and clawed at her hair, scratched at the skin of her cheeks, her neck, her scalp.

And Mary stood in her kitchen and her breath went in and out of her, and the shells hung at the window and the sheets steamed in front of the stove.

Clockwork Shark

Adam helped Mumma bring the broken sections of shed up from where it had fallen. She was planning to rebuild it. There was still no sign of the bench, and when she talked about it, it was as though someone had died. He watched her pick over the landslide, ignoring the danger notices. She wobbled about with a wheelbarrow, trudged up and down the steps with bags and boxes full of rescued bits and pieces, until the remaining garden, and all the spare corners of the nursery across the road, were covered with rows of stuff waiting to be sorted and cleaned and reinstated.

People from the council came with those plastic name things round their necks and sheaves of papers. Mumma shouted and swore at them and stomped about banging things when they had gone. 'Who do they think they are?' Fist on the table. 'It's my bloody land.' A kick at the stove. 'None of their bloody business.' A thump against the wall that made the shells in the window rattle against the glass.

A week after Hannah Bird's body was found, it snowed all night. And on Friday morning, there was a hard, sharp frost. Adam crunched over the beach, where a thin scattering of snow had settled near the foot of the cliff. He wore his hoodie under his big coat, his wellies, and a pair of Mumma's fingerless gloves. Gulls stood hunched near the water's edge until he was almost level with them. Then one would lift and wheel round, landing a hundred metres further on, and the others would follow, only to repeat the process when he caught up with them again. Eventually they changed direction, and flew back over the sea to where they'd started from.

Mumma had given him a list for the supermarket and two twenty-pound notes. She normally did the shopping in the car, but she hadn't been driving much lately, except for a few visits to clients. There wasn't much work for her in the winter. Good thing, really, as she was spending all her time rescuing her own garden, and most mornings she made him help her.

He went up the steps by Molly's but the kiosk was shut. He crossed to the playground, where there were lots of older children as well as the usual handful of toddlers with their parents. It was the end of the half-term holiday. Quick check. No Danny. Good. The paths had been gritted, but the grassy areas were still blanketed in thick snow, and shrieking children threw snowballs with bits of grass sticking out, or made hopeful attempts at snowmen. The ice on the far side of the boating lake was already breaking into shards that floated free, like slivers of glass.

An orange boat chugged across the water. Adam looked

for its controller, finally spotting a boy of six or seven – a bit bigger than Hannah Bird, he thought, before thrusting her from his mind for the thousandth time. The boy was wearing a blue and red bobble hat, and a woman stood beside him, watching the boat.

'Iceberg ahead! Starboard turn!' she cried, and then, 'Phew! Missed it!'

Adam watched the children, with a familiar ache in his middle. He had never belonged. Mostly it didn't matter. When he was at school he'd had Miss Finlay, and he sometimes had Mark, who made him laugh and who knew a bit about fossils, but then on his work placements he had never managed to say and do the things you had to say and do in order to belong. He liked doing things on his own, though, and he had Mumma. They were all right, the two of them. They didn't need anyone else, Mumma always said. But sometimes, lately, he had started to wonder if this was really true.

The boy and his mother moved further round, to the far end of the lake by the sign that said the water was three hundred and eighty millimetres deep. A smaller boy with an identical hat leaned on the wall next to Adam. He was trying to wind up a clockwork shark, but his chunky blue mittens made it hard for him to get a grip on the key.

'Do you want some help?' Adam said.

The boy looked up at him, hesitated, then handed the toy over. The shark's mouth was wide open, dark red inside, and the teeth were sharp and white, unlike the black fossil ones Adam had found. The eyes had frowny lines, and the dorsal fin was huge. Adam turned the key until the clockwork was fully wound. Reluctantly, he handed the shark back to the boy, who leaned over the wall and let it go, shrieking as it zoomed through the water.

The shark ran out of power in the middle of the lake, bobbing on the water, bumping against the ice. Adam watched, and beside him, the boy watched too. Around them, children laughed and built their muddy snowmen. Others had made an ice slide over by the swings. Breath plumed in white clouds. Cheeks flushed. Boots stamped. But only Adam and the little boy in the bobble hat saw the shark come to a stop in the middle of the lake. Inside Adam, the ache faded. An invisible tie linked him to the boy, and he felt that strange warmth again.

That must be the boy's brother, there in the matching hat, with their mother, both intent on the orange boat at the other end of the lake. If Hannah Bird's parents had been watching her...

Three hundred and eighty millimetres. Adam looked at his boots. Probably not high enough. Should he take them off? Better than filling them with water. He turned to tell the boy not to worry, he'd get the shark for him.

But the boy wasn't there.

Adam's heart thumped and his throat felt funny. Then he saw the boy in the water, standing up one minute, falling forward the next, and the water splashed up around him as his arms and legs thrashed.

Someone else got in too, but Adam reached the boy first, scooped him up out of the water and carried him back to the edge, where his mother stood, her mouth open but with no sound coming out. She seized the boy and hugged him to her, and then she said, 'Oh, oh, oh,' over and over again. Adam climbed back into the lake and waded through the freezing water, picked up the shark and waded back.

'Here.' He handed it to the older boy.

'Oh, thank you so much,' the woman said to Adam. 'I can't think what happened. How did he…?' And then to the boy, 'I told you not to bring that. It's a bath toy. You were going to have a turn with the boat…'

'You're welcome,' Adam said.

Snatches of the story peppered the air around him. …*just climbed over…lost his boat or something…one minute he was…drown in a few inches…who was it…young man in wellies…rescued him… where…there…was it you?…* And then he found himself being clapped on the back and there were handshakes and smiles and his fingers felt like ice but the warm feeling inside him had taken root.

Someone offered to buy him a coffee, but he said no thank you he had to get to the supermarket as he had a list. He sat on the wall and took off his boots and tipped the water out. Then he put them back on and walked up the high street to the supermarket. He squelched round the aisles putting things in the trolley and ticking them off in his head. At the checkout he put the shopping in two bags. His feet were cold and wet, but a left-over warmth filled his chest. He thought of the little boy and how they had stood together at the side of the lake, watching the shark bobbing on the water. He remembered the weight of him in his arms, his wide eyes, his sodden, dripping clothes. That bond between them. And he couldn't help thinking about Hannah. Remembering. He tried to push the memory away, but it wouldn't go.

'Is there anything else?' the checkout assistant said.

'No.' Then he realised that what the assistant meant was please move away from the checkout to make way for the next customer. So he did.

His mind churned. He stood in the street with the shopping

bags at his feet, and put his arms up round his head. What if it happened again? What if he…? He felt his knees bend and he sank into a crouch. He mustn't think. He mustn't. A humming sound filled his ears and he rocked back and forth.

Eventually, he heard a voice. 'Are you all right, son?' It was Mr Bright from the hardware shop. 'Want to come and have a sit down? It's pretty nippy out here. Someone told me you'd had a bit of an adventure, eh? Quite the hero.'

'I'm going to go home now,' Adam said. He got to his feet and picked up his shopping.

'Okay, son. If you're sure you're all right.'

'I'm all right,' Adam said. When Mr Bright had gone, he remembered a joke. 'I'm half left,' he said to himself, but he couldn't smile. He made his way up to the top road. He didn't want to go back past the playground. It was further to walk, but he would go up past the church and then turn down the track that joined the coast path to the east of the town.

Hero, Mr Bright had said. That was it.

There were plenty of children in Holthorpe who might need a hero, if that's what people wanted to think. But he would have to be careful.

She's wearing a yellow jacket and blue spotty trousers and red shoes. Her hair is a pale frizz like a dandelion clock. This wind, he thinks, could snatch her up and blow her away.

'I was looking for holey stones, but I found this.'

Her voice surprises him. It's rough and grainy like the fudge from Molly's kiosk.

'It's a stick,' he tells her.

'No it's not,' she says. 'It's a stone, silly.'

'It's a fossil stick. Once it was wood, but now it's turned into stone. It's like magic, but really, it's science.'

'Oh.'

'He takes the shark tooth from his pocket, holds it in his palm for her to see. 'I found this today,' he says. 'It's a shark tooth.'

Razor Blades and Chocolate

Rachel lay on the sofa, staring at the ceiling. Christopher was talking about going back to school. He sat on the sofa arm, by her feet.

'I don't mind,' she said. 'You can if you want.'

She was frightened to close her eyes because of the images that played on a loop – she'd be running across the beach towards Jamie and the dog, telling Hannah to stay with Daddy, coming back to find her gone. There were other images too – Hannah slipping on the rocks, banging her head, someone pretending to be friendly, getting her trust, and then…the waves, the tug of the current, the water going into her lungs. Every moment was a battle against the pictures. She was tired. So tired.

'I think it would help,' Christopher said. 'Fill the days. You know.'

No, she didn't know. Fill the days? Maybe the pictures crowded his mind too. She hadn't asked. He and Jamie had both been off last week – it was half term. But Jamie had gone back today. Stick to his routine, people had said. The school had set up some counselling. Izzy had. That was her job.

'But,' Christopher said, 'only if you'll be all right on your own.'

She shrugged. 'All right? What does that even mean? Anyway, I'm not on my own. Janet's here.'

Janet kept things going. She cooked wholesome meals in modest portions, and cleared up as she went along. She shopped with categorised lists and Rachel had seen her wiping the tops of doors with a damp cloth. She ironed their underwear and topped up the air fresheners. She answered the phone and the door and organised things for Jamie and made endless cups of tea. If it was my mum, Rachel thought, we'd have muddled through with jacket potatoes and beans, but there'd have been plenty of baking – chocolate cakes and flapjacks and fat fruit scones. The shopping would have been haphazard and the house a tip. But Mum wouldn't have made that tight face when I couldn't get out of bed. She would have climbed in and held me and stroked my hair. She would have listened to my raging without telling me to calm down and stop upsetting myself. She wouldn't have been afraid to say Hannah's name.

'Look, Rach,' Christopher said. 'I'd stay if I thought we were doing each other any good. But I'm not sure—'

'Go to work if it helps. It's obviously what you want. Fine.'

'I'll go in tomorrow. Just for the morning. They've said things can be flexible to begin with.' He stood, put his hand on the door, waited for a bit. 'I know you think it was my fault,' he said at last. 'I lie awake thinking the same. But thinking about who is to blame won't do any good. We need to find a way to help each other.'

She stared at a corner of the ceiling. She didn't want to look at him. He was right. And Gail had seen it, too. She did blame Christopher... And herself. If she had turned round, checked... The one she blamed most of all, though, the one who could have stopped it happening, the one she had always trusted – was God.

Christopher stayed by the door, silent. Then he said, 'Lucy asked if we wanted to go and see the place where they found her.'

Rachel's body stiffened.

'Near Saltbourne Gap,' Christopher went on. 'They can show us exactly where.'

'I don't know.'

'We can think about it,' Christopher said. 'And I think planning the funeral might help. It's been over a week since they found her. We can't put it off for ever. It will be a way for us to work together.' He paused. 'Remember her together. Grieve together.'

'But the inquest.' There had been something about an inquest, hadn't there? A band tightened round her chest, and her breath wouldn't come. They'd already been told there were no suspicious injuries. Submersion in water. Accidental... Phrases thudded through her. The sock on the beach. The missing shoe. Would she ever find out what had really happened? Would she ever be free of this horrible guessing game? Would she have to go to Saltbourne Gap – see the place? Would it help her get what she wanted? She needed someone to blame so it didn't have to be her fault, Christopher's fault, God's fault.

'Adjourned. Remember? They told us. We can go ahead

with the funeral. Gail said she can come and talk it through whenever you're ready.'

Remember? Who had told them? The police? And how could anyone ever be ready to bury their child? Tears slipped out of her eyes, trickled down her face. Through her thick sock, she felt the pressure of Christopher's hand on her foot. He held it for a second or two, and then left the room.

Hissing and sizzling came from the kitchen, and a meaty, oniony smell. Rachel couldn't face another meaty meal. Her stomach was weighed down with it, tight and bloated. She got up from the sofa and went into the kitchen. Mince was browning in a pan, and Janet was poking it with a wooden spoon. In another pan, neat cubes of potato lay submerged in water.

'I'll give you a hand,' Rachel said. She opened the fridge, found some courgettes and mushrooms, a stick of celery and some bright peppers, orange and yellow and red. She took the chopping board from its hook, and found the good knife in the cutlery drainer.

'It's all right, dear,' Janet said. 'I can manage. I thought we'd have peas with it. I was going to do something with those vegetables tomorrow. You go and sit down.'

'I'm fine. I've been sitting down all afternoon.' She'd tramped across the beach in the morning, shouting into the wind and throwing stones into the waves, with the holy stone in her pocket and a rage in her heart that would not calm. She was exhausted, but restless. Itching to do things, but at a loss.

'Shepherd's pie. It was always one of Christopher's favourites. And rhubarb crumble for pudding.' Janet opened a tin of tomatoes and poured them over the sizzling mince. She put the lid on the pan and, holding the wooden spoon aloft, looked at Rachel. 'Jamie's looking awfully skinny. Is he eating enough?'

'He eats like a horse,' Rachel said. 'I'm afraid he's not keen on rhubarb, though. He'll have ice cream or something.'

Was he still eating, though? Rachel tried to think. There had been regular meals, of course. Janet had made sure of that, and Jamie had been there, hadn't he? They had all been there, sitting round the table, with their napkins and their glasses of water and their separate grief. But what of his appetite? She had no idea. The image of him was distant, shrouded in fog.

'I'm going to do a quick stir-fry,' she said. 'I'm sorry, Janet. I can't face the meat.'

'Well if that's what you want. You should have said. I could have done it.'

Rachel's skin prickled. Her stomach clenched. 'I am saying. And I want to do it myself.'

Janet let out her breath in an explosive sigh, turned back to the stove, lifted the lid and stirred. She lowered the heat and went out of the room. Rachel heard her go upstairs and say something to Jamie. Probably extolling the virtues of rhubarb crumble.

Rachel ran the vegetables under the cold tap, rubbing at the celery with her thumb, and scraping the dark earth from the pale flesh of the mushrooms. She chopped and sliced slowly, inexplicably fearing for her fingers, imagining a sudden slip and a vivid fountain of blood. She finished, and a bright heap lay in the bowl. She found an onion and some garlic, splashed olive oil into a pan and switched on the heat.

When everything was done, she added a spoonful of red onion marmalade and let it melt in. The mince was still simmering, and the smell made her stomach turn.

Janet came back and turned on the heat under the potatoes.
'He was eating chocolate,' she said. 'No wonder he's not
interested in crumble.'

Rachel didn't answer.

'And his bin was full of wrappers.'

Rachel clenched her jaw. Janet must be the kind of person
who never craved chocolate, never used it to numb her feelings.
She couldn't stop the words hissing out between her teeth. 'His
sister is dead.'

She scooped her vegetables into a bowl, took them up to
Hannah's room, and ate them with a spoon. She heard the
others in the kitchen and crossed the landing to Jamie's room.
She looked in the bin, riffled through the wrappers. Five or
six. Not exactly full. She found some tissues. Blood-stained.
Had his nosebleeds started again? Had he mentioned it? She
couldn't think. Her fingers closed around more packaging. Not
chocolate wrappers. Stiffer, smooth. She pulled it out. Razor
blades. A pack of eight. An expensive brand. He wasn't quite
twelve. What did he want with razor blades? It didn't make
sense. She dropped the box back into the bin.

She wondered what Christopher would say if she told him
she couldn't breathe with his mother there. She squeezed her
fingers against her palms. I won't tell him, though, she thought.
I need her. Everything will fall to pieces without Janet. If only
she would stay invisible.

The next day, Christopher met her in the hall when she got
back from her pilgrimage to the beach. Through the open
kitchen door, she saw Janet scrubbing at the inside of a
cupboard whose contents were lined up on the counter. Rachel
pulled her boots off, hung up her coat and sank on to the

stairs. She could walk for miles, but as soon as she came back to the house, exhaustion overwhelmed her.

'Izzy phoned at lunch time,' Christopher told her. 'You didn't have your phone with you.'

'Oh, I'll call her back.'

'She's at work. It's Jamie. He didn't turn up to the counselling session yesterday.'

'Perhaps he didn't feel up to it. I don't think I would.'

'And he missed his last lesson in the afternoon. This morning he told his form tutor he'd gone home early with a headache. He said you'd promised to call them but you must have forgotten.'

'He didn't come home early. Did he?'

'She said his head of year wants us to go in and see them.'

'Is he in trouble?'

'No, of course not. They're concerned for his wellbeing. They want to see if they can do anything more to help.'

Rachel sighed. 'Everyone says the same thing. *Is there anything I can do?* They've all got the same obsession.'

'It's not an obsession,' Christopher said. 'It's instinctive. It's human. They care.'

'But it weighs me down,' Rachel said. 'This pressure to appreciate all the gestures people make, all the kind things they say. Even the best of them can't help. And the worst of them make me rage. People who think they understand, or who tell me how I must be feeling, what I ought to be doing to pull myself together. I'm sick of it. All of it.' She put her hands over her face. Even Izzy, she thought. 'It's too much. And now...Jamie. I can't, Christopher. I just can't.'

'I can't bear to see you rejecting everyone's kindness. You're building a wall round yourself.'

From the kitchen, Christopher's phone buzzed. He went to answer it.

'Okay,' Rachel heard him say. 'Yes. Will do. Half an hour or so.'

'What? Are you going straightaway?'

'Yes. He's missed afternoon registration. They don't know where he is.' He paused, and when he continued, he spoke gently, pleading. 'Come with me. Or he'll think you don't care. That's probably why he's doing it. As a kind of test. He needs us both, Rachel. Please.'

He was right. The trouble was, no matter what anyone needed, it simply wasn't in her. Of course she loved Jamie. But she was empty. As if she had died too, and her body was nothing more than an empty shell, playing a part.

But she nodded and got to her feet, put her coat and boots back on and followed him out of the front door.

A police car pulled up outside. A uniformed officer got out of the passenger door and met them on the path. Jamie was in the back seat.

'What...?' Christopher said.

'Mr Bird? Mrs Bird? Can we go inside? I'm afraid Jamie's got himself into some trouble.'

He had been caught shop-lifting in Save-it on the high street. Two packets of razor blades and three Twirls.

'We understand your family is going through a difficult time,' one of the officers said. 'We're not going to do anything formal this time. But do try to get help. We can suggest some agencies.'

'His school has organised counselling,' Christopher said.

Jamie sat on the sofa, still in his coat, looking at the floor, his shoulders hunched. He was so small, so insubstantial. Rachel wanted to hang on to him, press him tight against her body. *What are you doing?* she would say. *Stay with me. Please stay.* But she felt her arms might close around empty air, and he would be already gone.

When the police had left, Christopher said, 'You need to try and talk about it, Jamie. If not to us, then give the counselling a try. Or if you need a few more days off school…'

Jamie flung himself from the chair and charged up the stairs. His door slammed.

'Why razor blades?' Rachel said to Christopher.

'Common, apparently. One of the most stolen items.'

'Is this really all about whether we care?' she said. 'How are we going to pass, if it's a test? I don't know what to do. Do you? I feel like I'm in the wrong world, or the wrong life, like my skin has turned itself inside out.'

Hard Hat

Mary marched from the house, shrugging herself into her jacket, climbed into her car and slammed the door. How dare they fob her off with links to policies and bylaws and schemes? How dare they keep her on hold for twenty minutes, passing her between departments, only to tell her they couldn't deal with her enquiry on the phone and she'd have to put it in writing? And how dare they ignore her emails? What was the point of an automatic message saying precisely nothing and labelled donotreply? It was their responsibility, for heaven's sake. Her land was being snatched from her, great chunks of it cascading down to the beach, and they just stood by and did nothing. Well, she was going to make them do something. She'd drive to the council offices in Cromer and demand to speak to someone in person. Not just any old receptionist or dogsbody either. Someone high up in coastal protection. None of this coastal management stuff. Management! That was the thin end of the wedge. It meant giving up. Protection. That's what the coast needed. And that's what she'd get. She could design the scheme herself if they wanted.

She started the engine. It was over a week since she'd driven anywhere and a fear she didn't want to acknowledge fluttered behind her breastbone. She didn't dare put her foot down to the floor like she used to. This eye thing was a bloody nuisance. Perhaps it was time to do something about it. There'd be a pharmacy in Cromer with a rack of cheap specs. She'd pop in on the way home. All she needed was something to clear that patch of fog in the middle so she didn't have to keep squinting at things. She reversed out of the drive into Wetherley Lane. Her neck hurt if she twisted too far, but there was never anything coming.

Nine metres. That's what the people from the council had told her. When the cliff edge reached nine metres from the back wall of her house, they would issue an eviction order. It was policy. They marched about with their fancy electronic measuring machines, and tapped away at their iPads. 'Ten metres at this present time,' they said, but when she measured it with a proper tape measure it was ten metres and fifty-seven centimetres. The storm must have taken a good four or five metres. A third of her garden. And before that, in less dramatic incidents, inch by inch, the land had disappeared. The coast path outside the back fence was closed when Adam was eight, and by the time he was twelve, the path itself had gone, followed by the fence a few years later. She had seen no need to replace it. In a way, it would have been better if the house was on the other side of the lane, where she had made her nursery out of a pony paddock. It would have given her more time.

'You should have a look at the Coastal Rollback Register,' the officials told her.

'What? That crackpot scheme? The clue's in the name. I don't want my clifftop rolling back. That's exactly my point. I want it protected. Defended.'

All the other residents of Wetherley Lane had gone. Had done deals with landowners inland who wouldn't have got planning permission otherwise. 'Every one's a winner,' Kevin-at-the-other-end had said. 'At least I recover some of the value of this place.'

'It's not about the money,' Mary said. 'This is my home.'

A queue of traffic built up behind her and in the end she pulled in to a layby and let them all pass. On her left, a low fence marked the boundary of a meadow – half of it ragged grass, and half standing water. A flock of birds flew in and she heard the unmistakeable eee-oop of the lapwing. Pie-wipes, people called them round here. They wheeled in across the slate sky, their wings black then white, black then white, landed in the water and stood there, as if on tiptoe, alert, watching, waiting. Beyond them, on the field's margin, a row of pollarded willows stood guard.

She was about to pull away when a flash of yellow caught her attention under the fence near the end of the layby. Was she seeing things again? Was it the umbrella lady in a new outfit, or one of the beetles with a different shell? No. She was beginning to realise that those visions were always clear, in perfect focus. But this – she had to concentrate on her peripheral vision to see it, so it must be real. It was a hat. A hard hat.

When he was small, Adam went through a phase of pointing out hi-vis jackets discarded at the side of the road, shouting out the colours – orange! green! yellow! – and keeping a running total for weeks on end. A hundred or more in one summer alone. What did people do? Throw them away after one job? Or did they take them off in mid-project, let them fly away like kites in the wind?

She arrived at the council offices but the only parking space was outside the police station, on the same site. It was a new building, with some kind of turf roof and solar panels. There was even a wind turbine. Eco-friendly. Doing its bit against climate change. Huh, Mary thought as she parked the car, that's what's causing all these problems – climate change. Storm after storm, melting ice and rising sea levels and the land crumbling away. We can't just let it happen. We have to fight it.

There was a painting behind the reception desk – a blur of blue and grey with darker lines.

'Can I help you?'

When Mary's attention moved to the receptionist, the picture shifted into focus and she recognised the broken sea defences on the way to West Runton. They stood against the sky like blackened bones.

'I want to see someone in Coastal Protection.'

'Coastal Management? Do you have an appointment?'

Mary squared her shoulders. This was going to be a battle.

She stood her ground, refusing to leave, and in the end a man who looked as if he should be still be in college came down to talk to her, bombarding her with phrases like *managed retreat* and *realignment* and *sustainable approach*, referring her to the Shoreline Management Plan and giving her details of how to access the Rollback Register. 'It's a great opportunity, Mrs Farthing. What has happened at Wetherley Lane is due to saturation of groundwater. The cliff is unstable. I understand your concern, but there's nothing I can do.'

'I know what it's due to, thank you. And I know what needs to be done,' Mary said. She gave up trying to be polite. 'And if you people cared about your residents you'd pull your bloody finger out and get it sorted.' She struck the desk with the flat of her hand.

The official's eyes widened and he backed away.

The receptionist pointed to a sign about not abusing the staff. 'I suggest you read this,' she said. 'That includes verbal. They're just doing their jobs. You were lucky they even agreed to talk to you, turning up here without an appointment. Now, do you want me to call security?'

Abuse? For heaven's sake, Mary thought. But there was nothing more to be done here. Not for the moment.

A man stood between her and the door. He wore big glasses and a blue scarf. He put his hand on her forearm as she reached past him for the door handle.

'I couldn't help overhearing.'

'What?' She stepped back, shrugging his hand from her arm.

'What you were saying about the cliffs and the sea defences. How he tried to fob you off.'

'And?' Rage bubbled in Mary's veins. Her skin itched. She wanted to punch someone.

'We've got a campaign group. Defend Our Coast. DOC.'

'Doc?'

'There's a public meeting this evening in the community centre.' He thrust a leaflet at her. 'You should come. Join the group. They don't listen to individuals. We've got more chance of getting somewhere if we fight this together.'

'Won't do any good.' She didn't take the leaflet. 'They're

not interested. Didn't you hear what he said? Managed bloody retreat.'

'But groups like ours can make a difference. They're obliged to take local views into consideration. It says so here, look.'

'Empty words,' Mary said. 'Jumping through hoops. Local consultation, then do what they were going to do all along. Waste of time. Excuse me.' She moved forward, pushing him aside, yanked the door open and went out to her car.

She tried a dozen pairs of glasses and settled on a yellow-tinted pair that seemed to improve things. Then she bought a cheese and ham sandwich and ate it in the car before setting off for home. Instead of feeling deflated by her encounter with the council official, she was infused with energy, fired up. Her skin was alive, her muscles charged. If they wouldn't help, she would take matters into her own hands. There must be a way she could stop the erosion. In the old days, people had tied up bundles of brushwood and piled them against the base of the cliff. She had studied the history of it as part of her degree. The authorities had even encouraged people to tip their rubbish over the edge. She would find a way.

Everything looked different with the glasses on, the landscape washed in pale gold and – was that middle patch clearer? She came to the layby where she had stopped before, saw a flash of yellow. Nothing was coming towards her. A quick glance in the mirror. She swerved sharply, pulled across and crunched to a halt on the gravel. She climbed out of the car. The lapwings had gone, but there was the hard hat. She picked it up. The yellow had come off in places, and there was dried mud caked on one side. She got back in the car and sat with the hat on her lap. She ran her finger across the three ridges on the top. It's a shell, she thought. Don't turtle shells have ridges like that? She lifted the hat and put it on her head, fastened the strap. It was an extra skull, outside hers. Stupid. What did she want with an extra skull? Hers was pretty robust. She threw the hat on the passenger seat, and drove off, with a sudden certainty that next time she went out on the landslide she would find her bench. And it would be a sign. A sign that she could save her piece of the land's edge.

The little girl grins when she sees the shark tooth. Both her top middle teeth are missing, but her smile is like sunshine.

'I know where there are more fossils,' he says. 'Special ones. D'you want to see?'

'Can you get me one?'

'No. They're part of the ground. The beach. Past the rock armour.'

'Rock armour?'

'That's what these blocks are called but their other name is sea defences and they're to stop the sea hurting the land.'

'I know about a king who tried to stop the sea. He was called King Canoe and his feet got wet and he couldn't stop it. It's in a book. But Mummy says he didn't really want to. It was about God being stronger than anyone.'

'Well, if he did want to stop it, he should have used rock armour. Come on, let's climb over. I can help you if you want.'

Bench

Izzy came with two enormous slices of carrot cake. 'This is the best cream-cheese frosting you have ever tasted,' she said. 'And I'm going to make you the best coffee. I've brought it all with me – even cream.' She continued, without a pause, while she laid things out on the counter – blue and white bone china mugs, a posh-looking packet of coffee beans, a grinder. 'I know you didn't like what I said about shutting your family out. And I'm sorry you were upset. Maybe I used the wrong words. But we're friends, and I care too much to keep quiet, Rach. And you being upset with me isn't going to hurt my feelings or push me away. So I'm going to carry on being truthful, and if I think you need to hear something, I'm going to say it. I'd expect you to do the same for me.'

Rachel shrugged and sighed. 'Okay, I suppose. But I feel so alone. I know that people are imagining what it must be like and it makes me want to scream. I don't know why. It's like I'm in a bubble and all the messages and wishes and platitudes are pressing on its skin and if it bursts everything will fall to pieces and I'll be lost.'

Izzy rummaged in her bag, brought out some crumpled, bright paper. 'The kids made cards.' She held out a green one, festooned with curls of blue and white and orange. 'This is Lenny's. He's just learned how to curl paper by pulling it through scissors. Our whole house is like a packaging factory.'

Rachel took the card, opened it up.

'He was all right until he wrote her name,' Izzy said. 'Then he couldn't stop crying. "I love her," he sobbed, over and over. Set me off, too. And this is Flora's.' She handed Rachel a pink envelope scrawled with brown felt pen.

Rachel looked inside.

'Oh, there's nothing in there. The envelope is all there is. She insisted. It's chocolate, all the brown.'

'These are the best cards I've had,' Rachel said. They wouldn't stand up, so she pinned them to the notice board in the kitchen.

'How's Jamie?' Izzy said.

'He was caught shoplifting. Razor blades and chocolate. Christopher thinks it's some kind of test, to make sure we still love him.'

Izzy squeezed her hand, and this time she didn't say anything.

Early one afternoon, a few days later, Janet stood at the ironing board, and fished something from the laundry basket.

'Are these yours, dear?' she said. 'Or are they Christopher's? They don't look like something he would wear.' She held up a pair of scruffy trousers, dark grey, with pockets on the legs.

Then a crumpled green cotton shirt.

Rachel didn't recognise them. 'I don't know.'

Christopher was taking things slowly, back at work, and they were continuing to be flexible. Jamie had said he didn't need any more time off. He'd been quiet and withdrawn, refused to engage in any conversation about the shoplifting, and spent a lot of time shut in his room. His head of year had phoned to say he'd attended a counselling appointment, and he hadn't skipped any more of his lessons. Rachel wondered if they had passed the test after all.

She was unable to focus on anything for more than a few minutes. She hadn't set foot in the church and when she tried to pray she didn't know who she was talking to. Everything she believed about God had been called into question. Christopher seemed to find some comfort in his long conversations with Gail, and maybe with God for all she knew. Sometimes she wanted to ask him, but what if he, too, turned out to be not the person she thought he was? Fear lodged under her skin, prickled against it. All she could do was move from home to the sea, and back again. A fierce need pulsed through her veins, pressed against her ribs, pushed at the inside of her skull. If only she could find out what had happened. If only someone could tell her whose fault it was. That was the only way she would ever make sense of things.

The iron hissed and Janet undid the buttons of the shirt and spread it over the board.

Rachel remembered then. Remembered the bungalow, perched on the cliff above the landslide. Remembered Mary, the woman who had rescued her from the sea, taken her up the steps and warmed her by the stove, peeled off her wet clothes. These were Mary's shirt and trousers. There was a jumper too, and socks. And somewhere, a belt.

As soon as Janet had ironed and folded the clothes, Rachel took them upstairs, found the rest of Mary's things, put them in a carrier bag, and stuffed it into her backpack.

A biting wind blew in from the sea, stinging Rachel's skin and whipping her hair around her face. She should have brought a hat. She wrapped her scarf more tightly, covering her mouth and nose and ears. The tide was up, and she trudged across the cobbles at the top of the beach. For the first time since it happened, she had a reason to go somewhere.

And there was Mary, standing on the slope of land that had fallen from the end of her garden, looking up at the raw edge of the cliff above her. Beside her, a spade was stuck into the ground, which had been dug over like a field ready for planting. Rachel climbed up the shallow slope, remembering the warning signs along the path. *Danger. Unstable cliffs. Do not climb.*

'Oh, it's you,' Mary said.

'I brought your clothes back.' Rachel took off the backpack.

'Right.' Mary pointed up at the cliff edge. 'I had a bench up there. I've rescued most of my shed, saved what I could of the plants, but I can't find the bloody bench.'

'Do you have another spade?' Rachel said.

'Up the top. In the shed.'

Rachel took the bag of clothes up and found the shed, though it was no longer complete. Planks had splintered, and there was no glass in the window. The roof was sound, though, and the floor. Everything was stored in piles of boxes and tubs on the floor. A scratched, yellow hard hat hung on a hook on the back of the door. Rachel dumped the bag of clothes and found a spade.

Back on the slope, Mary took a length of twine and some sticks from her pocket and marked out a long rectangle. 'You take this section. I'll do the next one. I've already dug this over once, but it must be buried deeper than I thought.'

They worked in silence. Rachel fell into a rhythm and began to warm up. She was almost at the last corner of her section when her spade hit something hard. She scrabbled at the earth, scraped it away from a long, smooth piece of wood. A burst of joy exploded inside her, but was quickly smothered by a wave of guilt. How could she, even for a second? How could she ever, ever? She closed her eyes, breathed in the damp, earthy scent, and let the pain reclaim her.

'Ah, that's it!' Mary knelt beside her, dug in with her bare hands. In the end, both out of breath, they pulled the bench from the ground. Like some massive root, Rachel thought, as the rusty earth fell away from the pale wood. Or like something newborn. Between them, they set it on the slope and sat down on it, side by side, facing the ocean.

Rachel listened to her own breathing as it slowed, and Mary's, too. It was marvellous, really, air going in and out of their lungs, their hearts beating inside their chests, their muscles recovering from the effort. She remembered standing in Mary's kitchen that day – the heat from the stove, wet clothes being peeled from her body, but she couldn't remember getting home. Had she walked back? Had Mary gone with her, or taken her in the car? Did Christopher know anything about it?

She smoothed the cool wood under her palm. Felt the solidity of the seat supporting her, fitting her curves, as if it was measured for her bones, aligned to her joints. Out at sea, white peaks raced over the surface, and the waves rolled in, building to huge arcs, and then flung themselves on to the beach in a burst of spray. Beyond, on the blur of the horizon, faint outlines of the wind turbines stood under the putty-coloured sky. Gulls cried, wheeling on the air currents, up and round, down and back again, before landing in a group on the stone-scattered sand, and standing there like sculptures of themselves, waiting for some mysterious signal to take to the air again.

'I knew I'd find it,' Mary said.

'In your bones?'

'Bones. Heart. Stomach. I knew. That's all. It had to be here. Somewhere.'

'I think it's my bones,' Rachel said.

'What is?'

'Where I feel things.' She paused, rubbed the wood under her thumb. 'Want things.'

'What is it that you want?'

Rachel thrust her hand in her pocket, let her fist close around the holy stone. She pulled it out. 'She asked me to look after this.'

'Hannah?'

Hearing the name made Rachel's breath catch, and there was a flutter behind her ribs. Hannah. The word inhabited the space between them. It grew, curled and spiralled like a smoke ring, spreading out until little dots of it were everywhere.

'A hagstone,' Mary said. 'I've got a few of those hanging up in the garden.'

'A hagstone?'

'A stone with a hole in. They're supposed to have magical powers.'

'Oh, you mean hag as in witch?'

'That's right. Adam brought me mine. He's mostly after

fossils, but he collects sea glass too and odd bits of metal. All sorts. He calls them treasures. And if he finds one of these he brings it home to me.'

'I think I've seen him. On the beach. Tall. Serious.'

'Yes, that's Adam. Daft great lump. But not a bad bone in his body.'

'Do you believe in it – the magic?'

'No. Load of rubbish. You have to make your own luck.'

'Hannah made a prayer bracelet and it got lost and then she found this and she was going to make a giant one. She went off to look for more stones.'

'She believed in the magic, then?'

'Not magic. Prayer.'

'Same thing, isn't it?'

'I don't think so. The opposite, really. I mean, magic is pagan. Pre-Christian.'

'Call it prayer, then. Do you believe in it?'

Rachel looked at the stone. Hannah's name still floated in the air. 'I'm training to be a priest.'

'I take it that means you do. Or think you should.'

'I did, but now I don't know.'

'Why?'

Rachel looked up, surprised. How could she ask that?

'Why?' Mary said again. 'Think about it.'

There was something in Mary's gaze, in her weathered face and her blunt tone that made Rachel feel exposed. 'Because he let it happen,' she said. 'I mean God. He could have kept her safe.'

'Why should he?'

'The same reason I would. Love. I believed in his love. His protection.'

'People die. In all sorts of ways. People suffer.'

Rachel looked out towards the sea, the white wave-crests and the smudged horizon.

'The thing is,' Mary said, 'nothing has changed.'

Pain twisted inside Rachel. Everything had changed.

'People suffer,' Mary said again. 'Accidents happen. Children drown. Whatever you believed about God, you believed it in a world where that happened. Just not to you.'

'My mother died,' Rachel said. 'She had cancer.'

They sat in silence for a while, and then Mary said, 'You say it's in your bones. So what is it? What do you want?'

'I want her back.'

'Yes.'

'The funeral is on Monday. Hannah's funeral.'

'In the church? Here?'

'Yes.' She paused. 'If you…No, why should you…?'

'No,' Mary said quickly. 'No, I don't go inside churches. Not any more. But I'd like to give… I mean, not flowers, but will there be donations for something? I'd like to.'

'Thank you. I haven't got my phone on me but if you give me your number I'll send you the link. It's giraffes.'

Mary laughed. 'Giraffes?'

The two women looked at each other now, and when Rachel smiled, she felt a loosening inside her and this time the guilt didn't pull her tight again.

'Hannah was besotted with giraffes. So we found a giraffe charity. They're endangered, apparently. Some species anyway.'

'I didn't know there was more than one kind of giraffe.'

'Neither did I.'

They sat, watching the sea and the sky and the birds, and after a while, Rachel said, 'Thinking about what I want, it's not just that I want her back. I want to know. If I knew what had happened. If I knew whose fault it was...' She paused, felt her feet press against the ground beneath her, this ground that had moved and rearranged itself, redrawn the boundary between land and sea. 'I need it to be someone's fault.'

'Does it matter whose?'

'I keep thinking it's me, or Christopher – my husband. Sometimes I blame God. But I don't know what happened, so I can't be sure.'

'You want to know what happened, so you can blame the right person?'

Rachel rolled her hands in the ends of her scarf, still cradling the hagstone in her fist. She looked at her feet in their dirty boots, then up at the sky. 'I keep thinking about her sock and shoe.'

'What about them?'

'When they found her, they said she hadn't been...hurt. But she only had one shoe and sock on. They found her sock by the sea defences. But...the shoe... She had these red shoes. They didn't find the other shoe. And I keep wondering why she was only wearing one. But how can I ever know?'

'Hannah believed in prayer, you said.'

'Yes. But that doesn't mean it works. She was praying for a dog, but we were never going to get one.'

'Maybe not, but what if prayer is all you've got? You're used to praying. Why give up now, when you most need it?'

Rachel stood. 'Look,' she said. 'Let's get this thing back up to the garden. Let's put it back where it belongs.'

Mary heaved herself to her feet. 'We can give it a go, but it's quite a weight. Let's hope you're stronger than you look.'

'Tea? Might have the end of a fruit cake left.'

The kitchen was warm, and Rachel took off her scarf and coat, hung them over the back of a chair. They had dragged the bench up the slope and set it next to the shed, a couple of metres from the new edge of the cliff. But the wind was bitter now and their fingers were raw and red.

'Thanks.' She wrapped her freezing hands round the hot mug. Why did it matter so much?' she said.

'What?'

'The bench.'

'I got the idea that if I couldn't find it, I might as well give up.'

'Give up what?'

'Trying to save my house, my garden, my cliff.'

'Do you have a plan?'

'Not yet. But I'm going to bloody think of one.'

They drank their tea and ate the last of the fruit cake, and Rachel put her coat back on. 'I left your clothes in the shed,' she said. 'In a bag. They've been washed.'

'Thanks. Oh, don't go without my number. For the giraffes.' Mary picked up a marker that lay with a tangle of garden twine on the table.

Rachel held out her hand. 'Write it on here. I'd only lose a piece of paper.'

Mary's skin was rough and warm on hers, and it seemed to Rachel that they exchanged more than a means of contacting one another. She found she couldn't bear the thought that this woman might, in the end, lose her battle with the sea. That she might have to give up.

'If you could get the stuff,' Rachel said, 'I don't know – hard core or soil or whatever – you could build the cliff back up.

Landscape gardening on a massive scale.'

'Huh! Where would I get hold of that much material? My God, woman, you are not only stronger than you look, but also crazier.'

Rachel walked back along the narrow strip of sand with the wind behind her and Mary's number written on the back of her hand. The hagstone bumped against her hip. It was almost dusk, and out at sea the light of a small fishing boat shone bright against the darkening water.

A Bag of Pebbles

It was like a new job. As well as being a fossil hunter, Adam was now a hero. Mr Bright had said so. He'd be busier in the summer, of course, when the beach would be jam-packed with wind-breaks and pop-up tents and dogs and picnic baskets and ball games and buckets and spades. Children wandered off, and parents didn't always pay attention.

But it wasn't only the beach. Adam worked out a circuit. He usually helped Mumma with her jobs first, then he'd patrol the beach, before going all the way round the playground, and across the green by the flats. Some of the children playing out on their own were very young. Too young for school. Running up and down the paths, or hurtling along on tiny bikes and scooters and not a parent in sight. So he kept guard. He picked them up if they fell, lifting them under the arms. Magic kiss, like Mumma. If they went near the road he shouted at them to get back, stay on the grass. He'd nip to Molly's for a pasty or a sandwich, and at home time he waited outside the school gates, just in case. And then back home along the beach, looking for fossils.

Sometimes, the keeping guard wasn't about keeping children safe. It was about not letting them get away with stuff. The other day he had seen a boy stealing things from Save-it. Two Twirls and some razor blades. So he had told the shopkeeper and the police had come and the boy had to face the consequences.

But mostly it was about protecting children who might be in danger. One afternoon he found a little boy on the beach. It was the first sunny day for a week. The boy had been watching some older children throwing stones into the waves, and when they went away, he followed them for a bit, looked around him and then started crying. Adam took his hand and they walked up the beach, all the way from the second lot of steps to Molly's, and then a lady came running out of nowhere and grabbed the boy and squeezed him tight enough to stop him breathing.

'There you are!' she said. 'I was going out of my mind!'

'He was on his own,' Adam said. 'I was looking after him.'

The lady said thank you but her face looked angry.

The Saturday after that, at the same time as buying his ham and tomato sandwich, he bought a bag of chocolate pebbles. He'd had them once before and the strange sensation of danger as he bit into them made his stomach do a kind of flip. He sat on the bench in the playground to eat his sandwich and had just finished it when he heard laughter. Not the happy, friendly kind. He was about to jump up and make a quick getaway, in case it was Danny and his mates, when he saw that it was coming from a gaggle of children – eleven or twelve years old

– clustered around the swings. A smaller boy was on the swing, and the others were pushing him, some at the front, some at the back. They laughed and shouted and he went higher and higher, and on his face was an expression of pure terror.

'Let's make him go over the top,' shouted a girl with a long ponytail.

'Higher! Higher!' chanted a couple of the boys.

'What's the matter? Not scared, are you?'

'Thought you liked the swings. The little kids' swings.'

Adam's insides scrunched together. He knew how the boy would be shouting inside his head, *No! Stop!* He knew how he'd be hanging on as tight as he could and on every swing up he would wish he could keep flying, could sail away into the sky. But down he would come again and another shove would send him lurching up.

Quite the hero, Mr Bright had said. But was he? He wanted to leap up and barge into the group, scattering them with his hero voice. But he couldn't. It was just like with Danny. His words were stuck, and his legs were glued to the bench.

There were several other people about, families, and a group of teenagers in the shelter, but no one else intervened either. In the end, the gang got bored and went away.

The boy on the swing was crying. He scraped his feet on the ground to slow the swing, and Adam, released from his paralysis, was there before it had stopped.

'Are you okay?'

The boy sniffed, wiped his nose on his sleeve.

'Don't worry. They've gone. I know what will make you feel better.'

'What?'

'Come and have a look. Over here.' Adam walked towards

the bench where he had left his bag and picked up the bag of pebbles. 'Have some.'

The boy hesitated, and then followed.

'Go on. They're not really stones. They're chocolate.'

The boy reached out, but Adam grabbed his hand, turned it over and tipped out pebbles until his palm was full.

'You should sit down for a bit before you go. Calm down. You don't want to go home with your face all snotty like that. Have you got a tissue or something?'

The boy wiped his sleeve across his face again and sat down.

'What's your name?' Adam sat next to him, not too close. He didn't want him to be scared.

'Luke.'

'It's okay, Luke. I told you. They're chocolate. Look, it says it on the bag. I'm not tricking you.'

'What do you think you're doing?' An explosion of sound. A woman with a roaring mouth and angry, frowning eyes. 'Sweets? Who are you? You leave my son alone. Come on, Luke.' She grabbed the boy's arm, pulled him up. Pebbles shot in all directions, rolled across the ground.

She marched him away, and Adam quickly stuffed the sweet bag in his pocket. There were still a few left. Snatches of the woman's crossness reached him. *Never talk to strangers…how many times…can't trust…* Odd, he thought, how the words were like Mumma's, but the voice wasn't.

When they'd gone, he became aware of people staring and whispering. The two women nearest him, both with toddlers in buggies, nudged each other and one of them said, 'We've seen you here before, hanging around. This is a kids' place. It's not for people like you.'

They turned and started off down the path, and a man

caught up with them. 'Good for you,' he said. 'He hangs about outside the school, too. And he hasn't got kids, so what's he doing there?' As they walked away, Adam thought he heard the word police.

He crawled round picking up the scattered pebbles. He could take them home and rinse the dirt off. Shame to waste them. Then he realised he might be picking up stones. The chocolate ones were so realistic you couldn't tell the difference. He dropped them back on the ground and watched them roll under the bench.

He thought he might take the day off tomorrow.

An Unlit Candle

What if prayer is all you've got? Mary's words echoed in Rachel's mind. *Why give up now?* But where would she start? How could she pray to God? She didn't know who he was any more. But Mary's words wouldn't go away. *Nothing has changed. What if prayer is all you've got?* She couldn't ask for answers yet. There was something she had to do first.

She went down to the sea defences again, where the robot stood, arms outstretched. Across the sea, the wind turbines pointed their propeller blades in different directions, like giant signposts to random destinations. Waves rolled in diagonally from the west, and the rippling patterns in the sand mimicked the mackerel sky. Turnstones busied themselves at the edge of the surf, and gulls stood in contemplation, their feathers ruffling in the breeze. A pair of oystercatchers flew over the water, with their bright splashes of orange and pink, and their whistle-blast cry.

She chose a dark, egg-shaped stone. She drew back her arm, gathered her strength. All that shouting into the sky, hurling stones into the waves, all those spasms of anguish and fury, face down in the sand – she wanted, now, to package it up, make a bomb out of it and fling it at him. Let it explode in his face.

When it hit the rock, a loud crack split the air. The stone ricocheted up, in a fast spin, and then rattled down the slope into the shadows.

The birds took off, wheeling away on the wind.

The day before the funeral, on an afternoon of watery sunshine and pale sky, Rachel walked to the sea defences and then climbed up the steps by Mary's bungalow. She turned off Wetherley Lane on to the cliff path and then took the track up to the top road. She stopped at the church. She hadn't been there since that meeting, the day before it happened. She turned the heavy, iron handle and pushed the door, stepped inside. The familiar, dusty smell hit her first, and then beeswax polish. She drifted past the font, with its worn stone carvings – the pelican, the lion, the grinning green man and the griffon. The blue carpet of the central aisle was soft under her feet and the light through the stained glass fell in diagonal columns, throwing jewelled patches across the pews and the floor. The flowers by the pulpit steps were fading, the gerbera drooping and the rose petals going brown. Tomorrow, there would be new ones.

They had left it to Janet – ordering the flowers. Rachel and Christopher had sat together with photographs spread on the kitchen table. Hannah as a baby in her first pair of giraffe pyjamas. Holding hands with Jamie when she'd just started walking. First day of school, her skirt hem below her knees and her jumper bunched up at her wrists, a huge grin on her face. Christopher had suggested making a slideshow on a loop to play on a big screen at the wake, with music, but she said no let's keep it low-tech. They chose six pictures, mounted them in a frame. They had given Floppy Rabbit to the funeral directors to put in with Hannah. Every night, Rachel took the holy stone from her pocket, on its frayed blue rope, and slid it under her pillow. They still hadn't found the prayer bracelet.

In the Lady Chapel, Rachel took a candle from the box, but the matches and lighters were all locked in the vestry. Fire hazard. Next time, she would bring some. But next time would be tomorrow. How would she get through the day? It was impossible to see herself coming out the other side. She sat for a while, holding the candle. Then she laid it on the side altar in a lozenge of sunlight. Even unlit, it was a kind of prayer.

They had agreed to wear what they had been wearing that day – jeans and everyday jumpers. They had asked people not to wear black.

It rained. Everything was grey, sodden, dull. The cars crawled up the high street, and on to the top road, the tyres swishing on the wet tarmac. One of the windscreen wipers squeaked. Rachel and Christopher sat with Jamie between them, clinging together, silent.

At the church, they waited in the porch. The bearers stopped at the lych gate, adjusted the little white coffin on their shoulders. The ground under Rachel's feet dissolved and her legs wouldn't hold her. She fell against Christopher and a low sound came from her throat. He clutched her to him, stopped her falling. Beside them, Jamie stood, his eyes like bruises in his pale, pinched face, his sleeves pulled down over his hands.

The church was full. A blur of bright colours, young faces. The sound of weeping. The adults from the parent and baby choir sang. Gail spoke about everlasting life, and about the loving arms of Jesus. Christopher read the eulogy and halfway through he broke down and Gail stepped in and finished it, her arm around his shoulders.

Rachel sat in the pew, her fingers tight on the order of service, where Hannah's beautiful face smiled on the cover. Christopher came back to his place and there were prayers. *Time of darkness...creatures of this earth...leave her in your care.* And then, finally, the Lord's Prayer. Voices murmured round the church. The order of service slipped from Rachel's hand, fluttered to the floor. *Your will be done...* She ducked to retrieve it from the dust...*our daily bread...* She remained bent over, her head on her knees. I could lie down, she thought, here in the dust. I could disappear... *Forgive us our sins...* The words swam in from far away, muted and muffled. She sat up, light-headed, and the praying voices boomed in her ears, as if she had come up from underwater... *As we forgive those who sin against us...forgive those...sin against us...* She brushed the dust from Hannah's face and pressed the paper against her breast, closed her eyes.

Only immediate family were at the burial. Rain pattered on umbrellas and whispered in the bare branches. There was no wind. The fresh, damp earth smelled strangely sweet. Earth to earth. Dust to dust.

By the time they arrived at the Scout Hut, everyone was

eating and drinking and there was a blur of faces, a buzz of conversation.

'I don't know if I can…' Rachel said to Christopher.

'Why don't I get you something? Do you want a drink? Or tea? Water?'

'Please don't. Don't leave me.' Rachel clung to his sleeve.

'I won't. I'm here. Let's sit down. Izzy…could you…? Tea, and a cake or something… I think Rachel's… Something sugary would help.'

Rachel sank on to a chair, laid her head on her arms on the table. She wanted to sleep. Perhaps forever. Why were people talking so much? What could they have to say? It was over. It was all over.

She drank some tea and ate something that was mostly chocolate butter icing. Later she found herself drifting round the room, arm in arm with Christopher, murmuring responses to endless words of condolence. She summoned a small smile and fixed it to her face. She had the absurd notion that she was dancing one of those slow and stately numbers from a Jane Austen drama. Sidestep, back and turn. Move on to the next couple. She almost expected them to bow, and she would dip a curtsey. But most of them wanted to touch her – hugs with back rubs, long hand holds, pats on the shoulder.

Let it be over soon. Oh, let it all be done.

In the morning, it was raining again. Rachel went back to the church with a box of matches in her pocket. She stood by Hannah's grave and listened to the rain, smelled the wet earth. As soon as she entered the building, the scent of the flowers hit her. She hadn't noticed them yesterday. Daffodils and irises and white tulips, tubs of purple and yellow crocuses, and the fragrance came from the freesias. Janet had made it feel and smell like spring. A rush of gratitude took Rachel by surprise.

On the side altar, the candle was lying where she had left it. She was about to pick it up when she noticed that the wick was black. Someone had lit it. She took out the box of matches and placed the candle in the small stand on the altar. She looked at the black wick and pictured someone lighting the candle, and for some reason, the picture was of Mary, even though she never went inside a church. Not any more, she had said, as if something had happened to make her stop. Rachel imagined the flame that had burned for such a short time, flickering here in the quietness. And she breathed her longing into that flame. Her need to find the truth. It was enough, for now. After a bit, she put the matches back in her pocket, took the unlit candle out of the stand, and laid it on the altar cloth. It was as if she was laying herself down.

It was a beginning.

When she arrived home at lunch time, she found seven missed calls from Izzy. And a voicemail.

Rachel, I need to talk to you. Call me as soon as you get this. I'm at work, but you can use this number.

She sat on the bed and called back.

'At last. Listen, Rachel. This would be best face to face, but I wanted you to know straightaway.'

'What? You sound… What's happened?'

'Are you on your own?'

'I'm in my bedroom. Janet's downstairs. What's wrong?'

'Where's Christopher?'

'At work.'

'I had to call social services. It's Jamie.'

Rachel's heart raced, and her fingers tensed. 'Is he all right? Where is he?' She was ready to leap into action.

'He's here, at school. He's safe. Listen to me, Rachel. I had to call them because it's a safeguarding issue.'

'What do you mean? What's he done?'

'They're on their way to your house now. They need to talk to you.'

'Does Christopher know? Have you called him?'

'Jamie made a disclosure this morning. He's made allegations of abuse.'

'Abuse? What? No!' Rachel's mouth dried and her chest tightened. 'What's happened? Is he all right? Who?'

'He told us that his father has been hurting him.' She paused. 'Christopher.'

Rachel crumpled, her face on her knees, arms cradling her head. Nausea flooded over her, saliva filling her mouth with a horrible, bitter taste.

He folds back the carpet, presses on one end of the loose floorboard and slides his fingers under the other end to lift it. He shoves the things into the hole in the floor and wedges the board back in place.

They eat in front of the telly, and afterwards, when Mumma has settled down to watch her detective programme, he takes a jar of nails and a hammer from the kitchen window sill. In his room he puts on some loud, bashy music – that's what Mumma calls it – and hammers the board to the bit of wood that goes across the floor underneath. Bang, bang, bang, in time with the thump of the bass. A row of nails all the way across.

There. Gone.

Now he can forget about it.

Earth

On the day they had found the bench, Mary discovered that Rachel had left her scarf hanging over the back of a chair in the kitchen. She picked it up – a loosely knitted, multi-coloured thing in chunky yarn – and hung it on the back of the door with her own wax jacket. Then she remembered the bag of things Rachel had brought back, and went out to the shed to bring it in. In her bedroom, she pulled out the clothes. Freshly ironed. Beautifully folded. She lifted the shirt to her face. Some floral scent. She laid them in the bottom drawer of the chest. Most of the things in there didn't fit her any more.

She sat on the bed and thought about what Rachel had suggested. Ridiculous, of course. It would take an enormous volume of material to build up even her small section of the cliff. She could try to move some of the stuff that had fallen, perhaps, but the sea would soon reclaim it. What was needed was extra material so that the sea could take it without encroaching on the land where the house was. And she would need to replenish it constantly, like feeding a hungry beast. But where on earth would she get hold of such a huge amount of stuff? And what stuff, anyway? The cliffs here were a hotchpotch – chalk bedrock in some parts, clay and sand, gravel and flint, all covered with layers of windblown sand. Perhaps it didn't matter what she used, as long as it did the job without causing any harm. As long as she could get enough.

It was impossible. But she couldn't stop thinking about it.

She'd have to get Adam to help her, of course, if she could persuade him to stop these long days out. She couldn't do it without him. It wasn't easy, admitting that. All these years, she'd looked after him, fought for him, protected him, and now, bit by bit, she was beginning to rely on him almost as much as he did on her. Did that mean she had been a good mother? She'd taught him how to look after himself, hadn't she? How to keep people at arm's length so they couldn't hurt you. But then she thought of that bloody Danny and how Adam wouldn't stand up to him. Perhaps, instead of giving him the tools to defend himself, she had made him too dependent on her, too cautious.

The next day, Saturday, he came home with a bag of those chocolate pebbles and a strange question. He'd got something into his head about being a hero.

He offered her the scrunched-up bag. 'They're chocolate. It's a sort of joke you can eat. Go on, have some.'

There weren't many left. Mary took a couple and bit into them. 'Delicious,' she said, as the sweetness spread over her tongue.

He took the bag from her and tipped the last few sweets into his mouth, dropped the empty packet on the table. Then he said, 'Mumma, you know if someone's a kind person, a hero?'

'Ye-es,' she said slowly.

'And how sometimes other people don't like it and get cross?'

'Absolutely.' Look what happened to Jesus, she thought, with a stab of surprise that he should come to her mind.

'Should the hero carry on doing the kind things anyway?'

'It would take courage. I don't think it can ever be wrong to be kind. But you have to be careful. I mean, you can't trust everyone. Are you going to tell me what this is all about?'

'I don't need to now you've told me the answer.'

'Well, you'll always be my hero, you daft great lump. Why don't you show me a bit of kindness and make me a cup of tea? It's hard work out there. My legs are killing me.'

It took several days of internet searching and emails and phone calls, but eventually she found a contractor who was willing, under the radar, to deliver several lorry-loads of clay soil from an excavation site.

'How many loads do you want?' he said. He didn't ask what she wanted it for.

'How many have you got?'

'Twenty. Thirty maybe, if you don't mind waiting. It's a win, win,' he told her. 'I don't have to pay through the nose to dispose of it. And you get it dirt cheap. Haha! Get it?' He said she could use his compacting machine, if he didn't need it at the time, and there was a micro digger too, if she was interested.

They arranged for the first delivery on Tuesday afternoon. If she got him to drive to the barrier at the end of the road, he could position his lorry so that he could tip the load over the edge. It would mean a lot of moving work down at the bottom, and she wasn't sure they'd be able to get a digger down on to the beach, even a micro one. But she had a couple of wheelbarrows.

Tuesday. The contractor was late. No text message. Nothing. Bloody nuisance. She was itching to get on with it, now that she'd got a plan. She checked her phone again. Still no message. She keyed in his number. Left a voicemail.

An hour after he was due, the phone rang.

But it wasn't him.

It was the police. 'Mrs Farthing, we have your son Adam here at the station.'

She pulled up outside the police station, opposite the council offices where she had met with such stupid bureaucracy, yanked on the handbrake and puffed out a breath of relief. She had forgotten her glasses and had driven all the way feeling as though she was holding her breath, gripping the wheel so hard that her fingers went white. Her head was pounding. What did they think he had done? They wouldn't tell her on the phone. It must be some kind of misunderstanding. She hoped he wasn't in too much of a state. He wasn't under arrest, at least. They'd said it was a voluntary interview, but since they believed him to be a vulnerable adult, he needed someone with him before they could proceed.

She had to wait a few minutes, and then she was shown into an interview room and then Adam came in with one of the officers who had come to the house on the day that Hannah Bird went missing.

'I'm DS Stone,' he said. 'We've met. Would you like a cup of tea? A glass of water?'

If only he didn't sound so kind, so reasonable. She wanted to feel cross with him, but she couldn't. She tried to focus on Adam's face, gauge his expression, but he wouldn't make eye contact, didn't acknowledge her.

'Are you going to tell me what my son is supposed to have done?' she said.

There were procedures and forms and they cautioned him and she had to sign that she was happy he'd understood the caution and then, at last, she found out what it was all about.

Some 'members of the public' had reported Adam for inappropriate behaviour with children. He'd been seen approaching pupils outside the school that afternoon, and one of the parents said he'd been telling children off for climbing the wrong way up the slide in the playground. He'd grabbed hold of one of them, and she'd almost fallen. And there was a report of him offering sweets to a child on the previous Saturday. She thought of the chocolate pebbles. And his question about being a hero.

DS Stone went through each incident separately, asking Adam if he had done those things, giving him the opportunity to explain his reasons, and giving Mary the chance to ensure he had understood.

'I grabbed her to stop her falling,' Adam said. 'She lost her balance. I was helping her. And there was glass on the pavement outside the school, so I was just telling everyone not to walk there. They could have got cut if they'd fallen over. And some of them didn't have their parents with them. The older ones. They walk home on their own, so they didn't have anyone to look out for them except me.'

Mary didn't need to rephrase any questions, and when all the paperwork had been checked and signed, she was free to take him home.

'You said I should carry on, Mumma,' Adam said as they got into the car. 'Being kind. Mr Bright said I was a hero.'

'Did he?' Mary felt a rush of pride, but she was uneasy. Should she explain how the world was suspicious, over-cautious, risk-averse? Where was he getting this desire to make things better for people? Certainly not from her. But did she really want him to be afraid of those around him, always worried about what they might think?

She clicked her seat belt and started the engine. 'Sometimes,' she said, 'when you do something kind, it can have consequences you didn't expect, good or bad.'

When you rescue a mermaid, for example, she thought. One of the unexpected consequences of saving Rachel from the sea that day had been finding herself inside a church. Not at the funeral, of course, but afterwards, when everyone had gone. She had shoved a box of matches in her pocket and driven up there. The dust and the silence and the clammy dampness made her shudder. A candle lay discarded on the altar. She lit it, held it while it burned for a minute or two, then snuffed it out and left it there.

'I know.' Adam's voice had become a whisper.

It was dark now, gone tea time. They would call in at the chip shop. That would cheer him up. Sausage and chips in front of the telly, and he'd soon be himself again.

But when they came to the house, Mary banged her foot on the brake and the car skidded to a stop, flinging them forward in their seats. There, covering the whole of the driveway and most of the patch of grass at the front, were three enormous mounds of earth. They were as high as the tops of the windows, yellowish grey, with great, sticky clods.'What the…? The bloody idiot!' She flung herself out of the car and charged up to the huge clay mountain blocking the drive, stood there with her feet planted wide apart, waving her hands about. 'The bloody, bloody idiot! How am I going to move all that?'

Adam appeared at her side with the wrapped package of food. The smell of salt and vinegar cut through the metallic, sweet smell of the earth.

'Come on, Mumma.' He put his hand on her arm. 'Let's go and eat our chips. You'll feel better then.'

She let her breath out in one exasperated sigh, and followed him into the house.

The big girls will be going on the bus to the high school in September, shoving and shouting, their skirts too short and their eyes thick with make-up and their hair all big and messy. Then, before you know it, they'll have lipstick and high heels and a go-away-leave-me-alone curl of the mouth.

Hannah Bird will never get the bus to high school.

Because of him.

The thought jumps on him from nowhere and there is nothing he can do.

Pelican

By the time the social workers came, the rawness of Rachel's shock had passed. Christopher was being interviewed at school, they told her, and Jamie was being looked after at his school until the initial interviews were over. He had confided in his friend to begin with, they said, and the friend had told the welfare officer – Izzy – and then Jamie had made his disclosure to her. They would need to interview her mother-in-law too, since she was staying in the house. They had photographs of the injuries, but they wouldn't show her. There was a small burn on Jamie's forehead, which he'd said was made by hair-straighteners, some razor cuts on his wrist and some bruises on his upper arms consistent with being grabbed. He had been vague about dates and times, and there were some inconsistencies in his story.

'Because he's making it up,' Rachel told the social workers.

'But I don't understand why he would say such things. He's always got on with his dad. He's always felt – I don't know – his dad was on his side.'

'Side? Against who?'

'Oh, I didn't mean that. It's just an expression.' Against the world, she thought.

They asked about the shoplifting, and about how Jamie had reacted to Hannah's death. Had he had any counselling? Had he and his sister got on well? Rachel answered as if it was not her children they were talking about. Not her husband. She felt like an actor. Or an impostor in someone else's tragedy. It was impossible to inhabit it as herself. She would fall to pieces.

'I think,' Rachel said, 'he must have cut his arms himself. I saw those cuts. He had stolen razor blades. And I found tissues in his bin, with blood on.'

All the time that the social workers were in the room with her, she insisted that Jamie had made it up. When they called Janet in, she went back up to the Crow's Nest and rummaged in the drawer for her straighteners. She hadn't used them for years. She pulled them out from under a jumble of old make-up and socks, unravelled the wire and plugged them in. She stood in front of the mirror, released her ponytail and separated a lock of hair, ran the straighteners over it. She stood, looking in the mirror, holding the hot surface close to the skin on her forehead. But she didn't let it touch. Then she unplugged the straighteners, left them on the floor to cool, and lay on her bed, staring at the patch of sky in the window. How could anyone burn another person? On purpose? It was impossible to think of Christopher like that.

But, she thought, what if he has been visited by demons? The same demons as the ones that visited me?

When Rachel had driven to Peterborough in the middle of the night, it was because Hannah was in mortal danger. She was certain of it. If she stayed in the house, she would harm her baby.

Night after night, day after day, bone-tired, tears sliding down her face, and longing for her mother, she battled to get her daughter to latch on to the breast. She cajoled and whispered, she stroked and pleaded, and in the end, despairing, she shoved the baby in her crib and ran into the bathroom and buried her face in a towel and squeezed her fingers into the soft, sweet-smelling fabric. Images snapped into focus in her mind. Unbidden, unwelcome, horrifying. Scissors, high windows, pillows. Kettles, stairs, bathwater. Or – and this was the hardest to bear – her own treacherous hands.

When Jamie was born, Rachel was instantly in love. And it was no different with Hannah. Love at first sight. A fierce, all-encompassing mother-love that would go to the ends of the earth. Or fight to the death. Anything to defend, to protect, to save. The love didn't go away. It wasn't that. If she loved her child less, the thoughts of harm would stay away. They were the mirror image of her desire to protect – seemed to spring from it, like a curse.

The feeding settled. The crying lessened. Nights were easier. But it made no difference. The images persisted. She was going under. Drowning.

In the end, desperate, weeping, on her knees, she begged for help. Diane, the health visitor, stepped in. Choir was a lifeline, and that was where she found Izzy. One or two from church played a part, overseen by Gail. Christopher did his best, but the struggle took its toll. He was drained, exhausted, often silent.

Janet, who was there much of the time, was most concerned about Jamie, how he had been pushed into the background. She had even used the word *neglected*, and tried to make up for it by giving him extra attention, playing games with him, reading him story after story at bedtime, baking him special, after-school treats. 'But it should be his mother,' Rachel heard her saying to Christopher. 'It's her he needs, and the sooner she pulls herself together, the better.'

It took a long time, but Rachel recovered, and Christopher found his true self again. Afterwards, she said, 'God held on to me when I couldn't hold on to him.'

Would he do the same again? Maybe if she couldn't hold on this time, she would fall.

She went in the car to collect Jamie from school. He slid into the passenger seat, pale and silent, and did not look at her. His hair must be covering the burn mark.

'Do you want to tell me about it?' She started the engine and pulled out of the car park. How had he become so separate from her? So *other*? It seemed impossible that he had grown inside her, had been nourished by her body for months. He had been utterly dependent on her and she had known him so completely. If I believe Jamie, she thought, then Christopher becomes unknown. But if Christopher didn't do it, then Jamie becomes someone else. My husband, or my son. One of them becomes a stranger.

'No,' Jamie said. 'They said you were being told.'

'They told me what you said to them. But they didn't tell me why.'

'I said I didn't want to talk about it.' He sounded bored rather than angry or upset.

'Right. Not now, then.' He must have made it up. Surely. Was it part of the test Christopher had talked about? She shouldn't interrogate him. Reassure him, instead. 'Perhaps you need to hear,' she said, 'that we love you very much. Dad and I. No matter what. Okay?' Once again she felt like an actor, playing the part of a proper mother.

Silence.

'Dad will be home before tea time,' she told him, wondering how social services decided such things. It was a last resort, she had heard, separating children from their parents. The child had to be at risk of harm. So they must have concluded he wasn't. 'Gran's making pasta. But we don't have to talk about… what's happened.' *What you've done*, she wanted to say, but stopped herself. 'Gran knows, by the way. The social workers had to talk to her.'

'I don't want anything.'

'But you—'

'They gave me a sandwich at school.'

She didn't believe him. It was only half-past three. She thought about the chocolate wrappers, his bone-thin arms and legs, the ribs you could count under his skin. But when had she last seen the skin on his chest, his back? They said he had bruises on the tops of his arms. The marks of fingertips and thumbs. Someone had grabbed him. Held him.

Christopher's car wasn't there when they got back. Jamie raced up to his room and shut the door.

Janet said she'd spoken to Christopher on the phone, and they both thought it best that she went home. She'd left a note for Jamie upstairs.

'The pasta's in the fridge,' she said. 'Put it in the oven for forty minutes or so. I'd already filled the freezer. And the washing and ironing is all up to date. I changed the beds a couple of days ago. Not Hannah's,' she added quickly. 'I left her room for when you… Anyway, if you can manage without me, it'll give you all a chance to…well…'

Rachel nodded. They hugged.

'He didn't do it, you know,' Janet said.

Rachel nodded again. 'I know.'

After Janet had gone, Rachel remembered the flowers in the church. The daffodils and irises and crocuses – the colours of spring. The beautiful scent of the freesias. She had forgotten to say thank you.

Christopher came home. They hesitated, then moved towards each other at the same moment and held each other. He smelled of sandalwood and cotton and, faintly, of sweat. She leaned against his chest and he hid his face in her hair.

'Oh, Rach,' he said. 'What is happening to us?'

She tightened her arms around him. She wanted to tell him she knew he would never hurt Jamie. But she couldn't say the words. 'We'll get through it,' she said.

'Is he here?'

'He's upstairs. Said he didn't want anything to eat.' *What if he's frightened of coming down? Because of what he's done. Or what Christopher has done.*

'Shall I go up?' Christopher said.

'He didn't want to talk about it.' *Perhaps he blames me for not stopping it.*

'But…sooner or later…'

'Perhaps in his time.'

'Have you any idea why he said it?'

She shrugged. 'Part of the test, I suppose, like you said.'

'Rachel, you don't…' He moved away from her, looked her in the eye. 'You don't think I did it, do you? Those things he's said. You don't think I would ever hurt him?'

'No, of course not. How can you even ask?' And she took him back into her arms and breathed in the smell of soap and sweat and felt the soft cotton of his shirt under her cheek.

'Remember when Hannah was a baby?' he said after a while, disengaging from the embrace. 'When you had those thoughts?'

'Christopher, please.'

'Did you ever feel like that about Jamie?'

'No. I wasn't ill then.'

'Look, Rachel. The social worker asked me about you. You and the children. I had to tell her.'

'Tell her what?'

'About you hurting Hannah.'

She flinched away from him, stared at him, her mouth open. 'Hurting Hannah? But I didn't. I was scared I would, but I never, never did.'

'You don't remember?'

'Because I didn't! What are you talking about? What am I supposed to have done?'

'It was the bath. She wouldn't feed and you thought a bath would soothe her. You made it too hot, scalded her legs and her bottom. You lifted her out when she screamed and I ran cold water over her and she was all right.'

'It's not true! I didn't!' Hot tears spilled over. 'Why are you saying this?' she sobbed. 'You're the one that's been accused of hurting our children, not me!'

Our children. Plural. There it was. Jamie. And perhaps, Hannah. She stumbled from the room, grabbed her coat, shoved her feet into trainers, and ran from the house.

She went back to the churchyard. It had stopped raining and the sun, low in the sky now, shone through the leafless trees, but with no warmth in it. She stood by Hannah's grave again, smelling the sweet earth. Could she have hurt her baby and then blocked it from her memory? Was it possible? And why would Christopher remind her? If it was true, did anyone else know? Janet? Izzy? The health visitor?

She wrapped her fingers round the holy stone in her pocket. A breath of wind in the branches echoed Hannah's words. *Look after it for me. Look after it.*

Inside the church, the flowers by the font were bright in the sunlight. Here is where we baptised her, she thought. Where we entrusted her to God. *Safe in Christ for ever. Shine as a light in the world.* And even back then, God knew what was going to happen. *He knew.* She could not fathom it.

On one of the font's four sides, behind the irises and tulips, was the worn stone carving of the pelican. The mother bird, her great bill pecking at her breast, drawing blood to feed her starving children. A symbol of sacrifice. I would do anything, she thought. Oh, I would give anything to know. My life's blood. Please, please, let me find the truth.

She closed the church door behind her, and set out along the track to the coast path. The sun had gone and the air was damp and cold. She couldn't stop thinking about the pelican and her sacrifice. What if prayer wasn't enough? What could she offer that would make him listen? It wasn't until she reached the cliff and turned west along the path that she thought of Jamie and Christopher alone in the house, and began to run. And she did not stop running until she was home.

Scarf

Mumma said there was some leftover apple crumble in the fridge that he could have for breakfast. He opened a tin of custard, emptied it into a bowl and put it in the microwave, pressed the numbers.

Mumma was on the phone, getting cross. 'Look. All I'm asking is for you to move it to where I wanted it. If you'd come when you said you were going to, I would have been here and I could have told you where to put it.'

It was those big heaps of earth. She'd wanted the lorry to dump it over the cliff, but as far as he could see, it would be better to take it through the garden. Tipping it down the landslide would be a lot easier than moving it along the beach and up the slope. When he'd told her this she'd given him a sideways squint and called him a daft great lump.

The microwave beeped and Adam took out his steaming

bowl of custard, poured it over the cold crumble, and sat down at the table.

'If you're just going to make excuses…' Mumma said, on the phone, then paused. 'Yes, I would. How micro is it? Will it go in my car? I could come and… No? Okay. Well, I suppose that's better than nothing. The earlier the better. I want to get on with it while the weather holds.'

She poured herself a mug of tea and flopped into a chair.

'Bloody idiot refuses to move it, but he's bringing his micro digger and soil compactor and we can have them till tomorrow morning. So we'll be at it all day. My goodness! You must have hollow legs.'

She got up again and put some bread in the toaster. All day, Adam thought. But what about my hero work? What about the children? His trip to the police station hadn't put him off. He was proud of how he'd explained things. He was being kind, keeping children safe. They hadn't asked about his daily circuit, so he hadn't told them. But he was used to it now, and he didn't want to let go of that warm feeling of being part of things, connected. And anyway, hadn't Mumma said he should carry on?

'I hope his timing is better today than it was on Tuesday,' Mumma said. 'And I hope the digger is micro enough for the side path.' She spread a thick layer of butter on her toast, and dolloped a spoonful of marmalade on top. 'And I'll have to dig up that patch of tree mallow, otherwise we'll never get the thing right to the edge.' She took a bite of toast, and when she had swallowed it, she said, 'I suppose you were right after all. Maybe it is better to tip it down from the end of the garden.'

Adam scraped his spoon round the bowl and devoured the last of the sweet custard.

He watched while the man showed Mumma how to use the digger and the soil compactor. The digger was so small it didn't even have a seat. You had to stand on the back to operate it and she didn't look very confident. Perhaps she would let him do it.

'You should wear gloves and proper boots,' the man said, 'and ear defenders, but if you've got some ear plugs, they'll do. I normally have a spare hard hat in the truck somewhere, but it's not there today. Sorry.'

'It's all right,' Mumma said. 'I've got one.'

Adam had seen it, hanging in the shed. He didn't know where it had come from, but it wasn't there before the storm. He'd never seen her wearing it though.

'Don't do too much compacting in one go,' the man said, climbing into his truck. 'A couple of inches at a time. In layers. I'll pick the machines up in the morning.' He started the engine and roared off down Wetherley Lane.

Mumma climbed on to the footplate of the digger, fiddled about with the controls.

'Don't forget the hard hat,' Adam said.

'Oh, never mind about that.' She started the machine, edged it towards the nearest mound of soil.

'Mumma!' Adam shouted. 'You have to. He said you have to wear a hard hat and ear plugs and you haven't even got gloves on and if you don't follow the rules and wear all the right stuff I'm not going to help you.'

She made cross noises, but she gave in and they worked all morning. She got steadier on the digger, although she kept going too close to the broken edge of the garden and Adam had to shout at her to stop. She was wearing the strange yellow-tinted glasses she'd started using for driving, but he could tell she still couldn't see properly. She was wearing a new scarf, too, in lots of bright colours – unusual for her – tucked into the front of her body-warmer.

It was almost lunchtime before they had moved the first mound of earth. But when they went down with rakes and spades and spread it out, you couldn't tell the difference. It was going to take a lot more than three lorryloads. And hundreds of hours.

Mumma found some rope and they rigged up a pulley to lower the soil compactor down.

'Can I do this bit?' Adam said. 'I'll wear the hat like the man said.'

But she wouldn't let him.

'Let me drive the digger then, while you do this. I know how to work it. I watched. I could get the second heap done.'

'Don't be daft. You can't tip earth over while I'm down there. Anyway, you know what you're like, all gangly limbs and getting over-excited.'

'I'd be safer than you. If it wasn't for me, you would have gone over the cliff.'

'Oh, don't talk rubbish. And that section isn't level. You need to rake it again before I get this machine on it.'

But Adam had had enough. He trudged down the slope to the beach and set off towards the town. 'You can do your own bloody job,' he muttered. 'I'll get back to mine.' Using her favourite swear word made him feel bold.

It was a calm day, without much wind, but cold and damp. The tide was low, but he didn't feel like looking for fossils. His heart wasn't in it any more. He tried not to think about the box of treasures under the floor, and what else was down there in the dust. But the memory kept ambushing him, making his heart beat too hard and his palms go sweaty. The things he'd found since he'd nailed the board down were safely stowed under his bed now – the blue sea glass, the belemnites and the old bottle. But he had to find a better hiding place.

He was later than usual, so he went to Molly's first and bought a ham sandwich and a packet of salt and vinegar crisps. She was wearing a red hat with a white bobble.

'You look like Christmas,' he said.

'Well, why not?' She laughed, and her eyes went all sparkly and the bobble on her hat danced about.

He wished he had thought of a joke on the way, to make her laugh even more.

He took his lunch to the playground and sat on the bench where he had given Luke the chocolate pebbles. The only children about were little ones and none of them was alone. He finished eating and took the path that led up to the flats and the green. Only another hour till the end of school. At one end of the green was a group of teenagers, four of them, perched on stationary bikes. Surely they should be at school. Then he spotted a little girl scooting up and down a walkway that led to a car park. On her own. She couldn't have been more than four or five years old. She had black hair and a big red hairband. She wasn't wearing a coat – just flowery trousers and a blue jumper. He walked towards her, working out the words in his head. Be kind. Don't frighten her.

A shout came behind him. 'Oi! Bird-brain!'

Adam swung round. Danny. There, with the teenagers. Now coming towards him. Which way should he go? Through the car park, or up to the school? Or give up the circuit and run down to the beach?

'Cops got you, then, did they?' Danny said. 'Give you a ticking off? You need to behave yourself. Weirdo. People are watching you, you know. Yeah, go on then, run off. We know where to find you.'

Adam headed for the playground and the beach steps. Forget the school. Forget the rest of the circuit. He had to get away. Running footsteps followed him. Then stopped. At the top of the steps, he looked over his shoulder. No Danny. He ran down the steps, climbed quickly down the cobbles and ran across the sand, then slowed down and checked again. No one was there but he still felt uneasy being so exposed on the beach. When he got to the dip where the pool was, he clambered up past the little waterfall. It wasn't exactly a path, but it wasn't too difficult to climb up.

He hoisted himself over a lip of land and there, in front of him, hung a rope ladder, pegged into the cliff face at intervals. He tugged at it. Would he dare? Would it hold him? He pulled again, let it take his weight. It felt secure. He began the climb.

When he came over the top, he found himself in a hidden saucer of land, invisible from both the road and the beach. In the middle, the rope ladder was attached to a huge metal stake, sunk deep into the ground, and, nestling against the slope, was an old shed. He'd forgotten it was here. He'd been here before, a long time ago, but he'd come from the top, where the stream came down a gully near one of the houses that had been pulled down. He didn't remember the rope ladder though. He pushed the door open. It was dark inside – there were boards nailed across the broken window. He stepped inside, letting the door swing to behind him. As his eyes adjusted, he made out a heap of dirty carrier bags in one corner and a blue plastic fishing crate in another. There was a smell of damp and rot and earth.

He stayed in the shed until he felt sure that if Danny had followed him on to the beach, he would have given up and gone away. Then he climbed up the gully and came out by the bend in Wetherley Lane where the coast path joined it. He hoped Mumma wouldn't be too cross with him. Perhaps there would be time to do a bit more cliff rescue work before it got dark. That would put her in a good mood.

He came to the front of the house. She'd made a start on the second heap of earth, but she hadn't moved much of it. If she had let him drive the digger he could have got on much faster. Sometimes she treated him as if he was still a child. He went down the side path to the back of the house. There was the digger, standing next to that bench she had made. The one she had dug out of the landslide and brought all the way back up, though he had no idea how she'd done it.

Perhaps she was inside, having a breather and a cup of tea.

He pushed open the door of the lean-to, went through to the kitchen. 'Mumma, I'm back.'

She wasn't there.

'Mumma? I'm back. Where are you?'

She wasn't in the house. He went back into the garden, down to the end, drew level with the digger and the rescued shed. He looked down at the fallen cliff. She had compacted a small section, and the machine stood there, abandoned. The tide had turned and waves were breaking on the line where the stony bank met the sand. He heard a sound behind him that made him think of cows mooing. He turned.

The first thing he saw was one of her boots, then her leg. She was sitting on the ground, leaning against one of her big plant pots, with one knee bent up in front of her and the other leg stretched out in the churned up grass. She was still wearing the hard hat, but not the tinted glasses. The coloured scarf was draped loosely round her, trailing across the front of her body, and she clung to it, her fist tight.

'Mumma, what happened?'

He ran across, crouched beside her, touched her arm, her shoulder, her face. Her skin was icy and she was shivering so much her teeth were chattering. 'What happened? Where are you hurt? Can you get up?' A knot of panic took hold, tight behind his ribs. He wanted her to stand up and stomp through the mud and call him a daft great lump. But she wasn't going to. She was hurt. She had been sitting here, waiting for him to come home. And now it was up to him. He thought of scenes on telly. Yes, she was breathing. And she was conscious. Two good things.

She groaned and tried to say something, but she was shaking too much.

Adam unfastened the chin strap and took the hard hat off her, then wrapped the scarf more snugly around her. It was thick and chunky – more like a blanket, really. The texture reminded him of the sheep cushion, but it smelled of flowers, not like the usual earthy scent of her clothes.

'We need to get you in the warm, Mumma. Are you bleeding? Have you broken anything? Can you get up? Come on, Mumma. Please. You can't stay out here. It's too cold.'

She didn't answer and she seemed out of breath, even though she was just sitting there.

'I'll call an ambulance, shall I, Mumma, if you can't get up?'

She shook her head again, more decisively. 'No, no.' Then she moved her arms and shifted her body a bit and groaned again. She closed her eyes.

'Open your eyes, Mumma. I'll help you up. We can do it. You and me. It's all right.' He had a vague idea that if she'd broken any bones he shouldn't move her, but he couldn't leave her like this, and if she wouldn't let him call an ambulance...

In the end, he dragged the bench across the garden and made her turn herself round into a kneeling position and hoist herself up, and then, with her weight partly on her good leg and a lot on him, he managed to get her into the house and on to her bed. He eased off her bulky body-warmer, and was about to take the scarf, but she hung on to it, rearranged it round her shoulders. It made her look different, but it wasn't just the bright colours. There was something else, but he couldn't work out what.

It wasn't easy getting the boot off, and she swore a lot, but he did it in the end. When she had stopped shivering, she told him how to bandage up her ankle, and he got her some strong painkillers from behind the biscuit tin, and a glass of water, and then he made her a mug of tea with three sugars.

When he looked at her from the doorway, he realised what had changed. It was the way she had draped the scarf over her shoulders, the way she was sitting up in bed, wrapped in a shawl.

She looked like an old woman from a fairy tale, and it made him afraid.

She said it was nothing to do with the machines. She had missed her footing, that was all, and it wasn't broken, just sprained. She didn't say if you hadn't buggered off into town I wouldn't have been sitting in the mud freezing to death and in agony for three hours.

But that was the truth of it. He had let her down.

The little girl turns, so he does too, following her gaze. Further back along the beach, a man is throwing stones into the sea, and beyond that a lady and a boy are running towards another group of people who are trying to stop some dogs from fighting.

She turns back to him. 'I don't need you to help me,' she says. 'I can climb all by myself.' And she can. She clings to the rocks and then scuttles over them like a crab, sideways on her hands and feet. They clamber down the other side and there are the layers of mudstone, spread out before them, flat and glistening and dark.

'Come on, quick!' He grabs her hand and they run towards the water.

Bead Things, Broken

Gail took them in her car. It was a pilgrimage – more sacred, Rachel felt, than the funeral. Certainly more private. It was not a place she wanted to see. It was a place she had to see. Christopher had made the trip with the police yesterday, so that they could show him the exact location. Rachel sat in the back, with Jamie. At first, he had said he didn't want to come, but changed his mind at the last minute, and ran out of the house without a coat.

It was four days since he had made his allegations. They had been told that it might take a week or two for social services to conclude the investigation, but since they didn't think Jamie or anyone else was in any immediate danger, everything could carry on as normal for now. Normal? None of this was normal. How could things ever be normal again? Social Services had spoken to Christopher's school, but there was no need for him to be suspended. They were talking to Jamie's teachers too, and Izzy, of course. Christopher still thought Jamie's behaviour was a test of their love. But to Rachel, it didn't make sense. Was it some kind of sign language? A distress signal? She wanted to reassure him, to make him feel cared for, loved, understood. And she did love him. Of course. But she didn't understand him and she couldn't leave it alone. Whenever she mentioned his accusations, he refused to make eye contact, or he left the room, his face closed and tight. And all the time, under the surface, simmered the possibility that he hadn't made it up. The three of them moved around each other like dancers who never touch, never look at each other.

In the car, she wanted to reach for Jamie's hand, to feel his skin, the warmth of his living flesh, his *realness*. She longed to heal his wounds. To smooth her fingers over the burn on his head, the razor cuts on his wrists, the fingerprint bruises on his arms. She wanted the marks to melt away under her touch, and for him to be whole again. Unblemished. Perfect. For his heart to mend.

But he looked out of the window, away from her. And anyway, she didn't have the power. How can one broken human mend another?

The car park at Saltbourne Gap was as near as you could get by road. It was mid-morning, but only one other vehicle was there, an old pick-up truck with lobster pots and plastic crates in the back. The cliffs sloped down to nothing here, and along the path to the shore, grey-green spikes of marram grass clung to the sand that blew in from the beach.

They climbed over the shingle bank, their feet sinking and sliding on the steep slope. A lone fisherman sat on a folding stool, staring out to sea, his line stretching out into the turbulent water. There was a fresh, blustery wind, peppered with fine rain, and the sea was dotted with white crests. White horses, Mum would have said. Their footsteps crunched over the stones. Waves crashed, and whispered as they washed back into the ocean. Gulls wheeled overhead, their plaintive cries drifting on the wind. Salt stung Rachel's lips, and the damp, cold air misted her skin. She smelled seaweed and rain. They didn't talk, except for Christopher, reminding himself how to recognise the place.

'There,' he said after about ten minutes. 'Where that bit sticks out. It's just before that.'

They made their way diagonally up the stony slope, Gail hanging back to let the family go first.

At the top, the shingle bank sloped down again towards the base of the cliff, creating a shallow dip, a bowl, two or three metres across. The sea would only reach this far on some tides. Rachel didn't know who had made the discovery – a dog-walker, a runner, a fisherman? – but she imagined the phone call and the wait – would the person have seen it as a vigil? – and then the crime scene tape, fluttering in the breeze. Or would they have put up one of those tent things?

She found herself gazing at plastic bottles, a splintered plank, bits of rope – yellow, turquoise, blue – and a tangle of weed and bits of driftwood. Rubbish washed up by the waves. Discarded, worthless items. Things no one wanted.

And here, the sea had let go of Hannah.

She would have lain here, in a pool, until the water drained away through the stones and the tide went out. A pool. A bowl of water. An image swam to the surface in Rachel's mind – the font in the church, with its shallow, round bowl. She had stopped in front of it the other day, remembered Hannah's baptism, contemplated the mother pelican piercing her breast, giving her blood to save her children. Oh, God, she thought again now, I can't save my child, but what do I have to do to make you listen? What must I sacrifice to show you how much I need an answer?

They stood in silence round the edge of the dip, with its washed-up debris. We should be holding hands, Rachel thought, but none of them made the move. Then Gail said some prayers and at the end her voice wavered and Rachel saw that she was weeping. They had brought flowers, yellow roses, and one by one each of them stepped forward and laid their offering on the stones.

Rachel lay on Hannah's bed again, curled on her side. Jamie had gone to Anthony's and Christopher had gone out on his bike, said he wouldn't be back till dark, if she was all right on her own. He kept saying that. What did he think might happen to her? And what did all right even mean?

She had not allowed Janet in here to fetch the washing or tidy up or change the bedding. How could she ever give up this refuge, where Hannah's books lay on the floor and on the bedside table, where her soft toys huddled together on a little wicker chair, where the smell of her skin lingered in the sheets? On the window sill stood a lighthouse made out of paper cups stuck with red stripes, with a battery tea light in the top. Beside it was an egg box adorned with long ribbons of purple and yellow tissue paper and a scatter of sticky-backed jewels. Bright drawings covered the wardrobe doors and paper birds hung from the ceiling. She needed to be here, to breathe this air, to feed on it. She buried her face in the pillow, put her hands underneath it and wrapped it round her head.

Something hard and knobbly pressed against her ear through the cotton. Something was stuck inside the pillow case. She let go, found the opening and felt inside. Her fingers closed around the object and she pulled it out.

It was the prayer bracelet. The bead things that Hannah had lost.

'Oh!' Rachel said, and she clutched them to her chest.

After a bit, she ran her fingers over the beads. Our family, she thought, reminding herself of Hannah's colour codes. And now, because she is gone, our family is broken. We are pieces that no longer fit together. We are strangers trying to find our way in the dark, and when we bump against each other it hurts.

The bracelet had been there all the time, lost inside the pillowcase. And now, as her fingers rested on the beads, she knew what she must do in order to persuade God to hear her prayers. Knew what her sacrifice should be. It was the only way to find out what had happened. Find out who was to blame.

She pulled the bracelet on to her wrist, and began the task.

She worked quickly, sorting and folding and packing and labelling, giving herself no time to change her mind, no time to linger over anything. No time to consider that tomorrow she might wake up and wish she hadn't done it. It had to hurt. Lying here in this room, with Hannah's things – this was her life's blood. And like the mother pelican giving her life's blood, this was what she must give up to persuade God to answer her prayers, to find the truth. What was the point of a sacrifice if it didn't tear you in two? She had to prove herself.

Two hours later, she was done. The room was spotless. Clothes and toys were boxed up, labelled, in the boot of the car ready for the charity shop. She had stripped the bed, and made it up with a plain blue duvet set. She took the lighthouse, the decorated egg box, and the stash of other craft projects found in a drawer, outside to the recycling bin. She flipped open the lid and let Hannah's handiwork cascade into the bin, an avalanche of colour, the result of hours of dreaming and cutting and folding and gluing, the magic of her little girl's imagination. A physical pain gripped her, and she bent forward, retching. When the sickness had passed, she banged the lid shut and stumbled into the house.

But she couldn't let it go. She ran back out, tipped the bin on to its side and then upended it. She scrabbled about until she had gathered it all up, armfuls of brightness – birds and flowers and puppets and snowflakes, maps and hats and a fantastic, jewelled dragon. Then she ran upstairs to the Crow's Nest and stuffed it all in the back of a cupboard. Please let it count, she begged. I'll never look at them. I promise.

Jamie came home as darkness was falling. Rachel heard him come through the back door and go upstairs. Anthony's dad had probably given him tea again. He'd missed a lot of Janet's meals, not being a fan of pies and casseroles and fruit-based puddings, and Anthony's family always ate early. That's what he'd told them anyway. She sat in the dark, with the curtains still open, hugging a cushion in front of her chest. She hadn't given a thought to what she and Christopher would eat. There were still plenty of Janet's specials in the freezer. She wasn't hungry anyway.

The emptiness of the little bedroom upstairs, directly above where she sat, made her think the ceiling might lift, carrying away the Crow's Nest, and leaving this room open to the sky, and then she too might float away, over the cliffs, the beach, the sea. It made her feel clean, washed and light.

A door crashed. Footsteps ran down the stairs. Jamie burst in, launched himself at her.

'What have you done? Why have you taken it? Where have you put it?'

His fists beat against her chest. His breath came hot on her face, her neck. Before she could grab his wrists, he grabbed hers. He tore at the bracelet. The knot in the elastic came apart and the beads flew off. Jamie dived to the floor, scrabbled about on the carpet, sobbing and shouting. 'Why did you have to take it? You always spoil everything.'

'Jamie, please,' Rachel said. 'I'm sorry. I didn't know you... I thought it was lost. Hannah said she lost it. And then I found it today when—'

'No! I found it. I found it ages ago and you're not having it.' He scooped up the beads and stood with them tight in his fist. His eyes flashed. 'And,' he went on, firing the words at her like bullets, 'you shouldn't have done that to her room. All her things. You don't care. You don't care at all!' He turned and charged up the stairs, and she heard a door slam above her. He had gone back into Hannah's room.

Christopher put his bike away and came in with a paper carrier bag – the sort you get in posh shops.

'I'm cooking,' he said. 'But I need a quick shower first. Where's Jamie? Does he want to eat with us?' He took out packages wrapped in greaseproof paper and stowed them in the fridge. He laid vegetables on the draining board – asparagus and huge mushrooms and curly kale – and a pot of fresh herbs on the counter. He put a bottle of Sauvignon in the freezer.

'He's upstairs,' Rachel said. 'I think he had tea at Anthony's.' She pictured him lying in Hannah's cleared out room, with its empty shelves, its bare walls, its clean, lemony smell. Hanging on to the beads. Why hadn't he told them he'd found the bracelet? She wondered if he lay there on the bed, remembering how he had laughed at his sister for praying for a dog, how he had teased her about the meat and the marshmallows.

'Just going up for a shower,' Christopher said. 'Food should be ready about eight. I hope you're hungry.' He put his hands lightly on her shoulders and gave her a quick kiss on the lips on his way past.

Rachel was baffled. What was going on? Less than twelve hours ago they had made their pilgrimage, and now, after a four-hour cycle ride, he was breezing in with exotic mushrooms and asparagus, and kissing her as if...as if what? As if things were back to normal. As if their family wasn't disintegrating. As if Jamie hadn't accused him of abuse. As if Hannah was still alive. It didn't make sense. What was he expecting?

She put a few bits in the dishwasher, wiped the surfaces down and poured a glass of water. The room was stuffy. She opened the back door and stood there, looking at the dark sky, until the cold air made her shiver.

He lit a candle. 'Honey pecan chicken,' he said, putting the plates on the table.

She had to admit, it smelled delicious.

He sat down, poured the wine. 'Cheers,' he said, and they clinked glasses.

'What's going on?' Rachel looked at him over the top of her glass. 'What's all this about?'

'I did some thinking. It was a long bike ride.'

'Hmm.' She sipped her wine.

'We can't go on like this, Rach.'

'Like what?'

'Not talking. Curling away from each other inside our prickly shells.'

Rachel didn't say anything. She picked up her knife and fork, cut a thin slice of chicken. She couldn't stop thinking about Jamie, upstairs in Hannah's bedroom, clutching the broken bracelet. *You don't care! You don't care at all!* Had she finally failed the test? Was it over?

'We'll never get through it if we don't talk to each other. We need each other. I see the way you're hurting and I can't reach you. You've locked yourself away and you won't let me in.'

'We have talked,' Rachel said. 'I have told you how I feel. Sometimes.'

'You've allowed me tiny glimpses. Opened the door a fraction and then pushed me out again. You keep going out on your own for hours at a time, and I haven't a clue where you are, what you're doing, what you're thinking. It's like you're going in one direction and I'm going in another and we're getting further and further away from each other. And Jamie's lost in the middle.'

It was true. But did she have to explain it? Was that what he wanted? She ate some chicken, speared a piece of asparagus on her fork. She found she was hungry after all.

They finished the meal. They drank the whole bottle of wine and opened another. They talked. They even smiled. But again Rachel felt as if she were playing a role that wasn't hers. They were trying too hard, both of them, desperate to retrieve their connection. But it would shatter, sooner or later. It was inevitable.

It was still early, but they went up to bed and when he kissed her, she found her body ached for his touch. She wanted his hands on her, his mouth, the weight of him. Her limbs were weak with desire. Waves pulsed through her, electric. It had been weeks. Not since…

In the end, Rachel gasped and cried out, again and again, and then her cries became great sobs, shuddering through her body. They lay together, their limbs flung over each other.

He buried his face in her neck. 'Oh, Rach,' he said. 'We will be all right, won't we?'

She clung to him. But she couldn't answer.

They showered together, standing under the hot water for a long time.

'There's pudding,' Christopher said. 'I got brownies. Is there any ice cream?' He dried himself and pulled on a pair of jeans.

Rachel turned the water off, heard his steps on the stairs. She stepped out of the shower, wrapped a towel around herself. She held her breath. Was Jamie still in Hannah's room? Was Christopher going in there? Silence. She waited, her fingers gripping the towel at her chest.

He thundered back up the stairs, stopped in the doorway, breathing fast, his face dark.

'How could you? How could you do that? All her things. This is exactly what I mean about you shutting me out.' He stepped towards her, raised both his hands, but didn't touch her.

'I had to do it,' she whispered. 'I had to.'

'My God, Rachel, you think this is just your tragedy. Didn't it occur to you that this was something we should talk about? Decide together? It's not all about how you feel, what you want. She was my daughter too.'

'I had to,' Rachel said again.

'Why? What have you done with it all? And what about Jamie? I went to check on him and he wasn't in his room. I found him asleep on Hannah's bed, holding those bead things. Broken. Did you ever think about him? What he might need? How can you be so selfish?'

'All right.' Rachel raised her voice. 'You want me to tell you how I feel. You want to know why. All I want is to know what happened. I can't think about anything else. I thought if I…I thought it would make God listen…' Her voice wavered. She couldn't continue.

Christopher let his hands drop, took a step back. 'What sort of God are you talking about? Sacrifices? Bargains? Is that what you believe?' He sighed. His voice became weary. 'We'll never know what happened.' He paused. 'Tell me what you've done with all her stuff.'

'It's in the car,' Rachel said.

When he had gone, she climbed back into bed, alone, still cocooned in the damp towel.

Pineapple

There was no chance of Mary agreeing to Adam's suggestion of calling an ambulance.

When Adam was six years old, Mary had collapsed while digging out a tree stump in a two acre landscaped garden near Cley. It was as though a huge weight on her chest had pinned her to the ground, and every breath was a struggle. She lay for twenty minutes with the spade wedged under her hip and rain falling on her upturned face. When the client found her, he put her in the recovery position, covered her with a blanket and called an ambulance. She was kept in hospital overnight, had not the strength to resist. She had no family, and her keep-everyone-at-a-distance policy meant she wasn't on close terms with any of the other school parents. So Adam went to a foster home, and for three weeks afterwards he clung to her night and day and didn't speak a word.

It had turned out to be nothing more serious than a chest infection that cleared up with a course of antibiotics, but it left Mary with an overwhelming dread of being forced to abandon her son, of matters being taken out of her control. He might be officially an adult, but the police interview had reminded her, as if she needed reminding, that he was vulnerable. She'd promised she would always look after him. She couldn't risk another hospital stay. What if they took him into some facility or other? He'd be a wreck. Besides, this was only a sprain, and she knew what had to be done. Proper bandaging, keep it up for a few days. She'd be fine.

It was barely light when the builder came back for his machines in the morning. She heard him laughing with Adam outside. There were supposed to be another three lorry loads tomorrow, and they were going to borrow the machines again. Not much point now she was out of action. She'd phone him later to rearrange. Her ankle was agony, worse than yesterday. She heaved herself up enough to swallow some more painkillers, sank down against the pillows and went back to sleep.

The banging of the lean-to door woke her up. Eventually, she forced herself out of bed. She'd vegetate if she stayed there. She arranged herself sideways on the sofa, with her legs stretched out and a cushion under the injured ankle. Adam fetched her long-handled dibber from the shed to use as a walking stick, and she could hobble between the sofa, the bathroom and the kitchen. Good thing they had no stairs.

Adam wandered from room to room, and he must have gone out to the garden and in again a dozen times before the morning was even half over. Then he clattered about in the kitchen – cupboard doors, the fridge, cutlery. He came in with a tray. A sandwich, a packet of crisps and a KitKat. And a big mug of very milky coffee.

'I'm going out now, Mumma,' he said. And then, without waiting for a response, 'I know it's not lunchtime yet but I made this so you didn't have to get up and do it yourself. I'll get pastics for tea and maybe butterscotch buns because Molly usually has them on a Friday and will you be all right?'

'Of course I will. Will you?'

'Yes.' And he was gone.

She took a sip of coffee. It was barely warm, but she drank it anyway, then reached for the TV remote. There was bound to be some quiz or other.

The roar of a lorry woke her the following morning, and the rumble of tipping earth.

'Shit!' She threw off the covers. She had forgotten to phone that bloody builder. He was here, tipping another load of soil all over her drive when she could do nothing with it. She hobbled round the bed and yanked the curtains aside, blinking in the light. Adam was already perched on the back of the digger, wearing the yellow hard hat, and as she watched he started it up and moved slowly forward towards the mound of earth nearest to the side path. The soil compactor was standing by the fence. What was he thinking? He knew she didn't want him using the machines. Did he think that just because she was out of action, he could do what he liked?

She banged on the window, but neither Adam nor the contractor took any notice. The truck bed tipped back to its flat position, and then the truck drove off with a beep-beep on the horn. Adam loaded the bucket of the digger and she watched him disappear round the corner of the house. By the time she had made it to the door of the lean-to, he was halfway down the garden. She hung on to the door handle and shouted. He didn't hear her. He manoeuvred the digger to the edge of the garden, and then the bucket lifted, hung in the air for a moment, its outline blurry against the sky, and then it tipped and let go of its load over the broken cliff, as easily as spooning sugar into a cup of tea. Adam didn't hesitate. He reversed and turned and came back up the garden, looking as if he'd been driving micro diggers all his life.

She shouted again, and this time he switched off the machine, jumped from the footplate and marched over to her. His face was a smudge in the centre of her vision, but she adjusted her gaze and his wide grin came into focus.

'I'm doing it, Mumma. If I work all morning today and tomorrow it'll get done and I'll still have time to do my circuit and Matt's bringing another two loads today and three on Monday and he says there's more than he thought and do we need any pallets or sleepers because he can get a good deal on most things. And did you see me drive that digger? I told you I could do it.'

'Matt? Circuit? Sleepers? What on earth are you burbling on about? Did I see you? Yes, I bloody did. And did you hear me? I told you I don't want you on that thing. Not the other one either. It's too dangerous.'

'You're the one that had an accident.'

'I told you. It wasn't the machines.'

He looked at her. The grin had gone. 'I know why it was.'

Mary tightened her grip on the door.

'It was because you can't see properly.'

He didn't sound like Adam. He sounded like someone who knew about more than where to find the best fossils and what their Latin names were. The worst thing, and perhaps the best, was how gentle his voice was. It made her want to shout and cry at the same time.

'There's something wrong with your eyes, Mumma,' he went on. 'You need to go and see an optician. Get proper glasses.'

'I've got glasses.' It wasn't strictly true. Not any more.

'Where are they?'

She didn't answer. He was right, though, about why she had fallen over. Stupid bloody eyes. After Adam had stormed off across the beach that afternoon, she had finished a layer of compacting and was almost back at the top of the slope when the ground broke up into moving waves, like the sea. Hummocks of grass rose up and then vanished. Troughs and pot-holes and chasms opened up and it was as if she was searching for stepping stones across a flooded, unstable landscape. There was a fleeting glimpse of the umbrella lady in a miniature boat. She flung her arms out to keep her balance. Then with a sickening wrench her ankle went over and she was on the ground. A fiery pain shot through her and she cried out. She rolled into a sitting position, but could do no more. A wave of nausea hit her as the pain took hold. Was she going to have to sit here in the damp and cold and wait for Adam to rescue her? Stupid bloody useless glasses. She ripped them off and launched them over the broken edge of garden. Then she had wrapped Rachel's scarf more closely round her, leaned against a plant pot and closed her eyes.

She sighed, now, let go of the door and limped back into the house. Adam followed her into the living room, where she sank back on to the sofa and heaved her legs up. She couldn't be bothered to get dressed. Not yet.

'Can you get me a blanket or something?' she said. 'And I could do with a cup of tea. Please.'

When he brought the tea, he was still wearing the hard hat. It made her think of when he had counted all those hi-vis jackets, shouting out the colours from the car. He looked like a little boy dressed up as a builder. Except he didn't. Not really. He wasn't little. He wasn't a boy.

'Okay,' she said. 'I suppose it will help if you carry on with the work. But be careful. Don't let that digger get too close to the edge. And not too long at a time on that other thing. It can't be good for you, all that shaking about.'

'Okay, Mumma.'

His enthusiasm made the air sizzle. She switched on the television. It was in the middle of a re-run of *The Weakest Link*. She took a sip of tea. Hot. Not too much milk. Just how she liked it.

Each day, he brought her lunch on a tray, but never stayed to eat with her. He kept his habit of walking along the beach to town every day, but he hadn't mentioned any new fossils for a while. She'd seen those bullet things on his shelf a while ago, with some bits of blue glass, and that old bottle. She wasn't sure if they were still there, though. She wondered what he'd done with all his ammonites, and didn't he say he'd found a sea urchin a few weeks ago? She had never thought he'd give it up. He'd treated it like a proper job. But still, she began to wonder if he had some other reason for going to town every day.

The next delivery arrived as planned on Monday, and by late morning on Tuesday, Adam was on the last trip with the digger. Mary's ankle had improved. The swelling had gone down, the bruise had changed from purple to yellow and had sunk to a line along the side of her foot. She no longer needed the dibber walking stick. It was time, she decided, to venture to the edge of the garden and inspect Adam's work. She put on some loose gardening clogs that she'd never worn – hand-me-downs from one of her clients – and then noticed a letter on the mat by the front door. She went into the kitchen and found her magnifying glass.

It was from the council. It had come to their attention that there was some building work in progress at the property which did not have the necessary planning permission. All works must cease immediately. An application could be submitted, but if it was refused, a demolition order for the structure would follow forthwith.

After several attempts and many minutes on hold, Mary got through to someone in the relevant department. She would have driven straight over there if it wasn't for her ankle. She'd made the journey to inspect the so-called works, but she dared not venture on to the uneven ground of the fallen cliff. She had to admit Adam hadn't done a bad job. If you didn't know, you wouldn't be able to tell there was any imported soil there. She wondered who the tattletale was. Why couldn't people mind their own bloody business?

'I've a right to protect my property,' she said when she was eventually put through to someone in the right department. 'It's my land. I'm trying to get it back to how it was. If you lot had done your job, none of this would be necessary.'

They were immovable. Didn't listen. Kept repeating the same phrases. Managed retreat. Rollback Register. They said it wasn't their job to stop the cliff from falling into the sea. It was their responsibility to make sure their residents were safe, and that's what they were trying to do. In the end, she pressed the red button to finish the call and threw the phone at the sofa.

In the afternoon, when Adam had gone out, Mary decided to try the steps. There was a rail to hold on to and she could take her time. From the beach, the edges of the compacted sections looked unfinished, precarious, emphasising how her remaining piece of land jutted out from the rest of the cliff. If the sea ever came up this far, which it had done several times in recent storm surges, the material would wash away in a single high tide. She had to keep on fighting. But what else could she do? The eye thing was getting worse. She kept seeing things that weren't there, and now she could hardly walk. Certainly not on these great cobbles. She couldn't move from the bottom of the steps, except to go up again.

She bent and picked up a stone and hurled it towards the edge of her land. Then another. And another. Stone after stone flew through the air until she was breathless and her arms and shoulders ached. But she didn't stop. Energy pulsed through her and the burn of her muscles spurred her on. Every day, she thought. I could stand here every day and throw stones at my cliff to shore up the earthworks. After all, it was a recognised protection strategy – building a buffer of material between the beach and the cliff to absorb some of the wave power. If she made a habit of it every day, it could make a difference. She bent to pick up the next rock, and there, by her foot, was a large, brownish, egg-shaped stone, with a grooved pattern on it like a turtle's shell. Regular, raised squares with indented outlines. And a cylindrical knob on the end. She gasped. She had seen pictures of these.

A pineapple. That's what they had called them, in the war.

A hand grenade.

She stood still. The toe of her clog was almost touching it. What if she had thrown it, picked it up and lobbed it at her cliff?

Once again, officials in hard hats swarmed over the beach. Mary had struggled back up the steps and phoned the police. Now, the beach was cordoned off and a controlled explosion was carried out.

Mary sat in the kitchen with a cup of strong coffee. What if there were more pineapples down there? She'd heard of stashes of ammunition buried by the Home Guard in the war without proper records. There could be hundreds of the things. But you'd have to dig up the whole beach to have a chance of finding everything. And even then, you'd never be sure. What if she'd kicked it or stepped on it? She'd have been blown to pieces. It didn't bear thinking about.

There was a knock on the door, and then, before she got there, another knock.

'All right, all right,' Mary muttered.

It was a young man in a zip-up jacket and faded jeans. Even with her blurry vision she could tell his hair was a mess. Not a professional then. She had taken to making judgements like this because she found it so hard to see facial expressions. She tried, now, with her trick of focusing above the shoulder. Hmm. Good-looking. Hair not that bad after all. Friendly. Inquisitive. Eyes that reminded her of Evan, she realised with a sudden stab of loss.

'Hello. I'm Reuben Gillick. North Norfolk Post. I understand you found the explosive today.'

'Yes.'

'Can you tell me about it? What happened exactly? How did you know it was dangerous?'

'I can't stand here,' Mary said. 'You'd better come in.' She led him to the kitchen, where her half-finished coffee stood on the table. She sat. 'You can sit down if you like,' she said.

'Those shells,' he said, nodding towards the window. 'They look great, strung up like that. My nan made things with shells. Mirror frames and lamps and all sorts. We used to spend hours collecting them. Never found a bomb though.'

She told him about finding the pineapple, and how lucky she felt that she had come to no harm.

'Pineapple?' he said. 'I was told it was a World War Two grenade.'

'It was. They look like pineapples. That's what people called them.'

'I reported on a huge cache of bombs last year. They found them on a building site near Norwich. Forty of them. These bottle things with yellow stuff inside. Phosphorus bombs apparently. Like grenades I suppose. Throw them and the glass breaks and poof! Up they go.'

'Thank goodness I didn't throw the one I found.'

'Why would you have thrown it?'

'That's what I was doing – throwing stones.'

She thought again how like Evan he was – not the scruffy appearance, but his eyes and his voice and the way he made her want to talk. She knew she was being ridiculous, but he listened to her in a way no one had for a long time. Except perhaps Rachel. In the end, she told him about the landslide and how the council didn't care, about her earthworks and the letter telling her to stop, and about the threat of eviction if the cliff edge got much closer. She even told him about Adam, how she had moved in just before he was born, and how this fight was all for him.

'We're not going anywhere,' she said. 'This is our home and we've got a right to protect it.'

They went down the garden and he took photographs. The story would be in this week's edition, he told her, which came out on Friday.

It wasn't until he'd gone that she thought of the bottle on Adam's shelf. What had Reuben Gillick said? Bottle things? With yellow stuff inside? Bombs, he said. Phosphorus bombs. She rushed through to Adam's room, but the bottle had gone. He must have decided it wasn't treasure after all and got rid of it.

Red Paint

Adam's favourite room at Holthorpe Primary School had been The Hut, but it was no longer there. Separate from the main building, it had big windows and a blue square of carpet in one corner, and some squishy chairs. One spring, a family of foxes moved into the space underneath The Hut, and his teacher let them take turns filming them. Now, there was a new fence all the way round the school, and tall gates with a security key pad and a buzzer so you could talk to someone in the office.

Adam stood on the other side of the road, not directly opposite, but it didn't make any difference. Two of the dads crossed over, all frowns and jutting chins and tight mouths. One of them jabbed a finger at him, prodded him in the chest. Adam stepped back.

'What are you doing, hanging round here? You don't have a kid in the school, do you? Now get lost or we'll make you.

Got that?'

Adam walked away, looking straight ahead as he passed groups of waiting parents, pushed down the anxiety, concentrated on what he had to do. Why should he let anyone stop him doing his job? He tried to ignore the nudging and whispering, like Mumma would, but snatches and snippets buzzed around him, followed him as he quickened his pace... *dodgy character...mother's a weirdo...ramshackle bungalow...seen the paper...told the police...dumping earth...found a bomb...*

It was a few days ago, the bomb. He couldn't believe it was Mumma who had found it. It was a hand grenade from the Second World War, but Mumma said they called it a pineapple because that's what it looked like. He'd been coming back from his circuit and found police officers on the beach, and a line of tape attached to metal posts stuck into the sand. Unexploded device, they told him, and they wouldn't let him past, so he had gone back to the pool and climbed up the rope ladder again. He didn't go inside the shed, hidden in the dip, but found his way straight up the gully.

Adam hurried away from the pointing fingers and the gossip, past the posh houses, with their big metal gates and their lawns like carpets, and came to the alpaca farm. He watched the alpacas over the fence for a while. Bits of their coats were hanging off in tufts, and they looked dirty and sad. You could pay money to take them for walks – trekking, they called it – but it would be kinder to pay money for them to have a nicer life. After a while, he checked that the two men had gone, and went back to the school.

There was one girl still in the playground, with her teacher. It was a good twenty minutes after home time. She'd been in the group of bigger girls when he'd warned them about the broken glass on the path. They'd be going on the bus to the high school in September, shoving and shouting, their skirts too short and their eyes thick with make-up and their hair all big and messy. Then, before you knew it, they'd have lipstick and high heels and a go-away-leave-me-alone curl of the mouth.

Hannah Bird would never get the bus to high school.

Because of him.

The thought jumped on him from nowhere and there was nothing he could do. He stood, staring, until the teacher said something to the girl and they both disappeared into the building.

He made his way to the crossroads and turned down the high street. In the fossil shop there were some things he hadn't seen before – a bit of mammoth tooth for seventy-five pounds, and some pairs of polished ammonites from Madagascar, with red and yellow swirls among the grey. He could never see the point of slicing them in half and polishing the flat faces.

Next door was the fudge shop that had closed last year. Theirs had never been as good as Molly's. It had been boarded up for months, but now the boards had gone, and the shop front had been painted bright red like a post box. A piece of cardboard stuck to the window had the words *wet paint* daubed across it in the same bright colour. Outside, a white van was parked on the double yellow lines, and as Adam turned away from the fossil shop, he saw Danny Goodrum's uncle loading a step ladder into the back of the van. He crossed over quickly, forcing himself not to turn round to see if Danny was there too, and went into the newsagent's. He could get a couple of Mars bars, and when he came out the van would be gone. He went towards the sweets at the back of the shop next to the post office counter.

And saw Mumma on the front page of a newspaper.

He stopped and stared. There she stood, spade in hand, at the broken end of their garden, beside the shed, with the landslide below. Whoever took it must have been standing on something, to get that angle – the bench, perhaps. *Queen Canute Finds Bomb*, the headline said. And she did look like a queen, standing there, her hair blowing in the wind, holding the spade as if it was one of those royal sticks. She stared out to sea, with her usual I'm-in-charge expression. Adam picked up the paper and began to read. The first bit was about the grenade and her lucky escape and the controlled explosion, but there was more. He read about how the cliff had collapsed after the recent storm, about how Mary Farthing, *Queen Canute*, would protect her home from the sea at all costs, for the sake of her son. There was a bit about her experience in coastal engineering, her gardening business, even her blunt, no-nonsense manner. A wave of pride and affection spread through him. Mumma. Queen Canute. She was… He struggled to think of the right word.

'Magnificent,' he said aloud.

'Hey, are you buying that, mate? One pound fifty.'

'Yes, I am.' He handed over the money and was halfway down the high street before he remembered the Mars bars.

The sun came out. Adam strode across the narrow strip of sand, full of energy. High cloud streaked the sky, and the sea sparkled. *Queen Canute*. Magnificent. *For the sake of her son. Fighting to save her home.* Okay, so she sometimes got cross with him and she bossed him about a lot, but that was just her *no-*

nonsense manner. Everything she did was for him. She'd said so to the news reporter. And now that this story was out there, surely the council would do something about the cliff. Public opinion, it was called. Everyone who read this would stand up for Mumma. *Queen Canute.* He couldn't wait to get home and show her the paper.

Mumma was up a ladder positioned against the front of the house, as if she was cleaning the windows or clearing the gutters. What was she playing at? First, she went down the beach steps on a sprained ankle, and now, she was climbing ladders with no one there to put a foot on the bottom rung to steady it. She had a broom in her hand, and a bucket hung on the ladder hook, and she was scrubbing the wall.

'Mumma? What...?'

Huge red letters, scrawled across the front of the house, over the patchy grey render and even on the window glass. LEAVE TOWN PERV.

Adam's mind flashed to the red lettering daubed on the cardboard sign. *Wet paint.* The white van. Danny. *We know where to find you.* And the jabbing, pointing fingers outside the school. *Get lost or we'll make you.* He wanted to curl up with his hands over his head. His body was starting to rock, and a humming noise began in his head. But Mumma was up a ladder. She had already had one accident. He screwed himself together and took control.

'Mumma.' He kept his voice calm and kind, but firm. 'Come down, please. I'll do it. Come off the ladder. Be careful.'

When she did, he saw that she'd been crying. Her face was blotchy and her eyes red.

'I wanted to get it off before you came back,' she said in a manner that was far from blunt and no-nonsense. 'They must have done it while I was down the garden. I didn't even hear a car. I didn't want you to see it. But this is worse than useless.' She threw the broom down. 'It needs proper paint stripper.' She sniffed, on the edge of tears again.

'Oh, Mumma, don't cry. Remember what you always say. Ignore them. I'll get some special cleaning stuff from Mr Bright in the morning. I could hire one of those steam cleaner things. I'll get rid of it, Mumma. Don't worry.'

'I'm sorry, son.' It was as if she'd given up.

Inside, he made her sit down. 'I'll make us a cup of tea. I forgot the Mars bars, but never mind. I've got something to show you.'

He pulled the paper from his bag, unfolded it and smoothed it out on the table.

She peered at it, frowned at the photograph, then pushed the newspaper across to him.

'Get the tea made,' she said. 'There should be some custard creams in the tin. And then you can read it to me. All I can make out is the headline. Bloody small print.'

By the time he had read the whole piece, she was furious. 'What rubbish! Makes me out to be an absolute nutcase. He made me tell him all that private stuff and then wove his own ridiculous story out of it.' She swept the paper off the table. 'Put it in the shed with the rest,' she said. 'Bloody Reuben Whatever-his-name-was.'

At least she sounded a bit more no-nonsense now. Bit more like Queen Canute. Bit more magnificent.

Adam went into his bedroom and fished his treasures out from under his bed – the sea glass and the belemnites and the old yellow bottle. He stood them in a row on the carpet, and looked at them for a bit. Then he slid them back out of sight. He would have to find a proper hiding place for them. If Danny – it must have been him, with his uncle's red paint – could scrawl horrible words on the front of the house, he was certainly capable of breaking in and stealing things from under his bed.

But where could he put them? Not with the others. There was no way he would ever lift that floorboard. He'd already ruled out Mumma's reconstructed shed, but thinking of it reminded him of the other shed. The one that was hidden in the invisible dip in the cliff. It had a good door. The latch wasn't that good, but he could get a padlock in the morning from Mr Bright when he went to get the paint stripper and the steam cleaner. He'd clean the graffiti and hide his treasures, and he ought to start being more careful with his job. His circuit. He would find a less obvious place to watch the school from. He'd work out which children had the most freedom, and where they were likely to go. Places that might be dangerous. Places where they might need a hero.

They stop short of the breaking waves. The wind has got up again. It's going to be another wild night.

'Where are they – the fossils?' she says, in her funny, gruff voice.

'Here.'

'But where? I can't see any.'

'Here. They're footprints. Look. Here's one. And here, look. This one's about your size.'

The dents are full of water – tiny, foot-shaped puddles, twenty or thirty of them scattered over the mudstone.

'Is it? I'm going to see.' She bends down and takes off her shoe. She pulls off her sock, stuffs it in the shoe. 'Here,' she says. 'Can you hold this?'

He can't tell if she believes him. He thrusts the shoe in his jacket pocket and puts his hand on his phone. He wants photos.

'Perfect!' she says. And it is. She stands there, laughing, with her back to the sea, and her little bare foot in the dent. The sun shines on her face, and the wind blows her dandelion hair.

Distress Flare

The morning after she had packed up Hannah's things, Rachel slept late, and woke up alone, with the towel tangled round her legs. She did not remember Christopher coming to bed. She went down to Hannah's room and pushed open the door. The boxes she had stowed in the boot of her car now stood in front of the empty cupboards, still sealed with parcel tape and labelled in bright blue marker pen. Soft toys, picture books, leggings and jumpers. When you buy tee shirts, age six to seven, you never think that seven is too much to hope for.

Christopher had stolen her sacrifice.

'I tried,' she whispered. 'Please let it count.'

She wondered if Jamie had slept there all night, and whether he had mended the bracelet.

She found him in the kitchen, eating brownies and ice cream, the pudding Christopher had planned for last night.

Where's Dad?' she asked.

'He's gone to church. Something about Lent.'

Rachel drifted to the sink, looked out at the garden, where the daffodils were still in tight bud. If she cut some and brought them in, they would open in a couple of days. She took a blue glass vase from a cupboard, held it against her chest. If Christopher had asked her to go to church with him, would she have gone? The only service any of them had been to since it happened was the funeral. The polite murmurings of a Sunday morning service were a world away from the way she prayed now. She marched across the beach or up on the cliffs, day after day, shouting into the wind. She lay on the sand, pleading, repeating the words over and over. Twice she had driven to the car park by the spit before sunrise, walked all the way to the end and knelt on the stones, begging. *Let me find out. Please let me know what happened. Please let someone…*

But, all the same, if he had asked…

She hadn't even been aware that it was Lent. The right time for sacrifices. She hardly knew what day of the week it was, let alone what season of the church calendar. She thought of the boxes, back in Hannah's room, and the bright paper creations stuffed at the back of a cupboard in the Crow's Nest. Would her sacrifice still count, now that Christopher had sabotaged it?

Jamie's spoon clinked against the bowl. At times, she wanted to gather him in her arms and hold him till he mended. But this lie of his, this unfathomable allegation, was a wall she had to demolish before she could reach him.

'Why did you say Dad had hurt you?' She kept her voice quiet, didn't look at him.

He was silent.

'Can you help me to understand? Or just admit that you

made it up?'

The chair scraped on the tiles, and she turned in time to watch him leave the room. She listened to his footsteps on the stairs. How long was he going to keep this up?

She sighed and put the blue vase back in the cupboard.

If it had been Izzy who asked about choir, she would have said she wasn't ready. If she let her voice loose, it would not dance up and down in obedient, measured phrases. Her throat, her breathing, her heart would not allow it. A raw, animal sound would leap out of her and her pain would fill the sky.

But it was Lenny who phoned, on the following Friday afternoon.

'Will you come to choir with us tomorrow, Rachel? And then we can get a cake at Molly's, Mummy says, and have a snack-nick on the beach.'

'A snack-nick?'

'A picnic snack.'

She pictured his gappy smile and the eager shine in his eyes. There he was, in his house, with his bones and his muscles and his skin, warm and living, the breath going in and out of his lungs, the blood pulsing through his vessels and his heart beating and beating and beating. How little it would take for all the life in his coltish limbs to be snuffed out, for his breath to ebb away and not come back, for his heart to give up and for the blood to stand still. How did children still walk and run in this world, jump and sing and laugh? How did they stay alive? It was a miracle. How did their little bodies keep going, when all it took was a moment?

'Oh, I'm not sure…'

'You can borrow me,' Lenny said.

'That's very kind, but what do you mean?'

'It's a parent and child choir, so you can borrow me. Mummy can have Flora.'

Rachel laughed, but her heart squeezed. 'Okay.' She surprised herself by agreeing, in spite of the pressure behind her ribs.

Izzy took over on the phone. 'Good,' she said. 'We'll knock on your door and walk together so you don't have to go in on your own. And listen, it was Lenny's idea, that you should come, and that you could borrow him.'

'He's such a sweetie.'

'He is, isn't he? Except when he's whining that the crisps are the wrong flavour, or wiping his nose on my tee shirt or breaking Flora's Lego inventions and calling her a scum-null.'

'A scum-null?'

'He means numbskull. Makes her cry every single time.'

It was a picture-book kind of day. Blue sky, fluffy clouds, bright sunshine and a sparkling sea. There was a fresh breeze, and white wave crests galloped across the ocean. A storm was forecast, due in a couple of days, but for now, it was perfect March weather. They passed the old lighthouse and the lifeboat station. Lenny bounced along, holding Rachel's hand, and his energy was enough for both of them. Flora skipped beside Izzy, chattering about earwigs and whales and her new spotty socks. Inside Rachel, the weight of her grief hung heavy and solid. It was a part of her now, but at times, without warning, it would swell and burst from its fragile skin, rip through her and take possession, stopping her breath and forcing her to her knees.

'Look!' Lenny pointed down to the beach.

'Ooh,' Izzy said 'Canoeing. That looks fun.'

'They're kayaks, Mum,' Lenny said. 'Double paddle, see?'

'Oh, yeah.' Izzy shrugged and smiled at Rachel over the top of his head.

They stood and watched as the two kayakers launched their bright orange vessels from the beach, through the breaking waves, and out to sea.

'When I grow up, I'm going to be a pirate,' Flora said. 'And have a parrot and a stethoscope.'

'You mean a telescope,' Lenny said.

'I don't because I'm going to be a pirate doctor actually.'

Rachel could see her, in a white coat and a pirate hat, with a parrot on her shoulder. All grown up. A spasm shot through her. Hannah wanted to be an artist. Or a bookshop owner or a hatter but not a mad one or, if there was frost in the air, a knitter of stripy blankets.

In spite of the weight of her grief, and the spasms that gripped her, Rachel was comfortable being with Izzy. When she was with Christopher or Jamie, everything stretched taut – the questions and the doubts, the guilt and the blame, the fear of exposing her own wounds, when she knew she could not bear to look on theirs. It was true, what Christopher had said, about her not letting him in. But how could she? Her pain was hers, lodged inside her, pressing against her bones, her skin, pushing itself into every part of her. She had no space to let in someone else's pain. Hers would mutate, expand, split her open.

Morag, the choir leader, touched her arm. 'Don't force it,' she said. 'It's not all about the singing. Tap your foot, if you want, or hum, or just listen. Let the music in if you can. It's great that you're here.' Her voice was gentle and her smile warm.

Rachel was always grateful for the healing she had found here after the dark days of mourning her mother's death and the terrible depression that had overwhelmed her. Perhaps there would be a measure of comfort now. Thanks to Lenny, she had found the courage to come, but she was glad Izzy had picked a place for them near the door. The buzz and chatter, the burst of laughter and the air of happy expectation – it all felt like a world where she had once belonged, but now she was a stranger and she didn't recognise the language.

After a bit, she found she could let Lenny's enthusiasm carry her through. Beside her, he swayed and clapped and his clear, bright voice made her skin tingle. When he smiled up at her, his eyes shining, she said to herself, you were lucky, Hannah, lucky to have such a friend. The thought soothed her, like cool ointment on a sore, and she was glad to be here.

Until the last song.

'Let's do one we know to finish with,' Morag said. 'With all the parts and twiddly bits and the actions. 'He's Got The Whole World In His Hands.'

Rachel stiffened and her skin went cold. The door was right there. She could reach it in two strides. There was an expectant rustle and the piano played the introduction. Her pulse beat loudly in her ears. She couldn't get her breath. *In his hands.* She had believed it, but if it was true, then why…? She tried to push the question away. She couldn't let herself think like that. But how could she carry on praying if she didn't believe? The fragile thread of her faith was slipping through her fingers. She mustn't let go. The voices began – the lively, lilting melody, with the harmonies twisting through.

She closed her eyes.

Izzy's hand gripped hers. 'It's all right.' Her voice was low

and calm. 'We can go if you want. I'm sorry. I didn't think…
this song…'

The panic passed. Izzy's warm, strong hand enclosed hers,
the blended voices filled the space, and the rhythm of the song
pulsed through the air. The room was full of smiles, of joy,
of life. It was a good place to be. She had to face her doubts,
become acquainted with a new and perhaps uncertain way of
looking at the world. Sometimes, ointment on a wound had to
hurt before it healed.

Although the breeze was strong, there was a feel of spring
in the air, and the sunshine had brought people down to the
shore. There was a long queue at Molly's, and Rachel spotted
the fossil collector, Adam, at the front, with his oversized
jacket and his thick, unruly fringe. He had a rucksack on his
back, reminding her of when those boys had pushed him over
and run off with his bag. She thought of Mary, sitting next to
her on the bench. *Daft great lump. Not a bad bone in his body.* Molly
laughed at something he said and he beamed as he took the
paper bag she passed him.

'I'll get in the queue,' Izzy said, 'if you want to take them
down to the beach. Doughnuts with sprinkles, you two?
Coffee, Rach? Cake?'

'Mmm. Please. Flapjack, if she's got any. Thanks.'

Rachel went down the steps with the children, and held
Flora's hand while they climbed down the steep bank of
cobbles to the sand. People sat in groups, sheltered from the
breeze against the wooden groyne. The tide was creeping up
the beach and in less than an hour there would be no sand
left. Several castle projects were underway, though, and Rachel
noticed Adam on the fringe of one of them – two small

boys and an older girl, with a huge red bucket and heavy-duty spades. He stood with his rucksack on his back, one hand in his pocket, and the other clutching his paper bag. Every now and then he looked up, scanned the beach and the promenade above, as if he was looking for someone. Then his attention would return to the sandcastle and its builders.

Lenny and Flora ran about collecting handfuls of red seaweed and stones, and made giant face pictures on the sand. Lively waves crashed in, and the spray sparkled in the sunlight. A yellow and white fishing boat bobbed on the water, and, further out, a ship passed slowly in front of the wind turbines, its blue and red containers like a child's wooden blocks.

Voices caught Rachel's attention. A man had joined the red bucket group and was talking to Adam. She couldn't hear what he was saying, but by the way his head was thrust forward and his hands jabbing at the air, she could tell it wasn't a friendly chat. Adam walked away and sat down on the edge of the stones. The man said something to the children and then came over to Rachel.

'You want to watch him,' he said. 'He's been in trouble for it before.'

'For what?' Rachel said.

'Put it this way,' the man said. 'He's got an unhealthy interest in kids. Hangs around outside the school, and in the park. Starts talking to them. Being too friendly. I'd keep an eye on your two.' He nodded towards where Flora was patting a layer of seaweed.

'Oh, he's all right,' Rachel said. 'I know his mother.' *Not a bad bone in his body*, she thought.

'Well, I'd be careful if I were you,' the man said.

When Rachel looked back at Flora, Lenny wasn't there. Her

heart jumped, but then she spotted him at the water's edge with a bucket in one hand. It was the red bucket belonging to the sandcastle group.

'Lenny! Not too close,' she shouted, jumping up, but Adam was already there, and grabbed Lenny's hand, pulling him away from the waves, and saying something to him. Lenny handed the bucket to Adam. The next wave broke and washed up the beach, and in one swift movement, Adam ducked down and filled the bucket without even getting his feet wet. He handed it back to Lenny as Rachel reached them, but as he did so, he dropped his paper bag in the water.

'Oh, no!' Rachel said. 'Your cake!'

'It wasn't a cake,' he said. 'It was two butterscotch buns and they were the last ones, Molly said. She saved them for me.'

'What a shame,' Rachel said. 'Anyway, thanks for helping with the bucket.'

'Yes, thank you.' Lenny carried the bucket of water back to the group.

'You're welcome,' Adam said, and trudged towards the steps.

Izzy appeared with the cakes and drinks and they moved up the beach and sat on the stones for their snack-nick.

'Is that one of those kayaks?' Izzy pointed. 'Can you see? There. Way beyond the fishing boat. Look at the size of those waves. I can't see the other one. Can you?'

Rachel scanned the sea, and had just spotted one tiny orange craft when a line of red smoke shot up into the sky some way to the right of it, and a fraction of a second later, there was a loud bang.

'Oh, my God!' Izzy said. 'Was that a distress flare? Should we call someone? Did you see where it came from? D'you think it's the kayakers?'

A voice came from behind them, loud and deliberate. 'Coastguard please...Holthorpe. Yes... A red flare... Just one.'

Rachel turned. Adam stood half way up the steps with his phone. She watched him finish the call and then he stood still, staring at the sea.

It couldn't have been much more than ten minutes later that the lifeboat sped out past the ends of the groynes, bouncing over the waves, its engine buzzing.

'Look!' Lenny shouted. 'Flora thought it was a firework, but it wasn't. It was one of those...what are they called?'

'It was a distress flare,' Rachel said. She got to her feet, made her way over the uneven stones to the sand and stood there, her fists balled in the pockets of her fleece. 'Please,' she whispered. 'Please let them be okay.'

Knots of people gathered on the promenade, eyes fixed on the speeding boat, pointing, calling out to each other. A woman at the top of the steps had a pair of binoculars. Hope hung in the air, as though everyone was holding their breath.

The lifeboat circled, appeared to come to a stop near the single orange kayak. It was too far away to make out individual figures, but it wasn't long before the lifeboat moved on and there was a cry from the woman with the binoculars.

'There it is! They've found it! Look!'

Rachel couldn't see anything at first, but then she spotted another splash of orange.

'I think there's someone in the water,' the woman said. 'Yes, it's okay. I can see. They've got them on board. They're coming back in.'

A cheer went up. Someone started clapping and everyone joined in. There were hugs and laughter. Lenny and Flora jumped up and down, holding hands. Rachel's throat tightened

226

and tears pressed behind her eyes. They watched until the
lifeboat headed for the slipway further along, where the trailer
would be waiting with the net in position for recovery.

'Come on, kids,' Izzy called. 'Time to go.'

When they came up the steps, Adam had gone.

No one was home when Rachel got back. She was exhausted,
and glad to be alone. In the kitchen, she took the blue vase
from the cupboard, filled it with water and set it on the table.
Then she took a pair of scissors, went out to the garden and
cut the budding daffodils until she had a thick bunch. Inside,
she placed them in the vase. They would be open in a day or
two.

Seedy Fences

Mary couldn't get the report out of her head. *Queen Canute.* Bloody check. She hobbled to the shed and fished the newspaper out of the crate, took it back to the kitchen and spread it on the table.

Adam had set off for town as usual. Said he'd get stuff from Bright's to clean the mess off the front of the house. Bloody hooligans. Vandals. The worst thing was that word they'd used about Adam. It made her feel sick to imagine that anyone would see him like that. She didn't want to think about it, but there it was, plastered in huge letters across their house. Their home, the place that should be their sanctuary. And even if it could be erased, she could never unsee it. The damage was done and the bruise darkened inside her. She had stood on the ladder with her broom and the bucket of soapy water, scrubbing at the red until it smeared like blood. I can't protect him for ever, she thought. Not from people like this. Not from a world where if you're different you're treated like rubbish. At least she had stopped crying by the time he came home. It wouldn't do for him to see her like that. He depended on her. Too much, perhaps.

She found her magnifying glass and sat down to read the report for herself. She hadn't missed the yellow glasses since she'd thrown them down the cliff. This was good enough.

She shouldn't have trusted that journalist. The very fact that he'd reminded her of Evan should have rung alarm bells. That charm. Those eyes. That gift of making her believe that her feelings and opinions had value, that ability to draw things out of her, giving the illusion of a connection built on trust and honesty.

In the days before Evan, she'd had relationships that had worked for a while and then fizzled out with little in the way of animosity or recrimination or even much hurt. She'd been in love with John, a Canadian oceanographer, but after three years together, he was offered his dream job back in Canada. He asked Mary to go with him, but as she pondered her decision, Fiona, her sister, suffered a breakdown, leaving her anxious and fragile. 'I can't abandon her,' Mary told John. She met him once more, when he came back for a conference in London, but the spark had gone.

On her fortieth birthday, she bumped into Evan on the stairs at work and dropped a homemade red velvet cake at his feet. He went out to buy doughnuts for everyone instead, and she invited him to her birthday bash at the pub. And that was that. It lasted four years, almost. And then, Evan and Fiona were gone, and she moved into the house on the cliff, betrayed, bereft, broken. But with a child on the way and a fierce determination to navigate her way through this fickle world on her own terms, and under her own steam.

She finished reading the report. *Queen Canute*. What did that say about his intentions? He wanted to make her a figure of affectionate fun. No matter how sympathetically he wrote about her plight – the landslide, the council's attitude, the threat of eviction – she was essentially to be laughed at, patted on the head and told to do the sensible thing, even though the reader might feel a tiny bit sorry for her. He hadn't taken her seriously. It was all a clever pretence, his admiration of the strings of shells hanging in the window, his twee little fairy tales about his grandmother's seaside handicrafts. She should have paid more attention to her first impressions.

After the interview, she'd had high hopes for a public outcry when the newspaper published the report, visions of the council being forced to back down, of the promise of a new plan for defending this bit of the coast. Or, at the very least, of public support for her right to protect her property, to continue with her scheme to rebuild the cliff.

But Reuben Bloody Gillick, that pathetic excuse for a journalist, had put paid to all that with this nonsense, which would turn the community against her, and no doubt fuel the gossip and lies about Adam. She wouldn't be surprised if they got blamed for the bomb as well. She scrunched the page of newspaper into a ball and threw it across the room, half hoping for an explosion.

It wasn't until she sat down with her lunch – two pieces of marmite toast and a cup of tea – that she glanced at what was left of the newspaper. Classified ads. It was amazing that papers still printed them, what with all the other ways people sold stuff nowadays. She picked up her magnifying glass and perused the gardening section. She could do with a couple more polytunnels for the nursery. She needed to think about her spring planting. But was there any point? If the council had their way, and the weather played silly buggers, she and Adam could be out in a matter of months. Rehoused in some small box on a soulless estate miles from the sea, with a view of rows of other small boxes. And then how would she manage her business, with the nursery no longer on her doorstep?

An advert in the next column caught her eye. *For sale: Four berth caravan. Loads of life left in it for an old crone. Dink to one rear corner. Viewing welcome. Two hundred and fifty pounds.*

A caravan. Now there was an idea. A caravan on the land across the road. Just in case they forced her out. Insurance. She read the ad again and laughed. *Loads of life left in it for an old crone.* Did that refer to the caravan, or the person who might buy it? It wasn't a bad price. She reached for her phone and keyed in the number.

She didn't need to view it, she told the seller. It sounded ideal.

They would bring it over on Monday. Cash on delivery.

Mary spent the first part of the afternoon emailing clients. She had to stay positive. The house could be safe for years yet. She discussed planting schemes and a couple of redesigns, as well as routine maintenance tasks. She updated her record books, checked through her seed packets and prepared some orders.

When she went out, she threw Rachel's scarf round her

neck, inhaled the now familiar perfume. That woman had got under her skin, unsettled her. Since that day when she had mistaken her for a mermaid, when she had tended her like a baby and observed her raw grief, they had been tied to each other. Rachel's loss had given a sharper focus to Mary's fears for Adam. If she could, she would have put the encounter out of her mind. But Rachel kept reappearing, and whenever she did, something stirred inside Mary – a reluctant pull towards this other woman, this mother, like her. It mattered to her that Rachel should come through her mourning, should learn how to live again.

She didn't look at the front of the house. But she couldn't put the graffiti out of her mind. LEAVE TOWN PERV. They should have reported it of course. Perhaps she still should, before Adam came back with the paint stripper. But what would the police do? She couldn't put Adam through another interview. Better to get rid of it and put it out of her mind. But putting things out of her mind was becoming increasingly difficult.

The steps were easier this time. Her ankle was almost back to normal, if she didn't think about it too much. Braving the stony bank, she made her way to the rock armour below the Bluff. When Adam was little, and she had told him these were sea defences, he had said it was a silly name. 'They're not fences,' he said. 'They're rocks. And they don't have any plants growing on them.' It had taken her a while to realise he thought she was saying *seedy fences*. She smiled now as she looked at the tumble of granite boulders, imported from Norway, and imagined, in their place, a huge fence, like the wooden groynes nearer town, but planted with seeds that would grow into a living wall, stretching out into the ocean. A seedy fence.

She turned and began the slow trudge back up the stones, but soon gave up trying to keep her balance on two legs, and climbed the bank on all fours. At the base of the landslide, she stopped in the place where she had found the pineapple. She picked up a rock, hurled it at the toe of the slope. Then another, and another. She kept going until her shoulders and back ached. She stretched, rotated her shoulders, surveyed the slope, wondering what would happen if she defied the council and continued her rebuild.

And then the slope moved. At first she thought it was slipping, another landslide. But then she realised it was another of her visions. The ground rose and fell in waves like the sea, or like a meadow of long grass in the wind, as it had when she'd tripped at the end of the garden. Tussocks sprang up and then vanished. Vegetation danced and swayed over the slope.

She stared, and the idea came to her. That was it. Like Adam said. Seedy fences. She could use seeds. Vegetation. Planting. Soft engineering. Her focus shifted and the vision disintegrated. But she knew what she had to do. And she wouldn't need planning permission.

She had to deal with groundwater and gravity. This would be about deep roots and planned drainage. Quick-growing plants to begin with, to stabilise the topsoil, and then something more shrubby – the cliff wasn't high enough for trees. Sea buckthorn had been used in some places, but she was reluctant to use a non-native species. Blackthorn would be good, though, and yarrow, and maybe some sort of grass. She'd check the nursery, and add to her order list if necessary.

After another bout of stone throwing, she climbed the steps, breathless, but with a new determination fizzing in her veins. When she came to the house, the graffiti took her by surprise.

Bright red hate, scrawled across the walls and windows. She clenched her fists, and marched round the side of the house. Nothing would stand in her way. She would make this work. She had to.

Padlock

When Adam arrived home, bursting to tell Mumma about the distress flare, he found her sitting at the kitchen table, counting the cash in the box. Papers and seed packets and envelopes lay in neat piles, secured with elastic bands.

'I called the coastguard, Mumma,' he began. 'And the lifeboat had to—'

'Shh!' She slapped a ten pound note on top of a pile. 'One hundred. Let me finish counting this. Ten, twenty, thirty…' She continued under her breath. 'Right. That's a hundred and fifty. One of us will need to get more cash on Monday morning. A hundred pounds.' She placed the notes back in the cash box and put the lid on. 'What were you saying?'

'There was a distress flare and if you see a flare you have to call the coastguard even if you think it might be a firework and it was all right in the end because the lifeboat rescued the person in the water and I dropped the butterscotch buns in the water but Molly said they were the last ones.'

'You called the coastguard?'

'Yes. Because of the flare. It was a red flare and I filled a bucket with water for a little boy and the lady said thank you and she didn't get angry like some people do and Mr Bright is bringing his pressure washer.' Adam took his coat off, hung it on the back of the door with Mumma's new scarf, and sat down at the table with her. 'Tomorrow. He's going to help me clean the paint off.'

'What on earth did you tell him for? You can do it yourself. You don't need him. It's bad enough having that vileness plastered all over the house without inviting all and sundry to come and ogle at it.'

'I told him I needed to buy paint stripper and hire a pressure washer and he said you had to be careful with chemicals and why did I want it so I told him.'

'I hope you didn't tell him what it said.'

'I did and he said it was an absolute disgrace and what were neighbours for.'

Mumma made a clicking sound with her teeth and then sighed. 'Oh, he means well, I suppose, but you should have said no. We've always managed, haven't we, the two of us? We don't want to start relying on people like Mr Bright. It'd be the thin end of the wedge.'

'People like Mr Bright? You make him sound like a bad person, Mumma, but he's not. He's a good person. He's kind. And he said I was a hero, remember. And what wedge are you talking about?'

'You daft great lump.' She reached across and rubbed his hair. 'Anyway,' she said. 'Guess what? We're getting a caravan.

It's coming on Monday. That's what we need the cash for.' She beamed.

'A caravan? What for? We don't need a caravan.'

The coast path went through a caravan park on the other side of Saltbourne. From the beach you could see sheered-off slabs of concrete embedded in the slope – caravan bases that had gone over the edge when the cliff gave way. What did Mumma want with a caravan? A burst of apprehension filled his chest. 'Are we going on holiday?'

Mumma had taken him to Yorkshire once, when he was twelve. They stayed in part of a farmhouse, not a caravan. Bed and Breakfast it was called, but they had their tea there too. Yellow potatoes and thick gravy. Puddings made with jam. He remembered sheep and rain and hills and sleeping in a bed with the wall on the wrong side. They had spent an afternoon trailing round a country house with one of Mumma's friends from university, who called him young man and laughed too much and wore a tight top that made him look at her chest all the time even though he didn't want to. That evening Mumma insisted on climbing the hill behind the farmhouse at a quick march all the way to the top even though it was raining again. They were both out of breath by the time they reached the summit.

'Bloody so-called friends,' she said, banging a gate behind her and scattering a huddle of threadbare sheep.

He had never seen the point of going on holiday. Wetherley End was where he belonged. Why would he want to be anywhere else?

Mumma stood up, and piled the papers and the cash box on the shelf. 'Holiday?' she said. 'Absolutely not. I won't be towing it anywhere. It'll be parked up across the road, and there it will stay. Having a caravan on that bit of land will be a kind of back-up, in case the worst comes to the worst.'

It wasn't until Adam was back in his bedroom that he thought of the treasures under his bed and remembered about the padlock. He had meant to buy one for the shed while he was in Bright's, but he'd been distracted because of the conversation about the pressure washer and the graffiti. If he took the treasures to town with him on Monday, he'd be able to hide them in the shed on the way back, once he had got the padlock. Better put them in his bag now, so he didn't forget. He fished them out, stowed them in his rucksack, clicked the fastenings, and pushed it under the bed.

On Sunday morning, Mumma went out on the slope before Mr Bright arrived. Said something about raking it over for planting. At least her ankle was better now and the prospect of the caravan had put her in a good mood. The weather was worse, though. Another storm was on the way. Wind gusted around the house, and the sky was low and grey.

'Your mother about?' Mr Bright said.

'She's in the garden,' Adam said.

'I just wondered…' He nodded towards the red words scrawled across the front of the house. 'Are you sure you don't want to report it? Is she sure?'

'She doesn't like the police very much,' Adam said.

Mr Bright laughed, though Adam wasn't sure what was funny.

Adam didn't mind when Mr Bright took charge of the cleaning. It was his machine and he knew what he was doing, and in the end it didn't take long. As he was packing the stuff back in the boot of his car, he said, 'Look, son, if there's any more trouble, let me know. Okay?'

A few minutes after the car had vanished down Wetherley Lane, Mumma reappeared. She came round to the front to inspect.

'Hmm,' she said. 'Not bad, I suppose. You can still see a bit of red there above the window.'

She pointed, but Adam couldn't see anything. He was surprised she could, the way her eyes were these days.

By Monday morning, the wind was howling in from the north east, straight off the sea. It wasn't raining, but as soon as Adam stepped outside, sea spray misted his skin and he tasted salt in the air. He'd heard Mumma banging about in the kitchen, having an early breakfast, and now she was wiping the car windows.

'I'm driving to town,' she said. 'I'll get the cash, so you don't need to worry.'

'But I'm going anyway,' he said. 'I don't care about the weather. You can trust me. I'll get the money.' What he really wanted to say was that she shouldn't be driving, but she wouldn't take any notice. He thought about the vanished yellow glasses, and the way she kept missing her footing, looking sideways at things. Didn't she realise how bad it had got?

'It's not that I don't trust you,' she said. 'I want you to get those paving stones laid before the caravan arrives. Come and look. Make sure you know what to do.'

She had marked out a rectangle on the far edge of the land across the road. The stones and a pile of sand were left from a path project she had never got round to.

'But that's miles from the house.'

'That's the whole point. Miles from the house equals miles from the cliff.'

Adam remembered those broken slabs of concrete stuck half way down the slope below the caravan site. 'Oh,' he said. 'I see what you mean. But they'll have to tow it all the way across the field. I hope they don't mind.'

'For two hundred and fifty pounds, I should hope they bloody don't,' Mumma said.

Adam finished the job before Mumma came back, tidied up, fetched his rucksack from under his bed, and, remembering the boards across the shed window, put in a torch. Then he left the house, climbed down the steps and crossed the sand to the water's edge. Huge waves rolled in, crashing on to the sand in a mass of swirling foam. The wind roared, hurling the gulls about the sky like scraps of paper. He kept his eyes down out of habit, scanning for fossils, but his heart wasn't in it. When he'd thought of hiding his treasures in the shed, relief had rushed through him, but it had turned to a mounting anxiety. Would it be safe? Was it too far from the house? What if anyone else knew about it?

He strode along, buffeted by the wind, his face and hands stinging. He turned up the high street and went to Bright's first, and bought the biggest padlock he could find, and then back down to Molly's.

'A beef and onion pasty and two butterscotch buns, please, Molly.'

Molly wore the Christmas hat again and a big purple scarf and fingerless gloves. Her nails were painted to match her bright red lipstick.

'You're lucky,' she said. 'I'm about to shut up shop. There's no one about and this storm's only going to get worse. The bad news is I've run out of butterscotch buns.' She paused, grinning. 'But the good news is your mum's already been by, and she took some, so maybe you'll get one when you get home.'

Adam took his pasty to the playground, and ate it sitting on the bench, but there was no one there. He walked round the edge anyway, and then across the green to the flats, round the other side and then down to the beach again. He didn't see anyone who needed his help, just a couple of small children, wrapped up in fat coats and woolly hats, but they had their parents with them.

The tide had covered the sand now, and the wind was even stronger. If he wasn't going to trudge over the shingle, he'd have to go up to the coast path and approach the shed from the gully. It seemed impossible that only two days ago, there had been children building sandcastles in the sunshine. On his way to the steps, he passed the beach huts. Some of them had long metal bars that went across the front, slotting into brackets on either side. He wondered if he should have bought one of those for his shed. That would have been much more secure. After all, any padlock, however big, was only as strong as what it was secured to.

He came to where the cliff path joined Wetherley Lane – the bend where the last house had been, and scrambled down the gully. He climbed over a rise, and then down into the secret dip where the big metal pin secured the rope ladder, and where the old shed stood. His new hiding place, that not even Mumma knew about. A shiver thrilled up his spine. Here, in this little saucer of land, the sound of the waves was faint and far away.

He lifted the latch and opened the door, let his eyes adjust to the dimness before going in. The wooden floor was covered with debris – stones, and splinters of wood, a couple of flattened drink cans. Had they been there last time he came? There was that smell again – damp and earth and rot. It seemed worse than before and he felt sick. Perhaps it was the fish crate. He would have liked to leave the door open, but he didn't feel safe, so he closed it, and switched on his torch.

He stepped towards the back, and swung his torch beam into one corner. He kicked at the heap of carrier bags. As far as he could tell, they were empty. He shone the light into the other corner, where the upturned crate was. He pulled it towards him, and lifted the corner.

There was something underneath.

A heap of fur and bones.

Adam dropped the crate and the torch and stumbled backwards with a cry. He lost his balance, and fell, putting his hands down behind him. A sharp pain shot through the palm of his hand. He brought his arm round to the front of his body, cradled it next to his chest. When he picked up the torch and shone it on his hand, the amount of blood startled him. He pulled his sleeve down and pressed the cuff against the wound, holding it firm to stem the flow. He sat, leaning against the side wall, his rucksack digging into his back. He directed the light at the floor. Broken glass – a beer bottle.

When the bleeding had stopped, he returned to the fishing crate, and lifted it again. What was that thing under there? A rabbit? A cat? Some sort of small mammal, with not a lot of flesh left on it. Some of the bones were sticking out. He had to get rid of it, but he recoiled from touching it with his bare hands. In the end, he scooped it into the crate using the old carrier bags, and then carried it out, round to the back of the shed where the rope ladder hung down to the next dip in the slope, and threw it down. Bits of it became detached as it fell, and he shuddered, thinking of Hannah Bird's little body being washed up on the beach.

He went back inside the shed, shaking and nauseous, dropped the carrier bags over the place where the dead thing had lain, and stood the crate up against the side wall, like a shelf. He took out his pieces of sea glass, the belemnites and the old bottle, and lined them up on top of it, wishing he could still display them on his shelf at home, like he used to. But, even here, could he leave them like that, in full view of anyone who opened the door? Perhaps he should hide them under the crate, as someone had done with the dead animal.

Someone. His hands went clammy. Someone must have been in here. Someone must know about it. Or could the animal have got trapped under there by accident? All the time, bubbling up under his anxieties, was the memory of what had happened that day by the sea defences. He couldn't put it out of his mind.

He remembered the golden light and the gusting wind. Her gruff voice and the gap in her teeth when she smiled. He remembered how she had scuttled over the rocks, sideways like a crab, and then the feel of her hand in his as they ran to the water's edge. He remembered her little white foot – a perfect fit in the dent in the mudstone. And the way she had laughed, with the sun shining on her face.

And afterwards, the numbing fear, as he stood, shaking, in his wet clothes.

He was scared to stay in the shed, and scared to leave. He couldn't carry on like this. He would go mad. Every time he woke in the night, the corner of his bedroom carpet loomed at him. His dreams were crowded with jabbing, pointing fingers. You'll pay for this. Weirdo. And all the time that he was watching the other children, he was thinking of Hannah. Hannah, and her dandelion cloud of hair and her smile that was like sunshine.

'Oh, Mumma,' he whispered, 'what am I going to do?'

If only he had told her everything as soon as it had happened. When he had climbed up the steps in the dark and come back to the house, he should have told her then.

But it wasn't too late. She would stand by him. She would never let him down. Everything she did was for him. That's what she had told the reporter. He would go home and tell her. Now. Straightaway.

He left the treasures displayed on the shelf, went outside, latched the door, hooked the heavy padlock through the loop and clicked it shut. He patted his pocket with the key inside, and climbed up the steep gully towards the road. His injured hand throbbed and his legs felt weak, but he had made up his mind.

Mumma would make everything all right.

Butterscotch Buns

'I'm glad you decided to come,' Christopher said.

They were walking to eight o'clock communion. He reached for her hand, and she let him hold it, pressed her palm against his, longing to connect without the undercurrent of blame, resentment, doubt. They fell into step and continued at a brisk pace up the hill towards the top road. A swirling grey sky had replaced yesterday's sunshine and cotton-wool clouds. The stiff breeze had upped its game, and a wild wind gusted round the chimneys and hurled itself between the houses. The full force of the storm wasn't supposed to hit until Tuesday. Rachel hoped the weather wouldn't spoil their trip this afternoon. They were going to High Trees, the new Outdoor Adventure Centre, for Jamie's birthday, taking Anthony with them. Christopher had promised they'd be home from church in time to make pancakes before they went.

'What made you change your mind,' Christopher said, 'about coming to church?'

'I realised how scared I am,' Rachel said. 'I've been blaming God. I've been angry.'

'I get that. But what are you scared of?'

'Not believing. Losing my faith, I suppose.'

'Not believing in God?'

'I don't know who he is any more, or if he even exists.'

'Because he let it happen?'

She sighed. 'Don't you feel that at all?'

'Suffering isn't new, Rach.'

'I know,' she said, 'but I trusted him. And even if God's still there and hasn't changed, my way of relating to him has. And it feels...' – she moved closer to Christopher and tightened her grip on his hand – '...it feels so fragile.'

The early service was always a short one, with only one hymn, and no sermon, and attended by so few that they sat in the choir stalls instead of the nave, facing each other across the chancel. Rachel let the familiar rhythms wash through her, lulling her into a kind of trance, like floating on the ocean. But when they came to the Psalm, the words broke through. *Hear my voice when I call... Do not hide your face from me... Do not reject me or forsake me, God my Saviour...though my father and mother forsake me... Be strong and take heart, and wait for the Lord.* The liturgy moved on, but she kept the Psalm open in front of her, repeating the words inside herself, over and over. *Do not hide your face...though my father and mother forsake me...*

Father and mother. It was true. They had forsaken her, her father through choice, her mother by dying before her time.

Rachel and her brother Tim had different memories about their father, Ed, leaving them. They had argued about it for years. Rachel remembered their father going to Tesco to buy new Christmas decorations and not coming back until the spring, when he turned up at the door with a new beard and a shaved head, and asked if they wanted to go out for pizza. She could replay both events in her mind – the arguments about what colour baubles to get – Cathy saying don't get black, Tim saying get lights for our bedrooms. Then how Ed looked like a stranger when he came back and how she ordered a meat feast pizza and felt sick at the first mouthful. Tim said he did come back with the decorations, including a life-size inflatable Santa, but stormed out after a fight with Cathy that same night, in which Cathy broke his nose.

'Mum would never have hit him,' Rachel insisted, 'and you invented the inflatable Santa as some kind of weird replacement. *Father* Christmas.'

'Huh, that's rich, coming from someone who's suddenly "found God".' He made quote marks with his fingers. 'If that's not a substitute father figure, I don't know what is.'

One way or another, their father had abandoned them, returned intermittently when he was sober, and vanished into an alcoholic fog for months or years at a time.

It was different for Cathy. She had not chosen to go. But neither had she fought it. She accepted it. She talked about heaven, her new life. Was that why the sense of being abandoned, forsaken, was still there? I needed her, Rachel thought, sitting on the narrow bench in the choir stall, with the words of the Psalm playing through her mind. I needed her, and she wasn't there.

Be strong and take heart… Wait for the Lord… Was God – if he existed – telling her he would answer her prayers if she didn't give up? If anyone else had told her to be strong, she would have exploded. But how long would the waiting go on? And did she have the strength – the heart – to keep believing?

At the end of the service, Gail put her hand on Rachel's arm. 'It's good that you're here.'

Rachel met her gaze, and longed, for a moment, to pour out her doubts and fears, the sense that her faith was on the point of collapse.

But what if Gail didn't have the answer? What if there was no answer?

Anthony had already arrived when they got back. Christopher made a mountain of pancakes and Rachel laid out three different syrups, blueberries, bananas, chopped nuts and sprinkles. All Jamie wanted was chocolate spread and ice cream. She found herself examining his facial expressions, analysing his body language, picking apart his conversation. What was going on behind it all? She longed to see him relax, laugh, enjoy himself. If only his pinched, closed face would soften and open up. If he would only look at her without that guarded narrowing of the eyes. She knew it was her fault he had become so withdrawn. She had coiled into her shell and shut herself off, leaving him to navigate his grief without her. And then she had nagged and nagged at him to explain his accusations against Christopher. This trip, she determined, would be the start of them going forward as a family. She wouldn't give up her quest for the truth, but she couldn't let it steal what she still had.

The first activity was the climbing wall. The instructor emphasised the importance of teamwork. 'Lots of encouragement,' she said. 'Positive feedback. You have to help each other. Don't let your partner feel stuck. There's always a way up.'

Exactly, Rachel thought, as she was clipped into her harness. Beside her, Jamie was ready to begin, and when he grinned at her, there was a fleeting glimpse of his old self. A glow of optimism warmed her.

She soon found which of the coloured handgrips were the easiest to grasp, and planned her moves, taking it slowly. Every time she stopped to take stock, though, Christopher shouted suggestions. 'That green one there... Put your foot on that one... Now, see the one above your head...pull yourself up...' And then an exaggerated 'Well done!' when she made a successful move. She tried not to let herself be irritated. He was doing what the instructor had said.

Jamie was faster than she was, responding to Anthony's prompts, but a couple of metres from the top, he came to a halt, a little ahead of her, and to the left. He had four points of contact, but his knuckles were white, and his arms were shaking.

'Jamie?' she said, quietly, so that those below wouldn't hear. 'Are you okay?'

He didn't answer.

Christopher's voice. 'You can do it. Come on. Try that pink one to the right of your knee.'

He must think she was stuck. But when she looked to the right, there was no pink grip.

'Take your time,' Anthony called. 'You need to get your left foot higher when you're ready. That green one, maybe?'

'Don't give up now,' Christopher shouted. 'You're nearly there.'

'I'm not giving up,' Rachel called back, without taking her eyes off Jamie. Then she saw the pink grip by Jamie's knee.

Christopher had been talking to him, not to her.

'Mum.' Jamie's voice shook. 'I can't...'

'It's okay.' Rachel hoisted herself up to his level. 'You're safe. If you want to stop, just tell the instructor. She'll get you down.'

'I can't move,' he whispered. 'My hands won't...'

From the ground, Christopher and Anthony yelled conflicting instructions until Rachel shouted at them to stop. In the end, Jamie unfroze and made it to the top, but it was a long time until his hands stopped shaking.

The Super Swing and the Air Jump were closing early because of the weather, but they made it on to the last sessions of both before ending up in the café. In spite of the buzz of good humour, there was still something guarded about Jamie's eyes, something tight and hollow in his expression. She tried to reconjure that flash of his old self when he had grinned at her, but the shield had gone up, and she wondered if she had imagined it. What should have been a healing family day out had ending up as a series of petty irritations and fizzled into nothing. When they got home, Jamie went to his room, refusing suggestions for watching a film, or playing the new *Catan Starfarers* game he had asked for. She had wanted to make up for locking herself away in her own grief. She had wanted a new start, but it hadn't worked.

The next morning, as soon as the others had left for school, Rachel took the holy stone up to Hannah's room and rummaged inside the pillowcase for the prayer beads, but they weren't there. She sat on the floor, leaning against the bed. In front of her were the boxes Christopher had rescued from her car. She couldn't remember if she had told him about Hannah's craftwork stuffed at the back of a cupboard upstairs.

She didn't want to look at the boxes and their sad, neat little labels, so she turned, knelt at the bedside, her hands clasped round the stone.

She didn't know how long she knelt there. Was God ever going to listen? All she wanted was to know. Surely it was her right, as a mother. She thought back to Hannah's first day of school, when she had fallen over in the playground and grazed her knee. Rachel couldn't bear the idea of her daughter hurting without her there. Holding Hannah close after they got home, she made her tell her the exact sequence of events until she felt she had been there. And now, if only she could find out what had happened, it would be as if Hannah had been in her arms all the time, as if she had carried her through everything.

And she would know whose fault it was. Although the police had assured them there was no evidence of injury, she couldn't shake off the idea that someone must be to blame. Someone must have done something. Hannah couldn't simply have vanished into the sea.

Downstairs, she found two used cereal bowls on the table and a heap of dirty laundry on the floor in front of the washing machine. She sorted everything out, made a huge batch of chilli that would last for two or three dinners, and ate an apple. Sometimes it took her by surprise that she could find satisfaction – pleasure, even – from doing normal, everyday things, and a rush of guilt would overtake her.

The other day, Gail had phoned to say the tutor had been in touch about resuming her course. Was she ready to talk about it? She said she needed more time, but in truth she couldn't see herself ever being ready. It was impossible, now, to imagine a future where she was a priest. She might go back to teaching, but how could she cure souls when her own was so lost? Deep down, too, she was beginning to wonder if she had ever been the right sort of person. She opened the back door and threw the apple core into the flowerbed, where the daffodils were prostrate, flattened by the wind.

It was just after twelve when she set out for the beach. She'd go all the way to Saltbourne Gap today, and come back across the cliffs, then turn up the track and stop at the church. A fierce, squally wind whipped up the waves, and huge breakers rolled in, seething with white foam. Layers of cloud raced across the sky, pale higher up, and dark and menacing beneath.

She marched across the stones, close to the water's edge, the wind blasting in from the sea. Perhaps the new start would only be possible once she'd found the truth. Maybe there would be no getting through it, as a family or any other way, until she knew what had happened. Sea spray stung her face. Always she came back to this burning need. She repeated the words of yesterday's Psalm aloud in time with the rhythm of her steps. *Hear my voice… Do not hide your face… Be strong and take heart… Wait for the Lord.*

She climbed on to the cliff at Saltbourne Gap, turned to the west and walked back towards Holthorpe. The coast path followed the cliff edge for a mile, and then, because of the erosion of the last twenty years, turned inland along Wetherley Lane not far from Wetherley End. Outside Mary's bungalow stood an enormous, mud-spattered Range Rover, and as Rachel approached, Mary appeared from the other side of it. The car reversed into the drive, narrowly missing Mary's battered old Volvo, and drove off down the lane.

'Hello,' Rachel said.

'Oh, hello. It's you. Bloody cheek, that woman. Car like that and argued over fifty pounds.'

Rachel raised her eyebrows.

'She sold me that.' Mary nodded towards the patch of land across the road that she called her nursery. On the far side stood a dilapidated caravan. 'It'll do, when I've cleaned it up, but you should see the state of the inside. I wouldn't give her more than two hundred and she took it in the end, but she made no end of fuss. Good thing I don't want to tow it anywhere. Probably fall to bits.'

'What's it for?' Rachel said.

'Insurance.'

'What do you mean?'

'The council. Once the cliff edge is within nine metres of the house, they'll evict us.'

'Oh dear. So…?'

'That caravan is a hundred and fifty paces from the house. And that's my land. So if the worst comes to the worst…' She folded her arms, stood there, grim-faced in her wax jacket and muddy boots, her grey hair blowing in the wind.

Rachel smiled, remembering the piece in the paper referring to her as Queen Canute, with the photo of her looking much as she did now.

'Come and have a look.' Without waiting for Rachel's agreement, Mary crossed the lane and strode along the rutted edge of her field, past the polytunnnel and the beds she had prepared for spring sowing. Rachel followed her. A layer of greenish-yellow covered the outside of the caravan, and the door handle was rusty. Inside, it smelled of damp and mildew and the cushions were spotted with black mould. Broken shelving hung off the walls and the windows were filthy. There were bunks behind a torn piece of curtain, and a fold-out bed arrangement over the table and bench seats. There was a tiny sink, but no bathroom. The caravan rocked in the wind as if it was about to take off. It began to rain, and the drops hammered on the roof.

'See?' Mary said. 'Terrible state. Probably not worth half what I paid for it. Still, I suppose it'll be okay once I've fixed all this and got it cleaned up.'

Rachel didn't know what to say. Did she mean she would move in here if she was evicted? With Adam? With no plumbing or heating? She couldn't have thought it through.

'Cup of tea?' Mary said. 'The rain might stop after a bit. You're like Adam, tramping about whatever the weather.'

'Yes, please,' Rachel said. 'And I could do with using your loo if that's okay.'

They trudged through the mud and wind and rain back to the house.

'You left your scarf,' Mary said, when Rachel came back from the bathroom and hung her coat on a chair. 'Here.' She unhooked it from the door.

Rachel draped it over her shoulders and sat down. The kettle came to the boil and Mary made two mugs of tea. She brought a paper bag and two plates. 'Got these this morning.' She opened the bag and offered it to Rachel. 'Butterscotch Belgian buns. One of Molly's specialities.'

'Thanks.' Rachel realised how hungry she was. All she'd had to eat today was an apple. She took one of the buns, put it on her plate, and licked a smear of icing from her fingers.

Mary wrapped her hands round her steaming mug. 'What about you?' she said. 'How are you?'

'I've been trying to pray. Like you said.'

'Is it helping?'

'It's a bit one-sided,' Rachel said. 'The trouble is I only pray for one thing.'

A door banged at the back of the house. They heard someone in the hallway. Rachel picked up the bun and bit into it. It was sweet and sticky and delicious.

'Adam's back,' Mary said. 'Incapable of doing anything quietly, that boy. Yes. I remember. You said you wanted to know what had happened the day Hannah died.'

'If I knew,' Rachel said, when she had swallowed her mouthful, 'if I could picture Hannah's last moments, as if I was there with her, it would give me some sense of...' She paused. She couldn't find the words. Then she said, fiercely, 'Someone must know something. We were told no one had hurt her, but...oh, it all comes back to wanting someone to blame. I keep thinking someone must have been there. I've got all this anger boiling over inside me and I don't know what to do with it, where to send it. So if I knew... Does that make sense?'

'Absolutely. I wish...' Mary hesitated and her face flushed. She shook her head as if she had changed her mind about speaking. Then, all in a rush, she reached across the table, took Rachel's hand and said, 'I wish there was something I could do.'

A sound came from the door to the hall. A low, stifled cry. They both looked up, startled. Adam stood in the doorway, one hand on the door handle and the other over his mouth, his eyes wide with dismay. The strangled sound came again as he stood, staring at them, and then at the mugs of tea and the half-eaten buns on their plates.

'Whatever's the matter?' Mary said.

He turned, let go of the door, and stumbled from the room. A moment later, the outside door banged again, and then there was silence.

'Well,' Mary said. 'God knows what all that was about. He's a good lad, but don't ever ask me to explain the inner workings of his mind.'

Rachel gave an uneasy smile, but Adam's horrified stare had unsettled her. What could have upset him so much? 'Will he be all right?' she said.

'Oh, who knows? He'll come back when he's ready. He always does. Daft great lump.'

Rachel sipped at her tea but it was cold. Here we are, she thought, two mothers, longing to make things work for the sons we don't understand, being there, trying our best to help them find their place in the world. But is that what I'm doing? Am I really trying my best for Jamie? Can I honestly say that any of what I've been doing is about him? A stab of guilt twisted in her chest and she closed her eyes.

'What's the matter?' Mary said.

'I don't know. It's Jamie. The way you are with Adam made me think. You just accept that you can't know everything about him. But with Jamie... I have been worried about him, but I've been so wrapped up in my own search. I've convinced myself I'm doing all I can for him, but I think I just wanted to feel in control. My family has been falling to pieces around me and I got it into my head that if I could get to the truth about Hannah, everything would sort itself out. I'd be in a place where I could start again, rebuild, and that would include Jamie. But I may never find out. This praying for answers could all be futile. What if I've put everything into this and I end up driving Jamie away? What if I lose him? Christopher tried to make me see it, but I wouldn't listen.' She checked the time on her phone, pushed back her chair and got to her feet. 'I have to go home. I might just make it before he gets in from school. I have to talk to him. Put things right. Before it's too late.'

The rain had become heavier, and the wind howled over the cliff. The house itself seemed to be moaning and rattling, shaking on its foundations.

Outside, Rachel put her hood up, wrapped the scarf round her neck, and set off down Wetherley Lane.

The light is on in the kitchen, but the back of the house is in darkness. He eases open the door of the lean-to, slips through the hallway and into his bedroom. The telly is on in the lounge. He can hear the jangly music of one of Mumma's quiz shows.

It isn't until he takes off his wet jacket that he realises he still has the shoe. He takes it out of the pocket. It is small but chunky, with a Velcro fastening. He turns it over. The sole has the outline of a unicorn cut into the heel. He pictures the little foot fitted into the dent in the mudstone. His fist scrunches around the shoe. He stuffs it under his pillow with the shark tooth, and changes out of his clothes, kicks the bundle of wet things into the corner.

Giraffe Pyjamas

Rachel hunched further into her scarf, quickened her pace. Rain slanted in on the wind from the sea, stinging her face. She wouldn't go up to the church – not now. She'd go straight home by the cliff path. She had to sort things out with Jamie. She couldn't bear to think of him alone in the house if he got back before she did. When he'd started secondary school, they'd given him a key to the back door, and he'd seemed happy to be on his own for half an hour or so if she was out. He'd never complained. But maybe he did mind. After what had happened to Hannah, she should have paid him more attention – been there. Of course she should. She should have tried harder. He spent hours shut in his room with his computer games, his phone, his anxieties, even his guilt. He'd said that what happened was his fault because he'd let Harvey run off. She pictured the cuts on his arms, like clumsy threads holding the bits of him together. He had been lost enough to steal chocolate for comfort and razor blades for the sweet rush of physical pain. Then there were his lies about Christopher, and his outburst when he had found her with the prayer bracelet on the day she had cleared out Hannah's room.

It wasn't a test. Christopher was wrong. Jamie was drowning. Like Hannah. And she wasn't going to let him go.

By the time she reached the house it was half-past four and the rain was easing off. He should be here by now. She went through the side gate and round to the back door, but found it locked. Her key was for the front door, so she went back and let herself in, kicked off her boots in the hallway, and threw her wet coat over the banister.

'Jamie!' She ran up the stairs to his room, tapped on the door then pushed it open. Pyjamas lay strewn across his bed, and a half-finished Lego truck stood on his desk, surrounded by the black and yellow bits needed to complete it. The room smelled stale and musty, and she opened the window. She checked Hannah's room. Boxes were still piled up against the wall, but an open one stood in the middle of the floor, with clothes spilling out from the top, tee shirts and pyjamas. Something clicked in her mind and she went back to Jamie's room, picked up the pyjamas from the bed. There was a pair of his – blue and green stripes, and then another pair – just the bottoms, but they weren't Jamie's. They were Hannah's giraffe pyjamas, her favourites, but the top wasn't here. She held them to her face, breathed in and felt suddenly weak, sat down on the bed. She remembered his rage, how he had thrown himself at her when he had found her with the beads on the day she had packed Hannah's things away in her attempt to win God over with a sacrifice. And Christopher's too, when he had charged back up the stairs and told her how selfish she was. She folded the pyjamas and left them on Jamie's pillow. She longed to explain, to tell him she was sorry, that things would be different from now on. She ached for him to stop shutting himself off, and instead to let her in to where she could love him again.

Love him again? she thought. What am I talking about? I never stopped loving him. But perhaps that's what it felt like to him. Did he think I cared only about Hannah, loved her more? She pressed her finger nails into her palms.

Downstairs, the sitting room and the kitchen were empty. She stood, listening. She knew Christopher wouldn't be here. He was never back this early on a Monday. The house was quiet. But it was always quiet now, an empty shell, echoing with Hannah's absence, even when all three of them were here. She ran through the house again, up to the Crow's Nest and back to the kitchen. She checked her phone, but there was nothing from Jamie. She messaged him, and, when he didn't reply straightaway, wished she hadn't. He was probably at Anthony's. At least he hadn't cut himself off from his friends. She scrolled her contacts for Anthony's dad, but hesitated. Better not. Jamie would resent her checking up on him.

Her trousers were damp, sticking to her legs. She'd have a bath, warm herself up, work out how to win back Jamie's trust. But what could she say that would change his attitude? Was she going to give up her search for answers? Her quest to find someone to blame? Her prayers? Was this the sacrifice she was meant to make? Is that what it would take to reconnect with Jamie? Would she have to choose?

She fished the holy stone from her coat pocket, took it upstairs and set it on the corner of the bath while she ran the hot water. She peeled off her clothes and let them fall in a heap on the floor. The skin on her legs was red and sore, and her ankles and shins were dotted with tiny bruises. She glugged scented bubble bath into the running water, swirled it into foam, and then stepped in. The water was almost too hot to bear, but she lowered herself in, holding her breath. She took the holy stone on its blue rope and lay back, cradling it in her palm under the water, by her hip, and closed her eyes.

'Oh, God,' she whispered. 'Oh, dear God. Please don't make me choose. I have to know. I need to know.' She remembered what she had said to Mary, that day on the broken cliff. *It's in my bones.* It was true. The need was inside her, in the marrow of her. How could she deny it? Even for Jamie?

She pushed the pad of her thumb against the hole in the stone. *Hear my voice when I call. Do not hide your face from me.* The words repeated themselves in her mind, like beads on a string. And again, the images flooded in – Hannah climbing on the sea defences, talking to a stranger, struggling in the waves, being held, being hurt, being lost.

Rachel lay in the water until it was tepid. Then she sat up, took the stone and rubbed it hard over her skin until it hurt, and when she stepped out of the bath she felt like something newborn.

Why should she choose? She had to keep going. Surely God would answer her prayers in the end. She had to keep believing. But nor would she give up on Jamie. Now that she understood how she had been neglecting him, she could be the mother he needed at the same time as finding the truth about what had happened to Hannah. There was no reason she could not do both.

It was gone six by the time Christopher came in, and Jamie still wasn't home. Rachel was mashing potatoes, while fat, herby sausages kept warm in the oven.

'Good timing,' she said. 'I've made Jamie's favourite.'

'Smells delicious.' He kissed her on the lips.

'But he's not back yet, and he's not answering his phone.'

'He's probably at Anthony's. I hope he hasn't had his tea there. Did you tell him what you were cooking?'

'Yes. I keep texting. But there's been nothing.' Rachel put the lid back on the saucepan to keep the mash warm, and took a tin of baked beans from the cupboard, stood with it clutched to her chest. 'I'm wondering what I've done, what I've said. Why he hasn't replied.'

'Perhaps his phone's out of battery. Or they're taken up with some game or other.'

'I'm worried about him, Christopher. You know how withdrawn he's been. And you said his behaviour was a test of our love. I think it's more serious. I don't think he's doing any of this on purpose, you know, with any kind of agenda. He's grieving. Like us. I found Hannah's pyjamas on his bed. He's... he's really missing her, Christopher.' Her voice cracked. 'And I haven't...'

Christopher took the tin of beans from her and put it on the counter. She put her hands over her face and leaned into his embrace.

'Of course he's missing her,' he said. 'We all are.'

'But I need to make sure I'm here for him. I know I haven't been. You were right about us facing things as a family. Let's talk to him properly when he comes in. Make him see that we understand, that it's okay to feel like he does.'

'We could call Anthony's dad,' Christopher said. 'I expect that's where he is.'

'But won't Jamie think we're—'

'Rach, it'll be dark in half an hour and the weather's getting worse. School finished hours ago. And he's only twelve. We ought to know where he is, at least, who he's with.'

Rachel picked up her phone from the table, found the number and tapped call. She felt the pounding of her heart, put her other hand on her chest. Her skin was still tingling from the bath and the rough stone.

'It's Jamie,' Rachel said to Anthony's dad. 'He hasn't been home, and he's not answering his phone. Is he with Anthony?'

'I don't think so. Hang on a sec.'

Rachel heard him call out to his son, waited while they talked.

'He's not here. Anthony doesn't know where he is, but he's going to show me some stuff Jamie's posted on their group chat over the last few weeks. I'll call you back in a few minutes.'

'Okay, thanks.' She ended the call.

'He'll be back like a shot once he knows what's for tea,' Christopher said. 'Don't worry. Look, let's have a drink while we're waiting, shall we?'

He opened the fridge, found a bottle, but Rachel shook her head.

'No, I don't want to. I mean, just in case…'

'In case what?'

'I don't know. I can't help thinking something's happened. Why wouldn't he reply to my messages? Why wouldn't he tell us where he is?' Rachel found she was shaking, and she couldn't stop.

Christopher put the bottle back in the fridge and put his arms around her. 'Come here. It's all right. Come on, Rach. He'll be back soon. I'll try calling him again.' He took her phone, but Rachel heard it go straight to voicemail.

When Anthony's dad spoke to them again, Rachel put the call on speaker.

'I'm sorry,' he told them. 'None of them know where Jamie is, but he's posted some things in their group chat that I think you ought to hear. I'm afraid it's a bit upsetting.'

'What? What is it?' Rachel said.

'Earlier this afternoon he said *I'm never going back home. Then they'll be sorry.*'

Rachel's legs wouldn't hold her. She leaned against Christopher and a noise came from her throat.

'Anything else?' Christopher said. 'Does he say anything else? Like where's he gone? Why he doesn't want to come back?'

'There's only been that one message today, but Anthony says there have been others, since Hannah died. Angry stuff. about how...sorry to say this...how his parents didn't care.'

'What about other people he's in touch with?' Christopher said. 'Has he mentioned any friends they don't know? Someone he just knows online? I mean, could someone be...you know... pretending to be...'

Rachel didn't want to think about it. Didn't want to let the words in.

'Anthony says Jamie's talked about someone called Fossil Boy. He's not one of their group though. I think he's older.'

'I know who he is,' Rachel said. 'He's called Adam, but Jamie used to call him Fossil Boy. He lives up on the cliff. He's harmless enough.'

'Anthony seems to think Jamie's got something against him,' Anthony's dad said.

'Okay, mate, thanks.' Christopher ended the call. 'It's time to phone the police,' he said.

Rachel crumpled against him, buried her face in his clothes.

Shed

Rain lashed at him sideways. A fierce wind flung itself around him. Adam ran round the side of the house, and along the path towards the beach steps, splashing through the potholes, his breath ragged, his heart hammering and his mind buzzing.

Why was that woman with Mumma? It was her. Her! The woman he'd seen on the beach on Saturday. She was the mother. Hannah Bird was her little girl. Hannah Bird, with her sunshine smile and her dandelion hair and her little white foot. But why was Hannah's mother in his house, in his kitchen, wearing Mumma's new scarf and eating the buns Mumma had got for him? Mumma never had people in the house. She didn't believe in friends. It was just him and her. The two of them. Always had been. They didn't need anyone else. It was what she always said. I'll always look after you, she'd promised. And now, there she was, sitting by the stove with…

He had been going to tell her. All the way home he'd been going through the words he would say, longing for her arm round his shoulder. They would sit on the sofa and he would lean his head against her and she would tell him it would be all right. He mustn't worry any more. She would take care of everything.

But how could he tell her now? Now that he knew Hannah's mother was her friend. Mumma's words echoed in his mind. ...*something I could do*. No, Mumma, he wanted to shout, it's me that needs you. Not her. Not that woman. She had said she wanted someone to blame. *I keep thinking someone must have been there. All this anger*, she said. *All this anger*. Her voice had been sharp and hard, like flint.

'You can't blame me,' Adam shouted into the wind as he stumbled down the steps and on to the beach. 'It wasn't my fault.' Rain dripped down his face and neck. His hands were red and raw, and the place where the glass had cut him was stinging. He made fists, digging his nails into his palms. He kicked at the stones, lifted his face to the sky and let the rain pelt his skin.

He hadn't thought about where he would go. It was automatic, coming down here. This was his place, this beach. As much his home as the house on the cliff. But where he really belonged was with Mumma. And now, what had she done? She had changed sides. Gone over to the enemy. Betrayed him. He was cut loose. Adrift.

He came round the bend to where he could see the pillbox, slanting up out of the sand like a shipwreck, almost within reach of the breaking waves. Surely the tide wouldn't get any higher. It must be on the turn by now. Was that the crunch of footsteps on the shingle? Footsteps other than his? He stopped. Swung round, hands raised. No one, but up by the cliff, he thought he saw a movement. A dark shape that was there one moment, and gone the next. And then... Was that a voice? Or was it the wind? What if it was Danny or his uncle or those men outside the school with their pointing fingers, coming to check he'd got the message they'd scrawled over the front of the house?

He held his breath and listened. Nothing. No more footsteps. No voices. He must have imagined it. He moved, now, scrambling over the banks of stones towards the pillbox. He had been inside it once. It still had its steel doors but they were stuck forever open in the sand, half buried, immovable. You had to crawl through the entrance, and even inside, you couldn't stand because the space was half full of sand and stones. Two of the tiny windows were above the level of the beach, letting in a small amount of light. It would be a refuge, somewhere to hide and think about what had happened. And about what he could do now that Mumma had betrayed him.

He slid down the slope, and was about to go round to the entrance, when he stopped. There it was again, in a lull in the wind, between the crashes of the breaking waves. That was definitely a voice, not talking though – more a moaning and a wailing. He looked round again, scanning the beach and the base of the cliff, but he couldn't see anyone. He wished, now, that he had gone along Wetherley Lane and down the gully to the shed. That would have been a better place to lie low. He wasn't sure exactly when the high tide was due. He could only remember once seeing the pillbox underwater.

On the other side, he crouched down and made his way along the tunnel-like entrance passage, then crawled through the opening. He heard a sharp intake of breath, and almost bumped up against the huddled figure in the corner.

'Get out! I'm in here! Get out!'

The voice was panicky, high-pitched. It wasn't Danny, or his uncle, or the men with the jabbing fingers. This was the voice of a frightened child.

Relief flooded through Adam, even when the figure lashed out with his arms. There was no room for either of them to stand, and Adam was between the boy and his escape route. Instinctively, he put a hand up to shield his face and head, backing towards the doorway on his knees.

'All right,' he said. 'Calm down.' He grabbed the boy by the wrists and his fingers closed round something hard and knobbly – some kind of watch or bracelet. 'I wasn't going to... I'm not going to hurt you. I didn't know you were in here.'

'Oh, it's you! Fossil Boy! Weirdo! Just fuck off out of here!' Then the boy stopped flailing his arms, wrapped them round his head, and burst into tears.

When Adam's eyes got used to the dimness, he saw that the boy was small and skinny, maybe ten or eleven years old. He wore a thin jacket, and his hair was soaked, plastered to his head.

'Sorry,' Adam said. 'I told you – I didn't know you were in here. What's the matter?'

'Just leave me alone!'

'But you can't stay here. It's not safe.' Adam slipped into hero mode, replaying Mr Bright's voice in his head.

'I don't care!' The boy was still sobbing and sniffing, his head buried in his arms. 'Why can't you just fuck off?'

'It's dangerous. Being here on your own.' What would a hero say next? 'I can walk home with you if you want. It'll be dark before all that long. And you could get cut off if the tide comes in much further.'

The boy sniffed, and lifted his head, wiped his hand over his face. 'What do you care? It was you that got me into trouble that day in the shop. The police came and my parents found out. No one would have caught me if it wasn't for you.'

Adam remembered then. The boy with the razor blades and the chocolate bars. Twirls. He had watched him put them in his pockets and head towards the exit without paying. So he had told the shop assistant.

'You should go home,' he said now. 'Your parents must be worried.'

The boy shook his head. He was shivering. 'It will serve them right if they are worried. I thought if I ran away they'd be sorry. It would make them realise what they…how I…' He shook his head. 'Anyway, I'm not going home. They don't care.'

Like Mumma, Adam thought, wishing there was something she could do for Hannah Bird's mother, taking her side, when he was the one who needed her. After all the promises she had made to look after him. She didn't care either.

Adam eased himself into a sitting position, leaning against the concrete wall. 'I know how you feel,' he said. Would Mumma be sorry for siding with that woman if he didn't go home? 'At least we're out of the wind here. But we can't stay. Ten minutes at the most.'

They sat in silence for a bit. Although they were sheltered from the worst of the weather, it was cold in the pillbox, and both of them were in wet clothes.

'If you really aren't going to go home,' Adam said eventually, 'I know a place that's a lot more comfortable than this. It would be safer, too.' He thought of the heavy padlock, and the key in his pocket. 'I could take you there, and I could get you some things. A sleeping bag, maybe, and something to eat.'

'I've got food.' The boy picked up a backpack that Adam hadn't noticed, unfastened the flap and pulled out a giant bag of crisps. 'Want some?'

'Not yet. Let's wait till we're there. Come on.' He crawled backwards out of the doorway. 'Come on,' he said again. 'You can't stay here.'

The boy stuffed the crisps back in the bag, put it on his back, and followed. The rain had stopped, but the wind was still strong. Just in time, Adam thought, looking at the sea. He led the boy up to the top of the beach, to the dip where the waterfall was. They climbed up past it, hoisted themselves over the ridge, and there was the rope ladder.

'Who put this here?' the boy said. 'Is it yours?'

Adam shrugged. He'd never thought about how it got there. 'I guess it was the man that owned the house up there.'

'Does he mind who uses it?'

'Oh, he doesn't live there any more. He's gone. They all have, except for me and Mumma. Come on, then. You go first. And watch out. It'll be slippery.'

They were almost at the top when the boy missed his footing and cried out. He grabbed at the rope but his hand slipped and a shower of stones bounced off Adam's shoulder and clattered to the beach below.

'No!' the boy cried, but then he steadied himself and leaned into the ladder, clinging on to the rope with both hands, with one foot on one rung, and the other on the next.

'Go on,' Adam said. 'We're nearly at the top.'

'I can't.' The boy's voice was small.

'Don't be silly. Course you can. You've got this far.'

'I can't,' the boy said again.

'You'll be all right. It's quite safe. I've done it loads of times.'
Silence.

Adam didn't know what to do. It wouldn't do any good to get cross, he knew that, but how could he make the boy feel safe? They couldn't stay here. What if the boy got so tired he couldn't hold on? What if he really did fall? Pictures raced through Adam's mind – the fall, the cry, the crumpled shape lying on the shingle, not moving. The silence. He screwed his eyes shut, forced the images away. Then took a deep breath and opened his eyes, made his voice stay steady.

'We can go back down if you want,' he said.

'I can't,' the boy said. 'I can't move.' His voice wobbled.

'It's all right,' Adam said, trying to make himself believe it. 'We can wait a bit if you like.' The ladder was nowhere near vertical, and just to one side there was a slope he could get on to with a ledge at the top. He edged himself over, and climbed up until he was level with the boy.

'Look. I'm here. Right beside you. And hey, I don't even know your name.' He tried to make his voice light, as if it was the most normal thing in the world to be stuck on a cliff in a howling gale with someone you'd found in a half-buried pillbox.

'Jamie.'

'Okay, Jamie. We're going to rest here for a moment, and then – see this rung here? I'm going to take your hand – this one, next to me – and help you move it from here, to here, and you can hold on tight. Okay?'

'Okay,' Jamie whispered.

Adam thought of the times Mumma had helped him do something that scared him when he was younger. He had taken a lot of persuading to go back to the park after Danny

Goodrum pushed him so fast on the roundabout that he was sick. And they'd been in a café once, where the toilets were upstairs and there was a huge deer's head that looked as if it was coming out of the wall on the landing. It was terrifying, with its staring eyes and enormous antlers, and he'd almost wet himself before Mumma covered his eyes and led him past it, talking in a soft, gentle voice that she didn't use very often.

He reached out to put his hand on Jamie's, but when he tried to release the boy's fingers from the rope, the grip remained tight. Adam let go, but his finger caught on the band Jamie wore on his wrist, and he felt it give way, heard things fall like the stones.

'No! Now look what you've done! Why did you have to do that?'

But Jamie's anger had unfrozen him, and he managed on his own until they reached the top, the dip in the tumbled slope left by a previous landslide, and where the rope ladder was anchored to the great metal pin buried deep in the earth. And there was the shed, hidden from the beach, and hidden from the cliff top.

A fleeting doubt made Adam's stomach flutter. This was his place. His sanctuary. Did he really want to share it? What about his treasures? He shouldn't have left them out on top of the crate. After all, Jamie had stolen those things from Save-it. But he was only small, and he didn't look very strong. If he tried anything…

Jamie approached the shed door, touched the padlock. 'Have you got the key?'

Adam made up his mind. He took the key from his pocket, unlocked the door, and they went inside.

The door clattered in the wind, blowing open and shut.

Adam found a piece of old nylon rope on the shed floor, threaded it through the latch outside, brought it to the inside and tied it round a nail on the inside wall. The door still rattled, but it was better than nothing.

'Those are my treasures,' he said, when he noticed the boy looking at the things lined up on the crate. 'I found them on the beach. Some of them are fossils, look. These are called belemnites and they come from things a bit like squids and some people call them sea bullets or devil's fingers and these are bits of sea glass which the sea has worn smooth. And I don't know what this is.' He held up the bottle. 'I found it where the stream comes out, where we climbed up. I think the glass must be quite old because it's all worn and a bit cloudy. The lid is sealed on, but I'm not sure what that yellow stuff is.'

'Looks like piss,' Jamie said, and smiled for the first time.

'I thought that at first,' Adam said. 'But why would someone do that, and then seal the bottle? I've found loads of other things too – lots of shark teeth, some ammonites and even a sea urchin, but they...' He stopped. He might as well never have found those things, not now that they were forever nailed under the floor in his bedroom.

'They what?' Jamie said.

'Nothing,' Adam said. An impossible idea crept into his mind. What if they weren't forever nailed under the floor? What if he dared to pull the nails out, lift the board? What if he dared...? He longed to be able to forget, to forget he was ever anywhere near Hannah Bird. To stop being haunted by the memory, the guilt, the fear. Could he? Would he dare? Now that Mumma had betrayed him, taking that woman's side, maybe it was time for him to manage things himself.

Jamie sat on the floor and opened his backpack. As he

pulled out the bag of crisps, a phone fell onto the floor, and he reached out for it.

'Watch out. There's broken glass,' Adam said. 'I cut my hand.'

'It's out of battery anyway,' Jamie said. 'It's Dad's old one and it's rubbish. D'you want some crisps? I forgot to bring a drink.'

'I'll get some when I get the sleeping bag.' Adam helped himself to a handful of crisps. He'd got the padlock, so he could make sure Jamie stayed safely locked in while he was away.

'Don't go yet.' The boy's voice had gone quiet again, and shaky. He sat huddled against the side wall, hugging his knees to his chest, his head down. 'I don't know if… Don't leave me here by myself…'

Fossil Boy

When Rachel had gone, Mary leaned her hands on the table and pushed herself up to standing. She rubbed the aching muscles in her back. She had wanted to offer Rachel a lift home, but in town that morning, she had narrowly missed scraping a car on the high street. The road had been clear in front of her, and then, out of nowhere, a line of parked cars materialised, and she swerved out at the last minute. Her head was pounding by the time she got home, but what most unsettled her was her unwillingness to get behind the wheel again. Only a matter of days ago, she would have brushed off the mishap and carried on as normal.

The door rattled in its frame, rain beat against the window, and the shells quivered on their strings. The house shook in the wind like a little boat on the ocean. Water rushed and gurgled outside – the gutters and drains were overflowing. She put the mugs and plates in the sink and went through the hall to Adam's room. She rubbed the fog of condensation off the window, looked out at the wind-battered garden and the rain over the grey, heaving ocean. It shouldn't be dark for another hour or so, but the light had already gone. The worst of this storm was forecast for tomorrow, but it was already wild. Adam was used to being out in all weathers, and she didn't usually worry about him, but she kept thinking about the way he had rushed out, the look on his face, the sounds he made. Something had seriously upset him. She could only hope that he would come back when he'd calmed down. And if he didn't want to explain – well, that was all there was to it.

She was about to leave his room when she noticed his phone on his bedside table. Daft great lump, she said to herself. What did you have to leave that there for?

In the living room, she switched on the television and flopped down on the sofa. Quiz or murder? Which would it be? She flicked through the channels and settled on an ancient repeat of *Who Wants to Be a Millionaire?* But she couldn't concentrate and what did it matter anyway? What did she care about the greedy fools who wanted to win a million pounds? She had no desire to be a millionaire. All she wanted was her place, here, on the clifftop, and for Adam to be safe and happy. It wasn't much to ask.

The contestant was phoning a friend. And all at once, Mary thought of Adam's phone, left in his room. Maybe he didn't take it because he hadn't gone anywhere. He wasn't in the house, but… Mary leaped up from the sofa, and without stopping for a coat, pulled on her boots, and lumbered across the lane and up the path to the caravan. It's the sort of place he would go if he was upset. When he was small he used to squeeze into the space under his bed sometimes, and once he'd insisted on eating his tea there. Shouting his name, she yanked the door open and the rusty handle came off in her hand. She hadn't brought a torch, but in the dimness she could see that the caravan was empty. The musty, mouldy smell was as strong as ever. She wasn't sure whether to latch the door when she left. Without a handle she'd need a screwdriver to open it again, but she couldn't leave it in this weather, so she slammed it and pushed herself through the buffeting wind back to the house.

It wasn't until after nine that she began to feel she ought to be doing something more to try to find Adam. But what? She was used to him staying out for hours during the day, but it had been dark for three hours now, and although the rain had stopped, a fierce wind was still howling over the cliffs. Where could he be? And what had made him go off like that?

At ten, she turned the television off, put on her coat and her boots, switched on all the lights in the house, and went out with her big torch. But which way to go first? Would he have gone down to the beach? The tide would be falling by now, but even with the torch, in this wind the steps would be more than she could manage.

She set out along Wetherley Lane. The wind roared in from the sea. She could smell the salt. Everything was a blur, with vague patches of light and shadow, and odd details swimming in and out of focus – the top of a hedge, a tree, a gateway, potholes and puddles and the roadside ditch. 'Can't see a bloody thing,' she muttered, holding her torch aloft. She stumbled, almost lost her balance. The ground was playing tricks again.

She found herself thinking of a night like this when Fiona had come to pick her up from somewhere, before Evan was on the scene, and the car had broken down in the middle of nowhere and they had stayed there all night, safe and dry, sharing the single tiny car rug, while around them the world was tearing itself apart. She shook the memory away. There was no point longing for something she could never get back. She had put a lot of hard work into forgetting.

When she reached the bend where the lane went inland towards the top road, and the coast path headed west along the cliff, she turned and made her way back, buffeted by gusts of wind that almost knocked her off balance. She'd never find him by walking about in the dark. And who could she ask if she made it all the way to town? No shops would be open. She didn't know what time the pubs closed, but he had never been one for friends or nights out. He'd probably be at the house when she got there, tucking into beans on toast or a bacon sandwich, watching some daft comedy. She would sit beside him on the sofa and he would lean against her and explain the jokes. He would have forgotten whatever it was that had upset him.

But he wasn't there. It wasn't until the early hours that she considered calling the police, and that was only because she knew it was what any other mother would do. But did they send out search parties for every twenty-year-old who stayed out till two o'clock in the morning? She thought of the times they had questioned Adam, the way they had warned him about the children and the school, and how they had looked at her, as if her parenting skills were somehow lacking. No, he would come back when he was ready. She'd looked after him on her own, all these years. They were all right, the two of them. They didn't need anyone interfering.

She went to bed in her clothes, and fell into a restless sleep, with the wind howling through her dreams, and the house shaking and groaning around her, and woke at dawn, cold and stiff, with a dry mouth and a headache.

She sat on Adam's bed to drink her tea, looking out at the choppy sea, and the dark clouds boiling up on the horizon. 'Where are you, son?' she said aloud and then felt her throat tighten and her eyes prick. She got up quickly, marched to the kitchen with her half-drunk tea and threw it in the sink. She yanked on her boots, grabbed her coat and went out.

From the top of the steps, she surveyed the beach. The waves swirled white around the sea defences, a seething mass. Wind gusted and tugged, unbalancing her. She didn't trust herself on the steps. She trudged back to the house and fetched her car keys from the kitchen, pushing aside the memory of yesterday's near miss. She would drive slowly along the top road and park at the top of the high street. From there she could walk all the way down and call in at Bright's and the fossil shop and the newsagent, and then go down to Molly's. Find out if anyone had seen him. He can't have been out all night in this weather. So where had he been? Who had he been with?

Something jolted inside her at the idea that he could have been with someone. He had never mentioned that there was anyone. Surely he would have told her if there was a girl. Or a boy. Someone he... She climbed into the car, switched on the engine and reversed out into Wetherley Lane. The only person he spoke about with any affection was Molly. But that was because of the pasties and the butterscotch buns and the fudge. Wasn't it?

She had never told him about Evan and Fiona. All he knew was that his father had died before he was born, and he'd never pestered her for more information. But perhaps she should have explained. As a warning. Perhaps she had let him be too trusting.

As she slowed for the bend where the coast path turned off, she noticed that the old garden hedge of the house where Kevin had lived was so overgrown now that the gateway had all but vanished. Hawthorn, blackthorn, beech and holly – it was twice as high and twice as wide as he had liked to keep it. Behind the hedge, unpruned, the branches of an apple tree stretched towards the sky. It had been on the local television news, the day his house was demolished. It was the last one, except for hers at the other end.

When she slowed to give way at the top road, a van hurtled past in front of her, spraying an arc of muddy water over her windscreen.

'Bloody lunatic,' she muttered, turning up the wiper speed and pulling out. A dark shadow shot out from the verge and before she had time to react, she felt the thud and bump as something went under the wheels. She braked hard, stopped, and sat with her hands gripping the steering wheel, her eyes screwed tight shut. But there'd be nothing she could do. She wondered what it was. Rabbit, probably. When the sick feeling had passed and she could open her eyes, she drove the rest of the way at not much more than a walking pace.

No one had seen Adam. Mr Bright said he thought he'd been into the shop yesterday, and then he said something about the graffiti, which she didn't want to think about. The man in the fossil shop claimed he didn't know who she was talking about. Molly made her sit down on a white plastic chair and have a cup of tea, and to be honest, she was glad to have a rest.

'You should call the police,' Molly told her, 'if he's been out all night. He might be in some kind of trouble. People can be so mean, sometimes. I've seen them, having a go at him. And he's such a gentleman. It's a shame.'

Mary finished her tea and then wandered round the children's playground and across the green, tramped along the beach a little way, now that the tide was falling, hoping she might see the familiar shape of her son loping along, his bag slung across his shoulder, his jacket flapping loose. But no one was about in this foul weather except for a couple in the distance with a big black dog.

She plodded back up the hill to where she had left the car. Even though the wind was behind her, it seemed much further on the way up than it had on the way down, and when she finally flopped into the driver's seat, she was out of breath and her heart was thumping against her ribs. She sat there, gathering herself for the drive home. Her phone buzzed. Ah, at last, she thought, but then remembered that his phone was sitting there, useless, on his bedside table. She squinted at the display, but it was a blur. She swiped to accept.

'Hello?'

'Mary?' It was Rachel. 'I'm worried about Jamie. He didn't come home yesterday and he's not answering his phone. Christopher's been out looking for him all night. We've no idea where he is, but… Can I talk to Adam? I think he might know…'

'He didn't come home either. Not since he rushed off when you were there. I've been all round the town looking for him but no one's seen him. I'm about to drive home, see if he's back. What makes you think he might know about Jamie?'

'The police keep asking about people he might be with. We've tried to contact all his friends and one of them said that over the last few weeks Jamie's been mentioning someone called Fossil Boy.'

'Fossil Boy? And you think it's—'

'It is. It's Adam. Years ago, Jamie called him that, when we'd seen him on the beach. We didn't know his name. But I don't know why he's talking about him now… Apparently he'd got something against him.'

'How do they know each other, do you think?'

'I don't know. But, Mary, they're both missing. It can't be a coincidence, surely. Something must have happened to them. The two of them. I'm worried. They could be in danger. Maybe someone… Look, I'm going to drive over. Christopher will stay here. One of us has to, the police said, in case he comes home.'

'Why? What can we…?'

But Rachel had ended the call.

He loses his balance, tips over into the swirling foam, goes under. Salt stings his eyes, his nose, his throat. Pebbles batter his skin. The current tugs. He can't find the ground. Can't breathe. Arms and legs thrash.

Then – back on his feet as the wave washes back. Breath heaving. Heart pounding. Another wave towers over him. He plunges back in, diving down with his eyes open, but he can't see anything. He comes up to breathe, shouts across the surging water. But there's nothing. It's hopeless.

At last, he crawls out, exhausted, struggles to his feet, and stands, shaking, dripping, staring at the empty sea.

Shoe

Mary had been home no more than a minute or two when she heard the car pull up in the lane. A door slammed, and then came a series of sharp knocks at the front door. 'Mary, it's me.'

As soon as the door was unlatched, Rachel, red-faced and breathless, launched herself in, along with a wild gust of wind that banged the door against the wall. Rachel fought to push the door shut behind her, grabbed hold of Mary's arm, and propelled her into the kitchen.

'What's going on, Mary?' Rachel said. 'You must have some idea where Adam went? Who he might be with?'

Mary backed towards the stove, shrugging herself from Rachel's grasp. The shells tapped against the glass of the window. 'I don't know. He doesn't have—'

'And why did he dash out like that yesterday? He seemed – not just upset – more shocked, horrified even. Didn't you think?'

'Yes, he did, but you don't know him. Sometimes he gets the wrong end of the stick – jumps to conclusions. He gets all het up about things he's misunderstood.'

'But what was it? He'd only just come home, hadn't he? We heard the back door, and then, the next minute, there he was in the kitchen doorway, looking as if he'd seen a ghost.'

'I don't know. Could have been anything. Look, you said Jamie had mentioned Adam – Fossil Boy – to his friends. What did he say about him? What is it that makes you think they're together, or in danger?'

'They couldn't remember exactly. They said Jamie seemed angry. Most of his posts were angry, apparently, after Hannah. Could Adam have seen them, do you think?'

Mary shrugged. 'No. Adam doesn't use social media. He's not interested.'

'And you're sure he hasn't mentioned Jamie? Is there anyone who's been threatening him, bullying him? Could he be in some kind of trouble? Something Jamie's got mixed up in too, or…? Oh, I don't know what to think. Or what to do.'

Rachel folded into a chair, pushed her hands through her hair. Mary remembered the day of the mermaid, when she had peeled wet, salty clothes from the shivering, helpless figure she had found washed up on the beach. She thought of Rachel's thin frame, her pale skin, the way she had clawed at her face and hair.

'They'll turn up,' she said. 'Let's get the kettle on, and start thinking logically.'

'But what if they are in some kind of trouble? Has anything been going on with Adam? He's…I mean, I know he's a bit of a loner, and years ago we saw some lads being mean to him. Is it still going on? The bullying?'

Mary filled the kettle and switched it on. She took two clean mugs from the draining board and dropped a teabag in each. She thought of the red paint, scrawled across the front of the house. *LEAVE TOWN PERV*. Whoever was responsible – could they have made some further threat? Done something else? Outside, something clattered in the garden and she heard the rain begin again, drumming against the windows.

'There is this Danny Goodrum,' she said, 'who picks on him a bit, but he's harmless really.' She wanted to believe it, but what was harmless about Danny's name-calling and taunting? They had no proof that Danny was to blame for the graffiti, but doubt crept in now, and, for the first time, a real fear began to squeeze her stomach, a fear that Adam may not simply come back when he was ready. Nausea rose in her throat, and she leaned over the sink, closed her eyes.

'What about the caravan?' Rachel jumped up from her chair. 'Have you checked the caravan?'

'Of course I've checked the bloody caravan.'

But Rachel was gone, leaving the front door banging in the wind. Mary watched her blurred outline run up the track past the polytunnel, reach the caravan and struggle with the door. Mary sighed, took a screwdriver from a jar on the windowsill, shrugged her coat on and strode out. Rachel wasn't going to take her word for it that there was no one there. She'd have to open the door.

'Satisfied?' Mary said, not unkindly, when Rachel had checked the place. 'Now come back and drink your tea. Let's eat something.'

'Eat? How can you…?'

'Because I know what helps in a crisis. Having enough energy inside you. Come on.'

She tucked her arm through Rachel's, more to be sure of her footing than to reassure Rachel, and, heads down against the weather, they went back to the house. The sky was a seething mass of grey and purple and a fierce wind howled over the cliff. The house stood smudged and blurred behind the sheets of rain, as if it was half way to being rubbed out, like an image you would wipe off misted glass with the flat of your hand. Mary tried looking at it sideways, adjusting her focus, but it was no good. The details refused to reveal themselves. A deep rumble like distant thunder came from somewhere beyond the house, as if the earth itself was shifting, unsettled, unhinged, coming loose from its foundations. Mary stopped and stared. The house gave a shudder. A loud crack split the air, and then another. The rumbling became louder, merging with the roar of the wind and the lashing of the rain.

Mary stumbled forward, past the corner of the house, round the side path. Another splintering crack, and a muffled crash. She reached the lean-to. Wind whipped at her hair. Rain sliced across from the sea. She blinked and squinted and tried to make sense of the scene before her. This couldn't be real. It was like the ship and the beetles and the umbrella lady, like when the solid ground had turned to rolling waves. Stupid bloody eyes. She blinked again, shook her head, clung to Rachel who had followed her.

'Oh, dear God,' Rachel said.

Mary couldn't move. It wasn't her eyes. It was her world, slipping from her grasp.

The lean-to hung over nothingness, its door swinging and banging against the splintered frame. Behind it, only a few metres from where they stood, what was left of Adam's bedroom teetered on the land's edge, gaping open, its innards on display, snapped floorboards and joists sticking out over empty air. And below, a tumble of raw, bright earth obscured the slope she had raked over for her rescue plan. Scattered over it, lay the smashed and mangled remains of the end wall of the house.

Something small and red was caught among the broken boards of Adam's bedroom, like a drop of blood from a wound.

Rachel gasped.

The object swam into Mary's focus. It was a child's shoe. Bewildered, she stared. Then it came to her. *She had these red shoes*, Rachel had said. *She had only one shoe and sock on… I keep wondering why… I need it to be someone's fault.*

'Oh, Adam,' Mary breathed. 'What have you done?' The wind whipped up her words and hurled them to the sky.

'He…he…' Rachel's voice was a trembling whisper. 'What did he do? My baby girl! What did he…?' Her voice rose, and words exploded from her. 'Monster! Evil! Your son! My Hannah!' She grabbed Mary by the arms, screamed into her face. 'Where is he? Where has he taken Jamie? What is he? What has he done?'

All the power had gone from Mary's body. If Rachel let go of her arms she would collapse like a rag doll. Her mind churned. Why was the shoe…? What had he…? And Jamie…? Where would all this lead? What would Rachel do? What would happen to Adam? The police…a court…they would take him away… She saw it all unfold in front of her and there was only one thing she could think of that would stop it happening. It was too late to save the cliff, to save her house, but she could still save her son. She looked across the remains of the back of the house to where Hannah's shoe lay among the splintered wood. What had he been thinking? Why would he have hidden it unless…? There must be some reason. He would never hurt anyone. If she could only get rid of it, there would be nothing to link him…no evidence. They'd never be able to prove… She had to get rid of it. It was the only way.

When Rachel let go of her to pull her phone from her pocket, instead of crumpling to the ground, she dived in through the swinging door, across the lean-to and into what was left of Adam's bedroom, where the broken boards cradled the shoe. Behind her, she caught snatches of Rachel's call. 'Lucy? Found Hannah's shoe… Wetherley End…the last house. Adam Farthing… I think he's got my son…' Beneath Mary's feet, the floor rocked and creaked. She lowered herself onto all fours and inched forward. Where the wall and window had been, the wind and the rain pelted in through a great, gaping hole. Adam's bed had gone. Half the roof was gone, and everything was scattered with plaster and dust.

All at once the floor tipped, and Mary felt her foot gripped from behind, and then Rachel was level with her, kneeling beside her, holding her shoulder, pulling at her, hissing into her face. 'You can't do this. I won't let you. I've told the police and you can't hide the fucking thing now.'

Mary tried to throw Rachel off, to pull herself away. The floor tipped again, towards the fallen cliff. Rachel's breath was hot on her cheeks, her grip tight on Mary's coat.

'What kind of monster is he, your precious son? I thought he was…he seemed so innocent, so vulnerable, and all the time he's… How could you not have known? And now you have to tell me where the hell he is, Where he's taken my boy.'

Mary's breath wouldn't come. Her heart slammed against her ribs. A rushing sound filled her ears, and the red shoe blurred and then she couldn't see it any more.

She had to reach it…had to…

Suddenly Rachel let her go, and edged back up the sloping floor. 'I have to find Jamie. No one will believe you. The police will be here before you can get rid of it.'

And she was gone.

The wind howled like a mad thing. Mary looked up. Clouds flew across the sky like bits of ghosts. Rain lashed in. She adjusted her position, lay on her stomach. She could see it again now, just there. If she could only… She could hide it, bury it, burn it, throw it in the sea to be washed up along the coast. It would be her word against Rachel's. She edged across the floor, creeping forward, inch by inch, until she felt something give beneath her. She froze, terrified that if she adjusted her weight, everything would tip. But she had to get to it before the police came. There must be a way to reach it. She could feel her heart pounding against her ribs. Her whole body ached. In front of her, caught in the splintered boards, open to the driving rain, hung the red shoe – Hannah's shoe. But even as she held it in her gaze, it vanished, reappeared, vanished again. She closed her eyes, tried to slow her breathing, and when she opened her eyes again, she saw, beyond the shoe, beyond the ripped end of her house, a figure down there on the beach, running across the stones. Rachel, looking for both their sons.

Mary lay balanced on the teetering floor, trying to slow her breathing, to gather her courage. When Rachel was out of sight, she stretched her arms out, and tried to find some purchase with her elbows to drag her body forward. Her weight shifted. The floor moved and there was a splintering crack. She felt herself tip and slide, and the board beneath her vanished. Her hands reached out, clawing at air, and as she fell, she heard her own voice shout his name.

Treasures

It had stopped raining, but the ground was sodden, sticky with mud. Rachel slid and stumbled to the top of the steps, but when she looked down she saw that only the top section remained and the debris lay scattered over the fallen cliff. The wind blew in from the sea, gusting against her. Was the beach the best place to start? She had called Christopher as well as the police and he'd said Izzy was coming to stay at the house so that he could join the search. He would go up to the top road on his bike. There were some outbuildings at the alpaca place, the church porch, that old garage.

Rachel climbed down the steps that were left, testing each one before she put her full weight on it, and then scrambled down the landslide to the beach. She ran, then, across the stones, suddenly thinking of the pillbox, remembering how Jamie and Hannah had played there.

Please God, please. Let him be all right. Please let me find him. I can't lose him. I can't. Her mind churned. That boy. That monster. Hannah's little shoe, caught in the bones of his bedroom, hanging there. What had he done to her? What was he capable of? He had seemed so vulnerable, so innocent, when all the time he was a monster. She thought of those lads knocking him over, stealing his bag, and of his call to the coastguard the other day. She had believed in his goodness. Not a bad bone in his body, Mary had said. Could you be that wrong about your own flesh and blood? Or did she know? Had she known all this time?

She had to stop running. The great cobbles were too uneven, but at last she could see the pillbox, its low concrete roof slanting out of the shingle, its brick shell worn and crumbling. When she got there, she stooped at the entrance, and then crawled through into the chamber. There was nothing inside but a heap of washed-up rubbish. She crawled out again, stood up and scanned the beach, back east towards the Bluff and the sea defences, and west towards the town. Clouds boiled in the sky, dark and thundery. The landslide at Mary's house was hidden from her view behind a chalky spur of the cliff. She pulled out her phone and called Jamie again. Still no answer. Oh, please, God. But what if God didn't answer either? All those prayers to find the truth…

And then, with a force like a punch in the stomach, she realised he had answered. The shoe. Adam. Someone to blame. Someone who knew what had happened, who had been there. That's what she'd begged for. So God was listening after all. He hadn't abandoned her. But what was it all for, if she was going to lose Jamie? She tightened her fists and set off towards town, climbed diagonally up the stony bank, so that she could walk along the top of the beach. Her thigh muscles burned and her ankles ached, but she welcomed the pain. She wanted her body to hurt. After a bit, she came to a place where water gushed from a broken clay pipe sticking out of the cliff face a few metres up, cascading into a pool. She'd never seen it like this before. Normally the outfall was no more than a trickle, and the pool no more than a puddle. The land must be saturated. No wonder it was collapsing. She kicked with the toe of her boot at a tangle of yellow rope, remembering the rubbish washed up in the dip where they had found Hannah's body. Among the stones, all shades of grey and brown, dotted with white chalk, was a bright blue pebble, an impossible colour. Sea glass, like Adam's treasures. She bent and picked it up.

It wasn't sea glass. It was a bead from Hannah's bracelet. Blue – the one she had chosen for Jamie.

Clutching the blue bead in her fist, she looked round quickly, scanned the beach again, and then looked up towards the pipe. He must have been here. Jamie had been here. To the left of the waterfall was a place where she thought she could climb up. It was steep and muddy, but not impossible. Was that where he had gone?

She put the bead in her pocket, and hoisted herself up. It's all right, Jamie, she whispered. I'm coming. I'll find you. She thought of the climbing wall, the brightly coloured grips and safety ropes and harnesses, and she wished she had a teammate to cheer her on. Even Christopher. Especially Christopher. *Come on*, she said to herself, imagining his voice. *That ledge there...find a handhold...now, pull yourself up. Keep going. You can make it.*

But how would Adam have persuaded Jamie to climb up here? He must have found a way to make Jamie trust him.

What lies had he told? Was that what he'd done with Hannah, too? Somehow made her trust him? To make her go with him, over the sea defences, and then…and then…?

Water dripped down the slope, seemed to sweat out of it. Behind her, the waves crashed on to the shingle. She grabbed at a protruding stone, but it came loose and she slid backwards, sending an avalanche of stones and loose earth to the beach below. Up, again, with the wind howling at her back, her fingers blotched purple and red. What if Adam had already hurt Jamie? What if Jamie was lying up here, alone, losing blood or tied up, beside himself with fear? She had to find him.

She heaved herself over a lip of land, and came up on her hands and knees into a dip in the cliff face. As she knelt there, recovering her breath, she saw, near her fingers, a small bone, bleached white – a tiny, fragile thing. She shivered, closed her eyes for a moment. But she had to press on. From here, the upward slope was steeper, but there was a rope ladder set into the cliff. Rachel scrambled up, putting all her faith in whatever was holding it at the top, beyond the next ledge. Her muscles ached and her hands stung. Up. There. She threw herself over the top, her breath hurting her chest, her heart hammering. This was a bigger trough of land. It must be where the land had slipped in the past. The ground was uneven, full of dips and bumps. In the middle was a huge metal peg, securing the ladder. And there, in front of her was an old wooden shed.

'Jamie!' she cried, launching herself at the door. 'Jamie! I'm here!'

It was locked, with a shiny new padlock hooked through the latch. She rattled the door. 'Jamie! Are you in there? Are you all right?'

She listened, her ear pressed against the door frame, but

all she could hear was the wind whistling around her, and the crash of the waves below.

She moved round to the side of the shed. Boards were nailed across what must have been a window. She peered through a narrow gap, but even with the flashlight on her phone it was impossible to make out any details of what was inside. At the back, though, where the wall abutted the side of this bowl of land, there was a hole where the wood had rotted. It was the size of a small animal, a cat perhaps, or maybe a fox. She knelt on the wet ground, called through, ripping at the planks, scraping her hands. 'Jamie? Are you in there?' She lay down on her stomach, held up her phone and peered into the dimness. At first she could see nothing more than shapes and shadows, but one of them, there by the wall…could it be a figure, curled on its side? 'Jamie! I'm here! It's all right. I'm coming in.'

She thought she saw a movement, and then she heard something. Breathing? Crying? She gritted her teeth, tugged at the board and at last it splintered and came away. One more piece and she'd be able to get in. She ripped another section, pulled herself through the jagged hole, and reached for the figure. But there was nothing there. No one. It was just shadowy shapes.

Where had Adam taken him? And why was the shed locked if Jamie wasn't here? She swung the beam of her flashlight round the interior. A heap of dirty carrier bags. Broken glass scattered across the floor, and, in the corner inside the door, a fishing crate standing on end, with a row of objects on top, set out as if on display. Blue glass glinted in the light from her phone. Sea glass. There were some fossils, too – bullet-shaped stones – and an old yellowish bottle. Adam's treasures.

Anger surged through her. She caught up a piece of blue

glass and flung it at the back wall, where it cracked against the wood.

'Fucking treasures!' she shouted.

Then another bit of glass. 'Monster!'

Then the bullet fossils. One by one they slammed into the shed wall. 'What have you done with him?'

Her muscles burned with a fierce energy. Rage pulsed through her, a white heat. Shaking and breathless, she snatched up the bottle, drew back her arm for the throw.

But then…a sound outside. She held her breath, listened. Someone was out there. She was about to call Jamie's name again, but some instinct stopped her. What if it was Adam? And what if he had Jamie? She didn't want to make things worse. The drop down to the lower level of the cliff was only a metre from the corner of the shed. There was no knowing what a monster like him would do. Still gripping the bottle, she crawled to the hole in the back wall. Her heart thumped against her ribs. She couldn't control her shaking. She eased herself through the gap, thankful for the sound of the wind to cover her movements. Then she crept to the corner furthest from the downward drop. She could smash the bottle and use it as a weapon if she had to. Her fist was tight around its neck.

The sound again. Movements, footsteps. Loud, panicky breathing. And now a whimpering moan. It didn't sound like Jamie. She crept up between the shed wall and the edge of the dip. It must be Adam. He must have heard her call Jamie's name. But if he was here, where was Jamie? She peered round the corner of the shed. There he was – Adam, shaking and whimpering, crouching against the slope, his arms bent over his head, and something clutched in his hand. No sign of Jamie. She leaped out in front of the shed, the bottle raised.

'What have you done with him?' She launched herself at him, grabbed his shoulder with her free hand, pulled him up.

'I didn't mean… They're coming to… They said I was—'

'Tell me where he is! You fucking monster!'

'But I'm not. I didn't—'

'I know what you are. You had her shoe. All the time. You had her shoe!'

He gave a cry and his hand shot out. Pain sliced across her chin, sharp and hot. Summoning her strength, she thrust him from her. He stumbled backwards, towards the shed and the top of the rope ladder, losing his balance.

'Your house,' she spat out. 'It's gone down the cliff. And the police will be there, and they'll find the shoe. There's nowhere left to hide. So tell me what you've done with Jamie. Where is he?'

Adam was on his hands and knees now, by the corner of the shed, and his words had turned to an incoherent wailing.

A hot fury engulfed her, and in the moment that she let the bottle fly, she heard another voice.

'Mum!'

The bottle flew over Adam's head and hit the shed roof. In a flash of white light, with a crack that split the air, the world exploded.

'Jamie!' A white ball of flame burst from the shed. Thrown backwards, Rachel landed hard on her back and all the breath left her lungs. Debris fell around her. Bits of wood and sparks shot into the sky.

She lay winded, unable to move. Flames hissed and crackled, and the echo of the explosion vibrated through the air. Eventually she caught her breath, and struggled to her knees. 'Jamie! God! What the…?'

She knelt there, in the mud. The fire roared and shadows danced. White smoke billowed. Her eyes stung, and she couldn't see Jamie or Adam. She crawled forward, but the heat was too much. 'Jamie!' Her voice was hardly there. Her chin throbbed and her throat was raw. 'Jamie? Where are you?'

She flung herself sideways, crawled towards the top of the ladder as far as she could from the fire. If he wasn't here when she'd come up over the ledge, he must have come down from above, but why hadn't she seen him? What if the blast had thrown him…? She didn't want to look, but she had to know.

She came to the edge, lay on her stomach, peered over. The ladder hung there, stretching down to the lower dip. No one was there, but the foot of the cliff was hidden from view. He couldn't have fallen. He would have landed there, at the bottom of the ladder.

'Jamie!' she called. 'Jamie!'

Behind her, someone groaned and when she turned she saw Adam, huddled on the ground, his hands over his eyes. She crawled back from the edge and almost fell into one of the dips in the uneven ground. And there he was. Jamie. Lying on his side, his knees curled up like a baby. His eyes were closed and he was holding something over his mouth and nose. Some kind of scarf or a teeshirt perhaps. Rachel let herself roll in beside him and her arms went round him and he was breathing. It wasn't a teeshirt. It was Hannah's giraffe pyjamas. His eyes flickered open.

'Mum.'

She held him to her and thought she would never let go.

Flint

Adam had stayed all night in the shed with Jamie, who was too scared to be left on his own in the dark. As soon as it was light, while Jamie was still asleep, he had set out to get the food and drink and sleeping bags. The path up the gully had become a rushing stream. He pushed and splashed his way up. When he reached the lane, jerky, unpredictable gusts unbalanced him. The waves crashed below, and the clouds hung dark and heavy and low. He kept close against the hedge, listening and looking over his shoulder every few seconds. Someone might be following him. They were probably keeping track of all his movements, so they could report him to the police. Or deal with him themselves. It would be one of those men from outside the school. Or Danny Goodrum or his uncle, or whoever had painted those red words all over the front of the house. Voices roared on the wind, accusing, threatening, mocking. *Oi, moron...brain-dead...weirdo. Leave town, perv...you'll pay for this...get lost or we'll make you.* Fingers jabbed at him, and shadows loomed at him from the hedges and the ditches. It was hard to breathe and his heart drummed against his ribs. He stumbled on, head down, but the voices grew louder until they filled his head.

He flattened himself against the hedge, then crouched down in the ditch, and felt about for a loose stone he could use to defend himself. A droning monotone came from somewhere in his middle. He found a piece of flint, sharp along one end, wrapped his fist round it, clutched it to his chest, and began rocking back and forth. Rain beat down and the wind howled.

He didn't know how long he sat curled up in the ditch under the hedge, shivering and whispering to himself, clutching the flint. Eventually, he crawled out onto the road and turned back towards the shed. What was the point of taking the boy a sleeping bag? He wasn't going to be in the shed another night. He trudged back towards the old overgrown garden at the bend in the lane. He slipped and slid down the gully, losing his balance several times and once falling heavily on his side and dropping the flint. He scooped it up again. It fitted his hand like it was meant to be there, firm and hard and powerful. He thought of ancient people and their flint tools.

Jamie would be wondering where he was. He hadn't meant to take this long. He checked his pocket for the key.

But the key was gone.

He must have lost it when he fell over just now, or when he was hiding in the ditch up at the top. What was he going to do? How would he get the shed open? He would have to smash his lovely new padlock.

And then he heard a shout. Someone was here. Jabbing

fingers again, roaring mouths, red paint, chasing footsteps and horrible names. He slid down the last bit of the slope and then his legs wouldn't hold him and he curled down to the ground, shaking, bent his arms over his head, and heard a moaning sound from somewhere far away. But he hung on to the stone.

And when she launched herself at him, grabbed his shoulder, yanked him to his feet, that's when he hit out with the flint. And then bang! Everything white. Flames pouring from the shed and smoke everywhere. Had she done that? His eyes were stinging and his throat felt raw. He'd rolled across the ground and then managed to crawl up the slope.

And now, he had to get back to Mumma. The house had gone, that woman said. Fallen down the cliff. And the shoe. She'd seen the shoe. So Mumma must have seen it too. And she would think... He pictured her, looking at him through the rain, strings of wet hair flinging themselves about her face.

'What have you done?' she would say. 'What have you done?'

He had to get to her. Had to explain. He climbed back up the gully, not caring about his soaking feet, and came to the lane. Oh, Mumma, what are we going to do? He forced himself to keep going, whispering inside his head. It wasn't my fault, Mumma. I wanted to tell you, only... He longed to cling to her, to hide his face in her chest. If only he could go back and make it all different. He wished he had never seen the million-year-old footprints or the girl with the dandelion hair.

It wasn't my fault. He wanted to shout it into the wind, to rip the sky apart and churn up the sea, to shake the land from its foundations until he had made the whole world understand. *I didn't mean to. It wasn't my fault. She just...* But the words got stuck and he found himself jabbing at the air and it was only then that he realised he was still gripping the flint. He had the feeling he might have hurt that woman with it when she hurled herself at him, screaming at him and calling him a monster. He threw the stone into the hedge, and broke into a run, splashing through puddles and slipping in the mud. He had to get to Mumma.

There was an ambulance and three police cars and blue lights flashing. He stood, helpless, watching. Mumma's face was covered in earth and blood and rain. Her eyes were shut. They put a blanket on her and he heard them say hospital.

Her eyes flickered open as they lifted her into the ambulance.

'I couldn't reach it,' she whispered.

And he knew that she had tried to save him.

A policeman told him to get into the car, put a hand on his head.

They were taking him away.

He put his hands over his ears but inside his head the wind roared on and the sea crashed against the cliff and the house creaked and groaned and splintered. A giant wave towered over him, black and shining, ready to break.

Driftwood

In the churchyard, the snowdrops were over, their flowers brown and papery. Primroses nestled under the wall, and fat catkins hung from the hazel. Tiny white flowers had sprung out on the blackthorn, and leaf buds were unfurling on the hawthorn. Yellowhammers trilled their 'little-bit-of-bread-and-no-cheese' song in the hedges.

It was only March, but it was warm enough for shorts and a tee shirt – a golden and blue day. A woodpecker drummed in the tall oaks on the other side of the tower, and, high overhead, a buzzard mewed. Rachel sat on the grass by Hannah's grave, leaned back on her elbows, looked up at the cloudless sky.

For more than a week, the police had told them nothing except that the investigation was ongoing and Adam Farthing was helping them with their enquiries. To begin with, Rachel had felt cheated out of a proper answer to her prayers. With the sight of Hannah's shoe, perched among the broken floorboards hanging over the cliff, God had offered her a glimpse of the truth, through a crack in the door, and then slammed that door in her face.

Now, though, the investigation was over, and they'd been offered a meeting. A meeting with Adam, where he would give them his account of events. She could have her answers.

But something held her back.

'You said you wanted the truth,' Christopher said. 'Well, now we can have it. We can find out what happened.'

'I'm not sure.'

'Why not?'

She couldn't explain it. It was instinctive. She was stuck, on the threshold. It was as if hearing his story would take her through a door, and once she was on the other side, she could never go back. The door would be locked behind her. She was frightened of what lay beyond it, but she didn't know why.

A fluttering in the hedge caught her attention. A pair of goldfinches danced around each other, flashes of yellow and red and black. A charm of goldfinches – one of those quaint collective nouns that stayed in the memory. A murder of crows. An exultation of skylarks. Did a pair count as a charm? Fairy tales had charms – magic and curses and spells, governed by their own set of rules. But was real life like that? Were blame and guilt and justice and truth governed by some kind of immutable law? And was it anything to do with God? Or was it all chaos, confusion, chance?

Churning these questions round and round was like stirring the pieces of a puzzle. Rachel sprang up from the grass and went inside the church.

Sunlight slanted in through the windows, creating jewelled

patterns of colour on the floor, and turning the floating dust to gold. The air was cooler than outside, and she shivered. Goosebumps came up on her arms. The comforting scent of wax polish overlaid the smell of old paper and damp plaster. She sat in the front pew, where she had sat for Hannah's funeral. Her memories of the day were blurred and disjointed, but a fragment flashed into her mind. She had dropped the order of service, scrabbled in the dust to find it. It was in the middle of the Lord's Prayer...*our daily bread*... She had wanted to lie down and disappear...*forgive us our sins*... She had sat up and brushed the dust from the photograph of Hannah's face...*as we forgive those who sin against us.* The words echoed in her mind now, as if she had come up from underwater. The puzzle pieces slotted into place and she understood. This was why she was unable to take the next step, the step that should give her everything she had longed for. *As we forgive those...* How many times had she said those words? This was the core of her faith. How had she spent all these weeks longing to find someone to blame without realising that whatever truth she found, she would have to forgive?

But how could she? If Adam had done something to Hannah...if it was his fault...it would be impossible. She slid to her knees on that same dusty floor, clasped her hands, pressing her fingers against each other. *Forgive us our sins, as we forgive those who sin against us.* I can't, she whispered. I can't. So what was the point of hearing his story? What if he had done this terrible thing, and she couldn't forgive? She would be lost. Without faith. Cast adrift.

She knelt there in the dust, with the sense that she was clinging to a fraying rope, and wondering if it would be easier simply to let go.

Eventually, she left, and set out along the top road, turning left down the track to the coast path, walking quickly. When she reached Wetherley Lane, she began to run, and didn't stop until she was at the top of the Bluff. She had passed what was left of Mary's house without looking at it. The remains would be demolished sometime, she supposed.

The police had told her about Mary's fall, and about finding the shoe among the debris on the beach, but she didn't know where Adam was staying, or whether Mary was still in hospital. She thought about Mary's plans for the caravan, with its mildew and rust and broken fittings. It's not my problem, she said to herself. Why should I care? I need to focus on my own family, now that we're starting to find each other again.

After the explosion, in their natural dugout, Rachel and Jamie had clung to each other, with no strength to move, waiting for the emergency services to arrive, while the fire burned itself out and a tired wind squalled over the cliff.

By the time help came – the police, paramedics, and Christopher – Adam had disappeared.

'Was he hurt in the blast?' a police officer asked, once Jamie and Rachel had been checked over by the paramedics.

'I don't know. But what was it?' Rachel asked. 'Some kind of homemade bomb?'

'We're not the experts,' the police officer said. 'You'll have to describe it again, and the explosion. White smoke, did you say?'

'Yes. Could Adam have made it?'

'He wasn't like that,' Jamie said. 'I was angry with him to begin with, because it was him that got me into trouble that time at the shop. You know, the chocolate and stuff. But it turns out he was cool. He found that bottle on the beach. He showed me his fossils and things. He called them his treasures, only they seemed to make him sad. I know he wouldn't have hurt me. Not on purpose.'

Rachel and Christopher looked at each other. They would have to tell him about Hannah's shoe.

It wasn't until they got Jamie home that the tears came. He fell in a heap on to the sofa and sobbed.

'I'm sorry,' he said at last, his face in a cushion. 'I'm sorry.'

'What for, love?' Rachel rubbed his back, feeling his bones, so sharp under his top that she thought they might puncture his skin from the inside.

Christopher sat on the floor, close to Jamie's head. 'Hey,' he said. 'It's all right...'

'I just wanted... It was just that you...'

'You're home now,' Christopher said. 'You're safe. It's going to be all right.'

'I don't mean about running away,' Jamie said. 'I mean about lying.' His voice was small and muffled, his face still buried in the cushion.

'You mean what you said about Dad?' Rachel said, gently. 'Hurting you?'

Jamie nodded and sniffed. 'I don't know why I said it.'

'We all do things we can't explain,' Christopher said. 'Especially when... Well, it's been a tough time. For all of us.'

'What about the social workers and everything?' Jamie sat up and rubbed his sleeve across his face. 'Will I be in trouble? Will I have to answer lots of questions? Because I don't...'

Rachel reached for a box of tissues from the coffee table, handed him one.

'Well,' she said. 'I think it would help you to talk to someone about all of it, when you're ready. What's the counsellor like, at school?'

'I only went twice. She was okay, I suppose.' Jamie held the tissue against his face, pressing at his eyes. Hannah's giraffe pyjamas were still round his neck, damp and grimy.

'Quick thinking,' Rachel said, touching the fabric. 'Putting this over your mouth and nose. Taking cover like you did.'

'I didn't think about it. It was kind of automatic. I don't even remember how I got in that hole.'

'Must be all those battle games you play,' Christopher said, with a smile. 'Or whatever they are. They've taught you something useful, after all.'

'What I don't get,' Rachel said, 'is where you were when I got to the shed. I shouted your name over and over. And then I heard you, but it was too late because I…' She shook her head. 'Oh, I can't bear to think what might have happened.'

'Adam said he was going to get me a sleeping bag and some food and stuff, but he locked me in and he was gone a long time, and in the end I found that broken bit at the back and I crawled out of the hole…'

'Wait,' Rachel said. 'You got out through that tiny gap in the wall? How did you…? It was hardly big enough for a cat.'

'And no way was I going back down the ladder so I found a way up. It wasn't really a path – more a stream – but then I heard you so I came back down and you and Adam were fighting. I saw him go for you with that stone and your face was pouring blood and I was scared and I didn't know what to do and then you threw the bottle, or bomb or whatever it was, and…'

His voice wavered, and he stopped.

Rachel reached out, touched his hairline. His fringe had moved sideways, revealing a fading red mark on his temple, like a tick made with a broad marker pen.

'Is that where…the straighteners?'

He nodded miserably. 'I just wanted it to hurt. Because then I…'

She knew. Because then the deeper pain would hide. For a moment, it would disappear.

Slowly, he pushed up his sleeves. The scars were thin and small, but there were a lot of them, angled across his arms between his wrists and his elbows.

Rachel's hand went to her mouth. 'Oh, Jamie, love.' The stolen razors, the blood-stained tissues in his bin. The hours spent on his own in his room. How had they not stopped it?

He pulled his sleeves down and crossed his arms, pressing them across his chest, his hands gripping the tops of his arms, pressing in. She thought of the bruises. The fingermarks. His own fingermarks.

He leaned against her and she held him and she knew they were going to be all right.

On top of the Bluff, Rachel looked out towards the horizon. The sea sparkled in the sunlight. A ragged skein of geese flew overhead, and the sound they made was more like laughter than anything else. She walked more slowly along the last section, and when she came to the car park at Saltbourne Gap, she half-ran, half-slid down the slope of shingle to the shining expanse of wet sand. She took off her trainers and socks, left them on the stones, and ran barefoot to the water's edge. On stormy days the sea was brown and opaque, but today it was clear, and, further out, a deep blue-green. She hadn't been in the sea since it happened, and the shock of the cold took her breath. Up to her ankles. Halfway up to her knees. Her skin was chalk-white, and the water distorted her feet. The tide was on the turn, and the waves lacked energy, breaking with slow, half-hearted sighs.

A little way out, a raised sand bar lay like the back of a huge sleeping animal. Rachel waded through the surf towards it, up to her thighs in the deepest part, and then shallower as she climbed the slope. And then she was there, standing on the tiny island, with the waves lapping around her, the sun warm on her skin, and the blue dome of the sky above her. Bird footprints marked the sand, trails crossing this way and that. Gulls hung on the air currents, then wheeled round and flew off. Beyond the sand bar, under the clear blue-green, the chalk reef gleamed white. On the edge of the world the wind turbines dazzled, like angels, their narrow wings uplifted. Rachel turned her face to the sun and closed her eyes.

Her feet were no longer cold. She felt herself sinking a little into the soft sand, almost losing her balance. She opened her eyes, lifted one foot and replanted it, then the other. She watched as sandy water gradually filled her empty footprints and smoothed them out until they were gone. The bird trails, too, were vanishing. As if they had never walked here, she thought. And when I step off this island, no one will know I ever stood here.

She took a step forward, towards the submerged reef, and then another, into deeper water, until the waves reached her thighs, her shorts, her waist. She stumbled against the uneven chalk, and slowly, with her arms outstretched, she let herself fall. The water closed over her head and the cold engulfed her. This is how it feels. Everything slows. Pressure. Ears. Lungs.

Strange sounds. A faraway roar.

A burst of energy, an instinctive kick, and she was up. A rush of air. She turned on to her back, and let the water hold her. Rocked by the rhythm of the waves, she stretched out her arms and legs, lay flat, balanced between two worlds. Drifting. A dark shape swam into the corner of her vision. Now there. Now gone. She turned her head to the side, frowning in the sunlight. Something was floating on the water. She bent her body, tried to stand, but found that she was out of her depth and had to tread water. The floating thing was the size of a child – bigger than Hannah, smaller than Jamie – but thicker, more solid. She kicked out, swam towards it. It was a broken branch, black, its rough bark saturated. Driftwood. She placed one hand on top of it, then hooked both her arms over it, raising herself a little higher in the water. She didn't need a float. She was a strong swimmer, used to these temperatures. The beach was easily within reach, and the sea wasn't rough. But she hung on. The cold was seeping into her now. Her fingers looked bruised, and her feet were numb. She began to be frightened. Spring. The coldest time of the year, for the sea.

If she held on, let the current and the tide take her, would she end up in the dip where someone had found Hannah? In that hollow at the foot of the cliff, among the bits of plastic and tangles of seaweed and blue and yellow rope? Would some early morning runner or dog-walker find her, with the child-sized piece of driftwood still clasped to her breast?

For a while, she floated, facing the wind turbines on the horizon, feeling the swell lift and lower her body, letting her legs drift and swing in the movement of the water. Salt stung her nose and mouth, and numbness was stealing into her. But still, she hung on. She listened to the plaintive cries of the gulls, to her own breathing, and in the ripple and splash of the waves, she heard a whisper. *Let go. Let go.*

A great calmness spread through her. She looked up at the sky. I don't see, she thought, how I'll ever be able to forgive. It feels impossible. But I have to be ready to start that journey. All I can do is believe I'll be given the strength. I can't carry on if I don't find out what Adam Farthing did. I have to know what happened to Hannah. And before I hear his story I have to be ready to let go.

Gradually, the current turned her, and the cliffs came into view, a narrow line of russet and brown, with patches of grey and white. Solid earth.

And, letting the driftwood go, she kicked out behind her, and swam towards the shore.

Wave

Adam was in the police station again, but this time it was different because he knew Mumma wouldn't come and they wouldn't get chips afterwards because she had fallen from his broken bedroom down the cliff and gone to hospital in an ambulance. There had been flashing blue lights and a red blanket. There had been a hand on his head and a police car and someone had called him son but it wasn't Mumma.

He had seen DI Sally Lincoln before. She had a smile that turned on and off like a light switch. She and the other officer – a man in a denim jacket with a stud missing – took turns to ask him questions. There was another lady there called Jackie who said she was his Appropriate Adult. She wore pink boots, and rings on her thumbs.

Some of the questions were about what happened to Hannah. Starting with why her shoe was in his house.

'It's not in my house,' he said. 'My house is—'

'Yes, I know what happened to your house.' DI Sally Lincoln closed her eyes when she said this, and then opened them again. 'And I'm very sorry,' she added, but the smile was switched off.

And some of the questions were about what they called his behaviour around children. They meant his hero circuit. He told them about the clockwork shark and the boy on the swing, and the glass outside the school. He told them about the men who had jabbed their fingers into his chest, and the red graffiti, and Danny Goodrum threatening to steal his fossils. He told them about locking Jamie in the shed.

'I didn't know it was him,' he said. 'I mean Hannah's brother. Not then. He said he didn't want to go home, so I was going to get him a sleeping bag and some food. I locked the shed to keep him safe. In case Danny or anyone… I was looking after him, you see. I was looking after all of them.' He paused. Then he whispered, 'To make amends.'

'What did you say?' DI Sally Lincoln leaned forward, frowning.

'To make amends.'

'For what? What you did to Hannah Bird?'

'I didn't… I told you what happened. It was…'

Hannah Bird. He thought of her sunshiny smile and her dandelion clock hair. Of her gruff little voice and the gap in her teeth. He thought of her little white foot fitting exactly into a footprint that might be a million years old. Something fluttered in his chest and his breaths went in and out too quickly. It hurt behind his eyes.

'I…I didn't look after her. I didn't save her.' It came out as a whisper and then his eyes were wet and he couldn't breathe properly. Oh, Mumma, he thought. Mumma-in-the-hospital, what will happen to us?

In the end DI Sally Lincoln stopped asking questions and her smile switched off and stayed off.

Jackie and another lady and a man in a hard hat took him back to the house to collect some things, but they wouldn't let him stay.

'There's a caravan,' he said, but they didn't even cross the field to look.

'We've arranged a room in a B&B,' the lady that wasn't Jackie said. 'For the time being.'

A B&B. Adam thought of Yorkshire. The creamy potatoes and the jam puddings. The bed with the wall on the wrong side. The rain and the sheep. His tummy felt funny. He wished he could stay in the hospital with Mumma. There was a chair by her bed, but if it wasn't visiting time you couldn't go in. She had a bandage on her head and her arm was in a cast, and she said they'd made her an appointment with an eye doctor. She wasn't very talkative though, so he just held her hand.

A week later she was in the room next to his in the B&B, making shouty phone calls to the council and grumbling about the sandwiches he got her. She cheered up a bit when Mr Bright came with sausages and chips.

Another lady came to talk to him. She looked a bit like Molly, with the same orange hair and bright red lips. Jackie came with her, and kept saying things like 'Adam, is that okay?' and 'Adam, do you understand?'

The Molly lady said that if he agreed to it, there could be a meeting. He didn't have to do it, but people usually found it helped. Mr and Mrs Bird, Hannah's parents, had said they wanted him to tell them what had happened on the beach that day. They would meet in a special room with chairs and a table and…

'Would you like to see the room?' Jackie said.

The chairs were grey with wooden arms and arranged in a square round a big, low table. There was a wide window with some grass and pine trees outside. Jackie's pink boots squeaked on the shiny floor.

'Sit down, if you like,' the Molly lady said.

He sat. Up to now, he had been desperate not to think about that day, to push the memory away, but it kept clawing its way back in, wouldn't leave him alone. At first he had said no, he didn't want to talk to Hannah's parents. What had happened had happened. How could talking about it make it better? It wouldn't change anything. That's what Mumma would have said. She was always ignoring bad things, pretending they weren't there. Then he thought about her sight problem. She had ignored that and it hadn't gone away. It had got worse. She wasn't right about everything. Maybe he should believe the Molly lady when she said it usually helped. So in the end he said he would talk to them.

It was strange to be remembering on purpose when he had spent all these weeks trying not to think about it. Where would he begin? With finding the footprints after the storm? Or when he first saw Hannah from the bottom of the steps?

She was poking at the mud with a stick, down by the jumble of sea defences – those great blocks of dark stone that Mumma called rock armour. The tide was on the turn and an orange light flowed over everything, like it had been washed in gold. It would be dark in an hour.

'Are you looking for fossils?' he said, when he reached her.

She was wearing a yellow jacket and blue spotty trousers and red shoes. Her hair was a pale frizz like a dandelion clock. This wind, he thought, could snatch her up and blow her away.

'I was looking for holey stones but I found this.' Her voice surprised him. It was rough and grainy like the fudge from Molly's kiosk.

'It's a stick,' he told her.

'No, it's not,' she said. 'It's a stone, silly.'

'It's a fossil stick. Once it was wood, but now it's turned into stone. It's like magic, but really it's science.'

'Oh.'

He took the shark tooth from his pocket, held it in his palm for her to see. 'I found this today,' he said. 'It's a shark tooth.'

She grinned. Both her top middle teeth were missing, but her smile was like sunshine.

'I know where there are more fossils,' he said. 'Special ones. D'you want to see?'

'Can you get me one?'

'No. They're part of the ground. The beach. Past the rock armour.'

'Rock armour?'

'That's what these blocks are called but their other name is sea defences and they're to stop the sea hurting the land.'

'I know about a king who tried to stop the sea. He was called King Canoe and his feet got wet and he couldn't stop it. It's in a book. But Mummy says he didn't really want to stop it. It was about God being stronger than anyone, even kings'

'Well, if he did want to, he should have used rock armour. Come on, let's climb over. I can help if you want.'

The little girl turned, so he did too, following her gaze.

Further down the beach a man was throwing stones into the sea, and beyond that, a lady and a boy were running towards another group of people who were trying to stop some dogs from fighting.

She turned back to him. 'I don't need you to help me,' she said. 'I can climb all by myself.'

And she could. She clung to the rocks and then scuttled over them like a crab, sideways on her hands and feet. They clambered down the other side, and there were the layers of mudstone, spread out before them, flat and glistening and dark.

'Come on, quick.' He grabbed her hand and they ran towards the water.

They stopped short of the breaking waves. The wind had got up again. It was going to be another wild night.

'Where are they – the fossils?' she said, in her funny, gruff voice.

'Here.'

'But where? I can't see any.'

'Here. They're footprints. Look. Here's one. And here, look. This one's about your size.'

The dents were full of water, tiny, foot-shaped puddles, twenty or thirty of them scattered over the mudstone.

'Is it? I'm going to see.' She bent down and took off her shoe. She pulled off her sock, stuffed it in the shoe. 'Here,' she said. 'Can you hold this?'

He couldn't tell if she believed him. He thrust the shoe in his jacket pocket and put his hand on his phone. He wanted photos.

'Perfect!' she said. And it was. She stood there, laughing, with her back to the sea, and her little bare foot in the dent. The sun shone on her face, and the wind blew her dandelion hair.

And then he saw it, a giant wave rolling in, twice as high as the others, huge and unstoppable, curling up and over, ready to slam into her back.

He lunged towards her. The wave crashed over them. He reached for her hand, but there was nothing there. He lost his balance, tipped over into the swirling foam, went under. Salt stung his eyes, his nose, his throat. Pebbles battered his skin. The current tugged. He couldn't find the ground, couldn't breathe. Arms and legs thrashed.

Then – back on his feet as the wave washed back. Breath heaving. Heart pounding. Where was she?

Another wave towered over him. He plunged back in, diving down with his eyes open, but he couldn't see anything. He came up to breathe. Shouted across the surging water. But there was nothing. It was hopeless.

At last, he crawled out, exhausted, struggled to his feet and stood, shaking, dripping, staring at the empty sea.

She was gone.

His wet clothes clung to him and weighed him down. Wind gusted around him and he couldn't stop shaking. Waves crashed, on and on, the sound that sent him to sleep every night. He rocked backwards and forwards, and a moaning sound mingled with the cry of the wind.

'Help. Oh, Mumma, help,' he heard himself whisper at last.

He couldn't stop shivering. He must have stood there a long time, because it was dark when he found himself at the top of the beach. The tide had already covered the mudstone. He heard voices. Silhouetted figures called to each other down by the sea defences, waving torches and poking about on the rocks. Blue lights flashed up there at the end of the lane. People climbed up and down the steps.

And then the fear hit. There would be shouty policemen and a prison van. He'd seen it on the telly. Angry crowds with roaring mouths. *You'll pay for this.* Holding up signs. Banging on the van. The police would ask him questions and he would get in a muddle and say things he didn't mean to say.

They would take him away from Mumma.

He crouched in the shadows at the foot of the cliff. At last, the blue lights had gone, and he crept up the steps to Wetherley End, hidden by the gorse.

The light was on in the kitchen, but the back of the house was in darkness. He eased open the door of the lean-to, slipped through the hallway and into his bedroom. The telly was on in the living room. He could hear the music of one of Mumma's quiz shows.

It wasn't until he took off his wet jacket that he realised he still had the shoe. He took it out of his pocket. It was small but chunky, with a Velcro fastening. He turned it over. The sole had the outline of a unicorn cut into the heel. He pictured the little foot fitted into the dent in the mudstone. His fist scrunched around the shoe. He stuffed it under his pillow with the shark tooth and changed out of his clothes, kicked the bundle of wet things into the corner.

'Adam, is that you?' Mumma put her head round the door. 'There's sausage and chips in the oven keeping warm. There's a couple of jam tarts left, too. What's the matter?'

'Nothing, Mumma.' His heart hammered. He wanted to tell her. The words jumped about in his head but he wouldn't let them out. Couldn't.

'What's this?' Mumma picked up his jacket from the floor. 'It's soaked. It's not raining again, is it?'

'I fell over.'

'Bring it in the kitchen and hang it up.'

'Okay. In a minute.'

When she'd gone, he closed the door and crouched by the loose floorboard. He folded back the carpet, pressed on one end of the board and slid his fingers under the other end to lift it. He fished the shark tooth and the red shoe from under his pillow, shoved them both into the hole in the floor, and wedged the board back in place. His hands were clammy with sweat. He closed his eyes, tried to slow his breathing, to stop shaking.

They ate in front of the telly, and afterwards, when Mumma had settled down to watch her detective programme, he took a jar of nails and a hammer from the kitchen windowsill. In his room he put on some loud, bashy music and hammered the board to the bit of wood that went across the floor underneath. Bang, bang, bang, in time with the thump of the bass, a row of nails all the way across. There. Gone. Now he could forget about it.

But then he remembered the sock.

He curled his fingers into fists, pressed his nails into his palm, replayed the sequence. She had stuffed the sock into the shoe, given it to him to hold. He had put it in his jacket pocket. But when he shoved the shoe under the floorboard, was the sock still inside it? He couldn't be sure. He looked under his pillow, checked his jacket, steaming on the rail in front of the stove.

When the police came, they didn't say anything about a sock. Did that mean they hadn't found it?

He went out first thing the next morning intending to retrace his steps and look for the sock, but from the top of the steps he could see that there were people everywhere and he didn't dare go down. A search party. That's what it must be. They were looking for her. And if the sock was there, they would find it.

Please let it still be in the shoe, nailed down under the floorboards. He imagined wrenching out the nails, levering up the board, rummaging in the dust, pulling out the red shoe. But a cold sweat prickled his neck and he felt sick with fear. He didn't ever, ever want to see that shoe again. He wanted to forget it was there. Forget the footprints and the little girl and her dandelion hair and her sunshine smile.

And the giant, unstoppable wave.

At first, it was hard to get the words out. He arranged them in his head, but they mixed themselves up and came out wrong.

'It's all right, Adam.' Jackie was sitting next to him. 'Take your time.'

On the other side of the table, Mr and Mrs Bird sat next to each other, but he could only see their knees because he had to give his full attention to a boat-shaped dent in the table in order to bring his words under control.

The Molly lady sat on a third side of the square, with a notebook on her lap. The big window was on the fourth side and the sun was shining through it, filling the room with a soft, yellow light.

After a bit, the words sorted themselves out and Adam told the story of what had happened that day by the sea defences.

'And I wish…' he said, when he had told it all. 'I tried. Oh, I tried to find her. But…' – he looked up then – '…I couldn't.'

Mrs Bird's face was all tears, and Mr Bird's hand was on hers. They made no sound.

'I didn't look after her,' Adam said. 'I wish I could have saved her.' And then his words came to a stop. He swallowed. His throat ached. He blinked and looked back at the boat dent in the table.

The room was very still. No one spoke. He listened to his own breathing. Outside, the sun shone on the pine trees and the grass.

After a long time, there was a whisper from Hannah's mother. 'Thank you.'

Startled, he looked up at her.

She met his gaze. 'Thank you,' she whispered again.

Then she stood, and Mr Bird stood too, and put his arm around her shoulders and they went out of the room.

Lighthouse

'Remember,' Jamie said, 'how she used to pretend she was a giraffe.' He lay down on Hannah's bed and spread the jungle duvet cover over himself, folding it over so that his head was at the top of the giraffe's long neck. 'I'm a giraffe, and I like to laugh.'

How like Hannah he sounded, mimicking her gruff voice and the sing-song intonation she used when she made up her rhymes. He's going to be all right, Rachel thought. His eyes no longer avoided theirs. The scars on his arms were fading and he had lost that pinched, pale, closed-off look. He had relaxed into his skin. It seemed to fit his bones in a more comfortable way.

In Hannah's room, boxes were open, their contents laid out on the floor – clothes and toys and books; everything that Rachel had packed up on that Saturday after their pilgrimage, in her desperate bid to persuade God to listen to her prayers. 'Let's go through it together,' she'd said. 'Like we should have done in the first place.' They had sliced open the tape, pulled out tee shirts and trousers, jumpers and dresses, picture books and teddy bears and a huge knitted scarecrow with no stuffing left in his neck.

Jamie emerged from under the duvet cover, opened a plastic box, and let loose a cascade of tiny dolls' dishes and plates, miniature sunglasses and hats, boots and belts and bits of Lego.

'Hey,' he said. 'I wondered where those were. They're from my police aeroplane. These blue bits.' He collected them up and put them in a heap on the window sill.

'So,' Christopher said, 'how about we each choose something? One thing to keep. Or more than that, if we feel like it. We could have a special box, maybe, or keep them on a shelf in here.'

'All I want,' Jamie said, 'is the blue bead that Hannah said was mine.' He looked at Rachel. 'I mended her bracelet before I ran away, and when it broke again I thought that was it. But you found my bead at the bottom of the cliff, and then…you found me.'

Rachel thought back to how he had wrenched the bracelet from her, his anger fierce and raw, how the beads had scattered on the floor, how their family had been on the brink of falling apart.

She reached for his hand, squeezed it. 'I've got the holy stone,' she said. 'You keep the blue bead.'

He nodded, and swallowed, but didn't say anything.

'I think I'd like to keep something she loved,' Christopher said. 'Before she got Floppy Rabbit, she trailed this funny-looking creature all over the place.' He picked up the plush puffin, with its bright, over-sized beak, and enormous orange feet. 'I think he should sit here.' He sat Puff-Puffin in the little wicker chair. 'What about you, Rach? Anything other than the holy stone?'

'Hang on,' Rachel said. 'There's more.' She jumped up, grabbed an empty box and ran up the stairs to the Crow's Nest. She pulled open the cupboard door, reached in for the bright heap of paper and wool and pipe-cleaners that she had rescued from the recycling bin, the things she had not been able to sacrifice. She filled the box and carried it down to Hannah's room, tipped it out on to the bed.

Once they had untangled the muddle, they found purple paper birds, puppets made of spoons and straws and paper plates, with bright wool hair and googly eyes. There were treasure maps and Easter hats, egg box monsters and jewelled butterflies, painted stones and strings of stripy knitting, dragons and snowflakes and tiny cardboard houses with doors that opened.

And there was the lighthouse.

Rachel picked it up. Hannah had made it not long after Christmas, winding the strips of colour and working out how to get the tea light in and out so that she could switch it on and off. It had been one of those dull, purposeless days between Christmas and New Year when meals merge into one another and daylight never breaks through. But Hannah was immune to the general lethargy. She had sat at the table, folding and cutting and gluing, with the tip of her tongue sticking out and a frown fixed on her face, until eventually, she switched on the light and inserted it into the transparent top of the lighthouse.

'Ta da!' she said, and her face shone. 'One lighthouse, at

your service, madam!'

And it had stood on the table as the centrepiece for their mix-and-match lunch of leftover festive fare.

'This is what I'm choosing,' Rachel said now. She took out the tea light, switched it on and put it back. Then she stood the lighthouse on Hannah's bedside table. 'We can't put it in a box,' she said. 'Whoever heard of a lighthouse in a box? Let's leave it there.' *Shine as a light in the world.* The baptism words came back to her.

In the end, they piled up the stuffed toys on the bed, just as Hannah had always had them, then re-packed the boxes together, taped them and stacked them against the wall. They were no longer a sacrifice.

'She doesn't need them any more,' Christopher said.

For the first time, Rachel had a tentative sense of Hannah existing somewhere beyond this life. Until it happened, she had always believed in heaven, and then the pain had consumed her, leaving no room for anything else. She remembered what Cathy had said about leaving the only world you've ever known and being born into a new one. Like a baby, leaving the womb.

She sighed. She would never be as sure as Cathy had been. But maybe that was what faith was all about. Learning to live with your doubts, and hanging on anyway.

'No, and we don't need them either,' she said. 'But I think Lenny and Flora would love to have the books. And actually, Izzy probably won't mind if Flora has some of the clothes. I think I'll go over there now. Can you help me load the car?'

'You mean we can have all these?' Lenny said. Three boxes of books stood open on the floor of Izzy's sitting room.

'To keep?' Flora said. 'They'll live here, with us?'

'That's right.' Rachel smiled. 'It would have made Hannah happy.'

'Wow!' Lenny said. 'We could make a library. We could let all our friends come and choose.'

'Wow and wow and wow!' Flora said.

Before long, both children were lying on their stomachs on the carpet, surrounded by books.

Rachel and Izzy sat on the sofa in the bay window. It was another bright, blustery, spring day and the magnolia in the patch of front garden was covered in fat, pale buds.

'Did you know the house has gone?' Izzy said.

'No. That was quick. Do you know where they're living? Is Mary all right?'

'In a B&B, apparently. I saw Molly in the post office. She said Mary broke her arm and some ribs, but she's got a plan. She wants to get permission for a static caravan on that bit of land she's got on the other side of the lane. A proper big one that she and Adam can live in. And Mr Bright's given Adam a job. Two days a week on the understanding that he applies for college in September.'

'She would have done anything to keep that place. It meant the world to her.'

'It was only a matter of time. The sea was always going to get it in the end.'

'I suppose she knew that, deep down. And I guess if Adam's all right, she'll be all right.'

'What about you, Rach? What's next for you?'

Rachel curled her feet under her, leaned her head back, looked at the ceiling and sighed. She had made up her mind, talked to Christopher, and to Gail. 'I'm not going on with the course. I can't, Izzy. I can't see myself as a priest. Not now.

How can I? I'm too…broken.' She felt her voice quiver, and was unable to say more. She couldn't talk about her struggle with forgiveness, and even now that she knew Adam wasn't to blame, there was a long road ahead.

Izzy stayed quiet for a moment. Then she said, 'You know I don't believe what you believe, Rach, but I don't think being broken disqualifies you. If you're in the business of mending broken people, doesn't it help if you…well, if you've been there?'

'Hmm. I don't know about mending,' Rachel said. They were both quiet for a moment. Then Rachel said, 'It's not just about being broken. And it's not just about doubts, although I do have them. After Hannah died, all I cared about was me. It's like I was stuck in my grief and the only way out that I could see was to find out what happened, for it to be someone's fault. And I couldn't think about anything else. Or anyone else.'

'Grief takes people in different ways, Rachel. Don't blame yourself for that.'

'But I am to blame,' Rachel said. 'Look what happened to Jamie. How is that not my fault? I shut myself off from everyone who was trying to help me. I wrapped myself up and made myself blind to what anyone else needed. Christopher, too. I couldn't help him, and I didn't let him help me.'

She paused. Outside, clouds scudded across the bright sky, and branches danced in the wind. On the floor, the children were still engrossed in Hannah's books.

'The thing is,' Rachel went on, 'I'm not sure it was the grief that made me like that. What if it simply brought out what was already there? I mean, even before, I always struggled with…I don't know. Is it empathy or sympathy? The day before Hannah died I was questioning whether I could do it. I told you on the phone – remember? The pastoral side of things. It's not that I don't care about people, but I can never seem to find the right way to show it. The right words, or the right kind of silence. I don't have the patience, you know that. And for someone who's going to be a priest…well, it wouldn't work. It wouldn't be right.'

'You've always been a good friend to me.'

Rachel smiled, found Izzy's hand and squeezed it.

'Are things better, now,' Izzy said, 'with Christopher and Jamie?'

'Yes. I think so.'

'You seem different. Last time I saw you, you were – I don't know – sort of intent. Restless. Like you were on a mission. You didn't walk, you marched. Now, it's like you've stopped to breathe.' She paused. 'Has something happened?'

'We met Adam,' Rachel said. 'Usually it's for victims of a crime, a meeting like that, but Adam didn't actually… Well, it was a chance for us to hear what happened. And a chance for him to tell his story.'

She was silent for a while, remembering the muted sunlight, Adam's voice, his clear, matter-of-fact tone – at least for most of his account.

'So,' Izzy said, 'what did he say?'

'He was showing Hannah some fossil footprints he found in the mudstone. I'd chased after the dog. Christopher thought Hannah had gone with me and I thought she'd stayed with him. Anyway, you know how wild it was that day. There was a huge wave. They didn't see it coming, and she just…disappeared. He tried to save her. Kept diving under.' She stopped speaking, imagining the scene again, the heaving sea, the orange light in the sky, the wind. Hannah – one minute there, laughing, and the next, gone. 'It was an accident, Izzy. An accident. No one's fault.'

Christopher had sat close beside her, holding her hand. Adam had stared at the table, his back straight, his hands on his knees, and his voice was strangely like a lullaby. She listened and a great calm came upon her. Then the lullaby became hers, and she was singing it to Hannah, holding her close, carrying her through. It was only when Adam reached the part about not being able to save her that his voice cracked, and his hands trembled.

'I felt like I'd been given a gift,' she said to Izzy. 'I can't explain it. A gift.'

Rachel drove home from Izzy's, but she didn't go inside the house. She needed to walk, to be outside under the wide, blue sky. She needed to hear the splash of the waves and the cry of the gulls, to taste the salt, to crunch over the sand. She needed to feel the tension in her muscles and the pounding of her heart, and the air filling her lungs.

The new landslide was a rust-red stain on the cliff, like a wound, and the place where Wetherley End had been was raw and empty, the blue sky bright above the broken land. Huge lumps of fresh, orange earth lay scattered at the foot of the cliff, and the cascade of smaller fragments reached halfway to the water. At high tide, it would be impossible to walk round the debris. Rachel stood at the toe of the new slope, and looked up. That was where the splintered floorboards had hung over empty air. With Hannah's shoe cradled among them.

She was about to move on, when she saw a figure at the top of the broken steps. Mary. Standing there, the one-time Queen Canute, her arm in a sling, her hair blowing in the wind, looking down at her. She felt a jolt in her chest, a sudden tightening of her throat. They stood for a while, neither of them moving. Then Rachel lifted her arm in a kind of salute, raised it higher, and waved.

Moments passed. And then Mary lifted her good hand, and waved back.

Rachel turned and walked down to the water's edge, continued in the direction of the sea defences. She climbed over the rock armour, as she had done before, but now she knew. She knew that Hannah had climbed over here with Adam. *I'm here*, she found herself whispering. *Hannah, I'm here. I'm with you.* At last she could carry Hannah through it all. This. This was what she had wanted. It didn't make the pain go away. The weight of grief was still there. It was impossible to imagine ever emerging on the other side. But perhaps now she could begin to believe that God had been with her all along, while she had shouted and ranted and begged and bribed, that he had been waiting for her to let him hold her close. That, just as she had longed to carry Hannah through it, he had been carrying her. She sighed as she climbed down the tumbled rocks. She wasn't sure. Would she ever learn to live with not being sure?

On the other side, smooth sand covered the mudstone. You wouldn't know it was there. You wouldn't know there were million-year-old footprints hidden under these tiny grains of sand. Maybe there weren't. Maybe Adam had made a mistake and they were just puddles, insignificant dents in the rock. Or maybe, one day, another storm surge would scour away the surface and they would come to light again. Maybe experts would come and measure them and take photos and make plaster casts to put in a museum. They would work out who had walked there, how many of them, how tall, how old, and how long ago they lived.

Rachel stood facing the sea, watching the waves build and roll in, their white crests whipped up by the wind, until they broke, crashing on to the shore, washing up to her feet, and then sucking back.

I'm here. I'm here.

She walked all the way to Saltbourne Gap, over the bank, and up the sandy path where the breeze whispered through the grass. At the top of the car park, she headed west up the slope. And now she ran, pounding all the way up to the highest point of the cliff – the Bluff – standing solid over the place where the sea defences stretched across the shifting sand. She stood, breathing hard, heart thumping, leg muscles burning. The wind had died down, and she was warm in the sun. She pulled off her jumper and tied it round her waist. The wind turbines, bright white in the sunlight, seemed close enough to touch. She held up her finger and thumb, shut one eye. In front of the turbines, a ship glinted red and blue, like a toy. White wave crests danced across the sparkling sea. From here, she could see all the way to the shingle spit that curled out into the North Sea. Holthorpe was hidden in its dip, with only the top of the church tower visible above a fold in the landscape. Clumps of gorse fringed the rough grassland to her left, the bright yellow flowers filling the air with the scent of coconut. At her feet, rosettes of dark green promised a burst of pink when the thrift came into bloom. She took a deep breath, tightened the knot in her jumper sleeves, and turned towards home along the land's fragile edge.

High over the cliffs, the skylarks were singing again.

Acknowledgements

A debut novel may have a longer list of acknowledgements than subsequent works because it's about the author's journey to this point, rather than just about one book. So my first thanks must go to my parents, Michael and Joy Smith. I grew up in a house full of stories and books, where my father, an expert at one-finger typing, wrote hundreds of articles for many publications, and occasionally allowed me to use a sheet or two of his pristine typing paper.

I'm grateful for the support of fellow writers on the Word Cloud (now, sadly, defunct), and the writing community on Twitter, in particular Philippa East, Fiona Erskine, Laure Van Rensburg, Jane Jesmond and John Taylor. This novel would never have been written without a Word Cloud challenge set by Alan Peabody. The resulting piece won a prize in the Bath Short Story Award, whose judge confirmed my sense that the idea could work as the basis for a novel.

One of the first people to encourage me to submit my short fiction was Philippa Johnston at the Winchester Writers' Conference. I've learned so much from the Jericho Writers' York Festival and their brilliant self-edit course taught by Debi Alper and Emma Darwin; also the superb workshops and salons run by Kellie Jackson at Words Away, and Stephanie Carty's invaluable Psychology of Character course.

Thank you to my daughter, Katy Smith, and my sister, Jacqueline Pumphrey, for their perceptive feedback after reading an early draft of *Sea Defences*, and to book doctor extraordinaire, Andrew Wille, for helping me to identify the true heart of the story, and for supporting me through its development.

Thank you to all the agents who have given me kind 'rejections'. They matter.

A serendipitous meeting with fellow author Jennifer Antill led me to my publisher. Thank you to the team, especially to Dan Hiscocks for believing in my work, to my editor Simon Edge, copyeditor Clio Mitchell, and Nell Wood for the beautiful cover.

Lastly, thank you to my husband, David, and the rest of the family for your encouragement and love on my long road to publication.

If you have enjoyed *Sea Defences*, do please help us spread the word – by putting a review online; by posting something on social media; or in the old-fashioned way by simply telling your friends or family about it.

Book publishing is a very competitive business these days, in a saturated market, and small independent publishers such as ourselves are often crowded out by the big houses. Support from readers like you can make all the difference to a book's success.

Many thanks.

Dan Hiscocks
Publisher
Lightning Books